A
Gentle
Feuding

by Johanna Lindsey

G.K.HALL &CO.
Boston, Massachusetts
1984

Published in Large Print by arrangement with Avon
Books

British Commonwealth rights courtesy of
Judy Piatkus Ltd.

Set in 16 pt. Times Roman

Library of Congress Cataloging in Publication Data

Lindsey, Johanna.
    A gentle feuding.

    1. Large type books. I. Title.
[PS3562.I5123G4   1984]   813′.54   84-12798
ISBN 0-8161-3750-1 (lg. print)

A
Gentle
Feuding

Chapter 1

Early May 1541, Aberdeenshire, Scotland.

A BRIGHT moon broke through fleeting clouds, lighting the Highland moors and casting five men into dark shadows. Five men waiting behind a steep crag far above the great Dee river. The river was a silver thread winding its way through the wide valley between the Cairngorm mountains and towering Lochnagar.

A burn turbulent with melted winter snow passed below, joining the Dee. This thick stream traversed Glen More, where MacKinnion crofts dotted what little fertile land there was.

All was quiet in the crofts. All was quiet in the glen. The five men heard only the melodic sound of water far below and their own ragged breathing. They crouched behind the crag, cold and wet from their river crossing.

They were waiting for the moon to reach its zenith, when it would cast no shadow. Then the tallest of them would set them on their task—a task conceived out of bitterness. His clansmen were as

1

nervous as he was.

"The moon is high, Sir William."

William stiffened. "So it is," he said, and began to pass out the green-gold-and-gray-striped plaids he had ordered made for that night. "Let it be done then, and done right. The cry will be the Clan Fergusson cry, no' our own. And dinna kill all, or there'll be no one left to say whose cry they heard."

The five men moved away from their hiding place and gathered their horses. Swords were drawn and torches lit. And in a moment, a blood-curdling war cry split the still night. Seven crofts were in their pathway, but the assailants expected to attack only three, for MacKinnion crofters were skilled warriors as well as farmers, and the few attackers had only surprise on their side.

The family in the first croft were barely awake before their small hut was put to the torch. Their home was quickly consumed. Their livestock was butchered, but the crofter and his family were saved the sword. There was no blessing in that, for imprisoned in their inferno, their deaths were more agonizing.

A newly married couple lived in the second hut, the wife fifteen years old. She woke to the war cry with terror, terror that doubled when she saw her husband's anguished face. He forced her to hide beneath their box bed, and then he went out to meet the attack. She never knew what happened to him. Smoke gathered in the thatched hut, suffocating her. It was too late to wish she had not defied her brother and married her beloved. It was too late for anything.

The third croft faired a little better, though not by much. It was a larger farm. Old Ian lived there with his three grown sons, a daughter-in-law and grandson, and a servant. Fortunately, Ian was a bad sleeper and was awake to see the newlyweds' croft set on fire. He called his three sons to arms and sent his grandson to warn their closest neighbors. Simon was then to go to their laird.

The attackers met resistance at Ian's croft, four strong fighters. Ian could still wield a mean cudgel, and he held out for precious time. One of Ian's sons was dead, another wounded, and old Ian struck down before anyone heard the war cry of the MacKinnions. At that sound, the attackers fled.

It was an angry young laird who viewed the devastating scene in those dark hours before dawn. James MacKinnion halted his huge steed just as his cousin and friend Black Gawain ran into the newlyweds' hut, a small cottage built only two months before to welcome the bride. Only the low stone walls and a little of the roof remained of a home so lately filled with laughter and teasing.

For Black Gawain's sake, Jamie hoped the hut would be empty, but it was a slim hope and he knew it. He stared at the body of the young crofter, lying just outside the blackened door, the head half severed.

These clansmen of his, on the borders of his land, looked to Jamie for protection. It was beside the point that his castle was far away, up in the hills, and he could not have reached these people in time. Whoever had done this simply did not fear The MacKinnion's wrath. Well, they would! By God, they would!

Black Gawain stumbled out of the blackened debris, choking from the smoke. He threw Jamie a look of relief, but Jamie was not convinced.

"Are you sure, Black Gawain?" he asked solemnly.

"She's no' there."

"But are you sure, Gawain?" Jamie persisted. "I'll no' be wasting time searching the hills. The lass would surely have come forward 'afore now if—"

"Curse you, Jamie!" Gawain exploded, but the hard look in his laird's eyes made him call to his own men and give the anguished order to search the hut, thoroughly this time, leaving no board unturned.

Three men went inside. All too soon they returned, carrying the body of a young girl.

"She was under the bed," a fellow offered lamely. Gawain took his sister and laid her gently on the ground, leaning over her.

Jamie tightened his grip on his reins. "At least she's no' burned, Gawain," he offered quietly, there being nothing else he could offer. "She suffered little pain."

Black Gawain did not look up. "No' burned, but dead nonetheless," he sobbed. "God, she shouldna have been here! I told her no' to marry that bastard. She shouldna have been here!"

There was nothing Jamie could say, nothing he could do. Except make those who had caused this horror pay for it.

Jamie rode on with the dozen men he had brought with him from Castle Kinnion. They saw what had happened to the first croft. The third croft in the line of damage was untouched, but two of its men were dead, old Ian and his youngest son. Many animals lay slaughtered, including two fine horses Jamie himself had given Ian.

He felt his anger becoming an open wound. This was no common raid, but unpardonable slaughter. Who could have done such terrible damage? There were survivors. He would have a description, some clue at least.

If Jamie had guessed countless names, the name given him would have been his last guess.

"Fergusson. Clan Fergusson, and nae mistake," Hugh said bitterly. "There were nigh a dozen of those cursed Lowlanders."

"You saw old Dugald himself?" Jamie asked tightly, his eyes flaming.

Hugh shook his head, but he did not waver. "The clan cry was clear. The plaid colors were clear. I've fought enough Fergussons to know their colors as well as my own."

"But you havena for two years, Hugh."

"Aye, two years wasted," Hugh spat. "Two years I could've been killing Fergussons sae I'd no' be mourning a father and a brother now."

Jamie said carefully, "It makes no sense, man.

There's many plaids resembling the Fergussons', our own included. I must have more than a war cry anyone could imitate and colors seen in the dark."

"It's doubt yer have, Sir Jamie, and none here are blaming yer." A crofter, one who had been warned by Simon, spoke up. "'Twas a cry I thought never to hear again after these two years of peace, but hear it I did as the cowards fled down the burn."

"I've been up the burn and seen the damage," another man stated. "'Tis what yer aiming to do about it we're waiting to hear, Sir Jamie."

Jamie was shocked by this challenge. Most of the men present were older. If his being only twenty-five wasn't bad enough, his boyishly handsome face made him seem even younger. Those close to him knew of his fierce temper and frequently harsh judgments, but these men had seen little of him in the two years since his father had died and he'd become laird of Clan MacKinnion. There had been no opportunity for them to fight alongside Jamie.

"You want me to lead you in revenge? I'll do that gladly, for whoever strikes at you strikes at me." Jamie returned their stares, boldly eyeing each man. None could mistake the cold resolve in his hazel eyes. "But I'll no' begin a long-dead feud again without good reason. You'll get your revenge, that I swear. But 'twill be gainst those guilty and no other."

"What more proof is needed?"

"A reason, man!" Jamie replied harshly. "I need

a reason. You all fought Fergussons in my father's time. You know they're no' a powerful clan. You know we outnumber them two to one, even when they're joined with the MacAfees. Dugald Fergusson wanted an end to the feud. My own aunt insists the feud never should have begun, so I agreed to peace when there was no retaliation after our last raid two years ago. We've no' raided them since, and they've no' raided us. So can one of you give me a reason for what happened here tonight?"

"A reason? No, but here's proof." Ian's oldest son stepped forward and threw a scrap of plaid at Jamie's feet. The plaid was several shades of green and gold, with gray stripes.

At that moment a band of thirty men appeared, crofters and their sons who lived close to Castle Kinnion and had been gathered by Jamie's brother.

"So be it," Jamie said ominously, slowly grinding the unmistakable Fergusson plaid under his booted foot. "We ride south to Angusshire. No doubt they will be expecting us, but no' so close on their heels as we will be. We ride now, to arrive at dawn."

Chapter 2

JAMES MacKinnion moved slowly. An enveloping mist still clung to the dewy ground, and he was sopping wet from crossing the second of the two Esk rivers. He was tired from lack of sleep and the rough ride south. They had had to ride more than a mile out of their way to find a shallow river crossing. All things considered, he was in a foul mood. And he couldn't squelch his disquiet. There was something wrong in all this, but he didn't know what it could be.

He was alone, having left his men shrouded in the dawn mist by the river's edge. Jamie and his brother and Black Gawain had separated in order to survey the area for signs of possible ambush. It was something he always did when a raid was expected, and this one surely was. And it was something he did himself, not as a display of courage, although, being alone, he risked being captured, but because the welfare of his clansmen was his responsibility alone. He would ask no man to do

8

what he would not do himself.

The mist swirled and parted before him in a gentle breeze, revealing for a moment a wooded glen not far ahead. Then the mist settled again, and the vision was gone. Jamie rode for it; the trees were a pleasant change from the barren moors and heather-clad hills.

He had never before been this far east on Fergusson land before. He had never raided Lowlanders in the spring before, either. Autumn was the time for raiding, when rivers were broad but shallow, and cattle were fat from summer grazing and prime for market. He had always crossed the river in direct line with Tower Esk, the home of Dugald Fergusson. The swollen water had made that impossible this time. But their delays were short ones, and he was confident they were less than an hour behind the attackers, even though he and his men hadn't found their trail. He would not give them time to celebrate their victory.

Jamie's anger warred with his common sense. He wondered about the wisdom of his decision to ride south without further reflection. He had reacted to what facts he had. In truth, he could not have done differently. Dead men demanded he ride to avenge them. A scrap of plaid demanded he ride south. Yet . . . why? He would have given anything for more evidence. The act bordered on insanity. Was he sure of what he was doing?

Not knowing for sure ate away at him and turned him sour on the task ahead. Dugald Fergusson could not fail to know that Jamie had it within his

power to wipe out his whole clan. The Mac-
Kinnions could do it alone, and they also had the
alliance of two powerful northern clans, through
the marriages of Jamie's two sisters.

More than five hundred men could be raised if
needed. Old Dugald must have known that. He had
known of the first alliance three years before, and
of the second just after Jamie's father died and Jamie made his first—and last—raid on the Fergussons as the new MacKinnion laird. Dugald had not
retaliated after that raid, even though it had cost
him twenty head of cattle, seven horses, and nearly
one hundred sheep. Dugald knew then he was no
match for the MacKinnions, and Jamie knew it, as
well.

There was no challenge in carrying on the long-
standing feud, so Jamie had let his Aunt Lydia
think she had convinced him to end it. It pleased
her to think so, and he liked pleasing her. She had
always been after him to marry one of Dugald's
four daughters in order to end the feud for good,
but he would not go that far. His one marriage had
ended so tragically. That was enough for Jamie.

He frowned, thinking how his aunt would react
when she learned where he had gone, and of the
total destruction his dark side called for. It could
very well make her retreat from reality and not return.

Lydia MacKinnion had not been quite right since
the MacKinnion-Fergusson feud had begun forty-
seven years before. She had witnessed the cause of
it—though she had never told what she saw or said

why Niall Fergusson, Dugald's father, had killed both of Jamie's grandparents, starting a vicious war that lasted ten years and wiped out half the men of both clans before it settled down to periodic raids that were solely for the lifting of livestock, a practice as common in the Highlands as breathing.

Perhaps Niall Fergusson had been insane. Perhaps insanity ran in their family and Dugald was insane. That was possible. And an insane man must be forgiven, maybe even tolerated. After all, wasn't his aunt just a little bit insane herself?

A calm settled over Jamie as he came to this conclusion. He could not punish a whole clan for the acts of a madman. His terrible upset about the whole affair was eased then. He would retaliate in kind, but not destroy them all.

The mist was rising steadily as Jamie entered the wooded glen. He saw that he could pass through it in a matter of minutes, the span of trees being no more than a hundred yards. He had ridden only about half a mile away from his men, but with no croft in sight he was beginning to wonder if he was even on Fergusson land, if they hadn't miscalculated and ridden too far downriver when they sought their crossing.

Then he heard a sound, and in a flash he slid off his horse and ran for cover. But when he listened again, he recognized the sound as a giggle, a feminine giggle.

Leaving his horse behind, he moved stealthily through the bracken and trees toward the sound. At that early hour, the sky was still gray-pink and mist still clung to the earth.

When Jamie saw her, he wasn't quite sure he believed the vision. A young girl was standing waist-deep in a small pool, the mist swirling about her head. She looked like a water sprite, a kelpie, unreal, yet real enough.

The girl laughed again as she splashed water across her naked breasts. The sound enchanted Jamie. He was mesmerized by the girl, rooted where he was, watching her play. She was frolicking and having a joyous time of it.

The water should have been freezing. The morning was cold. Yet the girl seemed not to notice the cold. Jamie didn't, either, after he had watched her awhile longer.

She was like nothing he had ever seen before, a beauty, and no mistake about it. In a moment she faced him, and he saw nearly all of her loveliness. Pearly white skin contrasted starkly with brilliant, deep red hair. Almost magenta, it was so dark and gleaming and long. Two strands waved around her breasts and floated in the water. And those breasts were tantalizing, round, high and proud in youthful glory, the peaks sharply pointed because of the caress of icy water. The tiny waist complemented the narrow shoulders and the taut belly, which dipped teasingly in and out of the water, revealing a gentle swell of hip as the girl moved around. Her features were unmistakably delicate. The only thing not clear to Jamie was the color of her eyes. He was not quite close enough to see, and the reflection of the water made them appear a blue so clear and bright as to be glowing quite impossibly. Was his imagination running wild? He wanted to move closer and see.

What he really wanted was to join her in the water. It was an insane idea, born of the strange effect she was having on him. But if he did move closer, she would either disappear—proving she was not real after all—or scream and run away. But what if she did neither? What if she just stayed there, let him come to her, let him touch her as he ached to do?

Common sense had fled. Jamie was ready to chuck his clothes and slip into the pool when the girl murmured something he couldn't hear. Suddenly there was a splash, and the girl reached for an object that came from . . . where? Jamie's eyes widened. Was she truly a sprite then, to invoke something and have it appear?

The object turned out to be a chunk of soap, and the girl began to lather herself with it. The scene was simple enough now, a girl bathing herself in a pool. The unearthly quality was gone, and Jamie's senses returned. But . . . soap falling into the water all by itself? He scanned the high bank opposite until he saw the man, or, rather, the boy, sitting on a rock with his back to the girl. Her guardian? Hardly. But the boy was watching out for her nonetheless.

Jamie felt the full weight of disappointment descend on him now that he knew he was not alone with the beautiful girl. The presence of the boy brought him back to reality. He had to leave. As if to point out his folly in tarrying, the first rays of sun broke through the glen, showing him the time he had wasted. His brother and the others would have all returned to the men by the river. They would all be waiting for him.

Jamie was suddenly sickened. Watching the girl, being transported to what seemed a sphere outside reality, he was appalled by the contrast between the lovely scene before him and the bloody one he would see in just a short while. Yet he could no more stop the one that was soon to happen than he could forget the one he was watching. Both seemed inevitable.

Jamie's last look at the girl was a wistful one. Beams of sunlight dotted the pool, and one touched the girl and lit her hair like a burst of flame. With a sigh, he turned away. That last vision of the mystical girl would be etched in his memory for a long time to come.

As he rode back to join his men, Jamie could think only of the girl. Who was she? She could be a Fergusson, some crofter's daughter, yet Jamie found that hard to believe. What man with such a beautiful daughter would let her bathe as naked as you please in an open pool? And he hated to think she might be a Fergusson. Even a beggar passing through Fergusson land would be preferable.

She might indeed be a beggar, he thought, bathing before she stopped at Tower Esk for a handout. The country swarmed with them, especially in the Lowlands where kirks were more numerous and the people more pious and charitable. But such a beautiful beggar? Possible, but doubtful. Who was she, then? Would he ever know?

The urge to go back to the glen and find out was strong, but his men were within sight, and now that the mist had cleared, Tower Esk could be seen in the far distance atop its fortified hill. Numerous crofts were visible, scattered over the moor. The time had come.

But Jamie was not as hell-bent on devastation as he had been earlier. The lovely girl had eased his anger, as had thoughts of his aunt and what warring would do to her. A wrong for a wrong would be exacted, but Jamie would be merciful. When he reached his men, he explained his change of heart. His word was law, so those who felt he was being too lenient could be damned.

Three crofts were destroyed that morning, the crops trampled, and all the stock lifted. But no women or children were killed. They were made to stand by and watch as their homes burned. The crofters who wanted to fight did—and died. Those who didn't fight were spared.

Jamie tarried at the scene of his vengeance, waiting for Dugald Fergusson to come if he dared. He burned crofts that could be seen from the tower battlements, but his band of men was large, and he knew Dugald couldn't afford to respond. It was really a challenge for vengeance, meant to humiliate his enemy. Once his men were satisfied with victory, he withdrew.

The feud was on again. Jamie was not pleased by it. He had enough troubles at home without bothering with the faraway Fergussons. The Fergussons had wanted this, and so it was.

But on the long ride home that day, Jamie was not planning future raids. He was thinking of a beautiful girl in a secluded glen, a mystical maiden with skin like pearl and hair of darkest flame.

Chapter 3

June 1541, Angusshire, Scotland.

S HEENA Fergusson stared out over the battlements of Tower Esk, gazing at the peaceful moor, her thoughts anything but peaceful. An early riser by nature, she watched the dawn sky brighten and challenge the pink heather below, and chafed because she was forbidden to leave the tower house, not even for a short brisk ride, not even with a dozen retainers riding beside her.

It wasn't fair. But nothing was going right these days, and all because The MacKinnion had decided, last month, to break the truce that had existed for two years. For two peaceful, carefree years Sheena had been allowed the freedom she had known as a child. The first of four daughters and Dugald Fergusson's favorite, she was always treated with the care of a treasured heir until the long-hoped-for heir finally arrived. After Niall was born, she was still the favorite daughter—but just a daughter.

Strange, but she had never resented Niall. She

had loved her little brother from the day of his birth. Six years old, a true hoyden, and spoiled terribly, she had been fascinated by the boy baby after the uneventful births of three sisters.

Their love surprised everyone. By rights, Niall should have been closest to his sister Fiona, for they were only a year apart. Yet it was Sheena he tagged after, Sheena he looked to for amusement, Sheena who gave him the love he needed as he grew from a wee bairn to a young lad. They were inseparable even now. Sheena was nineteen, long past a marriageable age, and Niall was only thirteen and still quite childlike most of the time.

During a moment of great maturity, Niall had agreed with their father that Sheena should stay within the tower walls. It was no longer safe in the countryside during the day. That was the most galling: the MacKinnions were the only clan to raid by day. All others, including their own, rode under cover of night. But the MacKinnions, ever bold, struck during daylight.

The fear that had prevailed this last month was disgusting, bringing all kinds of changes into Sheena's life—the loss of freedom, the threat of marriage, too many arguments. The fights with her sisters were nothing new, but the fights with her father were tearing her apart. And why must they fight? Was she wrong to want to marry a man she loved? Was it her fault she had yet to fall in love?

Oh, there had been talk, when she was a child, of a marriage that would create a powerful alliance, but that had stopped two years before, and she had assumed she would be allowed to have a love match. Her father had even said as much. He had taken her side every time her sisters pleaded with him to force her to marry so that they, in turn, could marry. Every one of them had her husband picked out already and was eager for marriage, even fourteen-year-old Fiona. They had had no problems finding love matches that were also powerful unions. Sheena had not had their luck.

But Dugald Fergusson had refused to rush Sheena. Nor would he allow any of his younger daughters to marry before she did, which would shame her. Now all that was suddenly changed. Now it was imperative that she choose a man from a powerful clan. And she must do it within the month, or her father would do it for her. Sheena was stunned. How could her father do that to her? He loved her. She was his pet, the jewel of Tower Esk, as he fondly called her.

But, deep down, she knew why. And although she hated it, she couldn't fault him, not really. He was protecting his clan, insuring their defense with powerful alliances. There would be a triple wedding. Sir Gilbert MacGuire had long ago asked for Margaret, after Sheena turned him down. Margaret, just turned seventeen, had been waiting a year and a half to marry Gilbert. And arrangements were also being made for sixteen-year-old Elspeth's choice, Gilleonan Sibbald, of whom Dugald heartily approved. It remained only for Sheena to make her choice. But there was no one she cared to spend the rest of her life with.

"I should have known I'd be finding you here, now that you canna ride off to chase the morning mist."

Sheena looked around, saw her mother's cousin, and dismissed him. Turning back to face the dawn, she said, "I dinna like your dogging me, Willie."

"I've asked you no' to call me Willie."

"William then." She shrugged. She was beginning to thoroughly dislike him, cousin or not. "What difference does it make? I'd rather no' be talking to you at all."

"Och, Sheena, you're a hard lass, and no mistake. And here I'm only looking after your best interests."

"Was it my best interests that made you tell my father I should be marrying now?" she asked sharply, her dark blue eyes piercing William with a look of pure venom. "I dinna think so, cousin. I think you had *your* interests at heart. But 'twill gain you naught, for I'll no' be marrying you!"

"I wouldna be so sure of that, Sheena," William replied coldly.

She laughed. The sound was altogether humorless. "You've done naught but defeat your own purpose, Willie. You've convinced my father well. He'll no' be letting me marry a MacAfee. We're already aligned with them, and he wants new blood in the family—thanks to you."

William ignored her bitterness, as he ignored all things not to his liking. "Dugald will agree to our marriage. I guarantee it."

"And how is that?" she sneered. "You have the

means to end the feud?"

"Nay, but Fiona's marriage can be moved up. She has her heart set on The Ogilvie's brother himself. Think of it, Sheena. An alliance with The Ogilvie is worth three with any other clans. It might even make the MacKinnions back down."

"Now you grasp at straws, cousin." Sheena's contempt was growing. "Nothing would make The MacKinnion run scared, and you know it as well as I. He's a savage Highlander. He lives to kill, as do all his clan."

William went on smoothly, "But your father would rest easy with an Ogilvie in-law, so he would have no objections to your marrying me."

"You always seem to forget I dinna want you," Sheena replied levelly. "Why is that, cousin? I've told you enough times. I told you earlier this year, I told you last year and the year 'afore that, but you never listen. I'm telling you again now, and I pray 'tis the last time. I dinna love you, and I dinna want a man nigh as old as my father for a husband. I dinna mean to hurt you, cousin, but your persistence makes me want to scream."

"Would you rather be marrying The MacKinnion then?" William shouted angrily.

The color drained from Sheena's face. "Are you daft?" she gasped.

"Nay, quite serious," William said, smug now that he saw her fear. "To marry The MacKinnion himself would end the feud, wouldn't it? Dugald would pounce on the idea if I encouraged it, for it has already crossed his mind."

21

"You lie!"

"Nay, Sheena. Ask him. Such a marriage would end the bloodshed and the lifting and even make the Fergussons prosperous for once."

Sheena's stomach knotted, for his reasoning was sound, awful though it seemed. And Dugald listened to William's advice much too often. But to marry The MacKinnion himself, a man so terrible that his first wife killed herself on her wedding night because of his brutal treatment! That was how the story went. Marrying such a man! She couldn't bear the idea.

"He wouldna have me," she said in a desperate whisper, shaking her head.

"He would."

"I'm his enemy, a Fergusson. He hates us all. He proved that by starting the feud again."

"The man would have you," William said firmly. "Any man with eyes would want you. The MacKinnion would no' just accept the offer of you, either. With his bold arrogance, he would demand you be given to him."

"You would do that to me, William?" she asked quietly.

William scanned her face, pleased that he had shaken her so deeply. "I want you for myself, Sheena. But if I canna have you, then aye, I would see you go to him to end this feud, for it kills MacAfees as well as Fergussons. Think about that, Sheena. And you think well, for soon again I'll be asking you to wed. I'll be expecting a different answer next time I ask."

Sheena watched his tall form walk away. She began to tremble. Of course she would choose her cousin over a savage Highlander, even though she couldn't bear the thought of marrying William. God, would her father really do that to her? Make her marry their terrible enemy? No, he wouldn't, not even to end the feud. Dugald loved her. He knew as well as they all did that The MacKinnion was an uncivilized brute. He had himself told her stories about James MacKinnion, terrible stories. The man had been raiding and killing since he was a child. His own wife had preferred death to his touch. William couldn't convince her father to condemn her to a life of beatings and cruelty.

Sheena left the battlements and went in search of Niall. He would give her courage. But . . . her problem still wouldn't be solved. She still had to marry someone—and soon.

Chapter 4

August 1541, Angusshire, Scotland.

SHEENA woke in the quiet hour just before dawn, and in only a few minutes she had braided her thick, long hair and donned the tunic and plaid that disguised her as a young lad. With a candle in one hand and a small bundle clasped in the other, she slipped from the tiny room that had been hers ever since she became estranged from her sisters and could no longer bear to share their much larger, more comfortable chamber.

Down a narrow corridor were five steps that led to Niall's bedchamber on another, higher level. There were several levels in Tower Esk, many small rooms and cubbyholes. There were only a few large chambers besides the hall on the second level, and the storage and dungeon below that.

Sheena's home was one of the newer tower houses that, more and more, across the Lowlands, were replacing large castles. Only a century old, Tower Esk was a family stronghold rather than a feudal fortress. Just a small fortified hall, really, it was designed simply and plain in appearance, although it did have little runs of crenellation on the parapets and balustrated galleries. Six stories high and taller than it was square, it was not as impregnable as a castle. But it would be no easy task to overtake it, either.

Sheena had grown up on the ever-disputed border between the Lowlands and the Highlands. The borderline was in dispute because, while the differences between the two areas were distinct differences in culture and language, the Fergussons were a mix of the two. The Highlanders were an uncivilized lot, a Gaelic-speaking people with perhaps one kirk per parish, sometimes not even that. They were hardly pious or God-fearing. And they thrived on war like no other people did.

The Lowlanders were more civilized because of their closer association with the English, their numerous royal burghs and grand abbeys. They were more pious, as well, with an abundance of kirks. Though, truth to tell, many of their Catholic priests and monks were not as devout as might be expected, their positions being mostly hereditary.

The Fergussons, in the middle, tried to maintain a balance. They spoke English because they were considered Lowlanders, but they knew Gaelic because they had come from the Highlands centuries before. And they had fewer dealings with the English or with royalty, and were less likely to forget the old tongue. They wore English fashions, true, and Sheena even had an aunt in Aberdeen who was a nun, but they were not pious, going to kirk perhaps once a month.

It was not pleasant being in the middle and being a small clan, ever troubled by the bigger clans and currently at war with a powerful Highlander. Lowlanders farther south lived in comparative peace. Not so the Fergussons. Sheena could certainly understand her father's hope for alliances and his need to use his daughters toward that end.

Opening the door to her brother's room, Sheena found him still fast asleep. But a quick shake altered that, and when Niall's eyes opened and saw the way Sheena was dressed, he groaned and ducked his head under the covers. She wouldn't have been dressed so if she hadn't meant to leave the tower.

"Come on now, Niall." Sheena shook him again.

"Nay."

"We'll be back 'afore the sun rises," she persisted, yanking his covers away. "You wouldna have me go alone, would you?"

Niall knew that determined tone well enough and could only grumble, "You'll be getting us both a skelping."

"Nonsense. No one's to know."

"I dinna like this, Sheena. No' for me, but for you. 'Tis dangerous to leave the tower these days. What if—"

"Dinna say his name!" Sheena snapped. "I'm sick to death of hearing that cursed name."

"That doesna change the facts, Sheena. He's raided five times in the last three months since he broke the truce. He rides our land as if it were his

26

own. How could I protect you if he came upon us on the moor?"

"That'll no' be happening, Niall, and you know it well. He doesna raid this early. He waits for the bright light of day for his dirty deeds, so there'll be no mistaking him for another.

"And what if he were to change his tactics?"

"He's too bold to resort to surprises," she scoffed. "Now dress yourself and be quick about it. Old Willie's the gatekeeper today, and he's blind as a bat, so there will be no trouble slipping past him."

A short while later, two small figures ran across the moorland. Horses would have saved time, but they would never have got out of the tower with horses. As it was, they had been delayed by the departure of an unexpected patrol. The five men would be able to do very little against a band of MacKinnions, but a party of scouts was better than no warning at all. That warning was becoming increasingly important, for Dugald feared more and more that the tower itself would be attacked, not just the crofts.

The sky was turning pink already, but Sheena would not let her spirits sink, even though her time in the glen would be cut short. Today was bathing day, and she planned to take impish pleasure in shocking her sisters by not bathing with them, for they would never guess she had already done so. It was just one of the little pranks she played on her sisters to get even for their constant nagging. Margaret was usually the first to call her wild and irresponsible, and to complain to their father that no man would have Sheena because she was slovenly, disrespectful, and much too bold.

Her father knew better. She wasn't really wild, and certainly not slovenly. He knew her love for swimming and riding, which was why he had forbidden her to leave the tower. She was a touch disrespectful, but only when her temper was riled did she dare argue with her father.

Sheena sighed. There had been a lot of that lately, especially the month before when he gave up expecting her to name a husband. He had done so for her. The only good thing about it was that it had put William out of the running.

"Will you join me this time, laddie?" Sheena asked as they reached the high bank that looked down on the little pool. "The water should be warm enough. Oh, it does look inviting!"

"And who'd watch over you, eh?" Niall shook his head and plopped down on his favorite rock. From there he could view the whole of the moor on this side of the glen.

"But you haven't swum once this summer, and I know you love it as much as I. In the spring you said the water was too cold, and then the trouble began."

"We shouldna have come here, Sheena," he said.

Sheena grinned at his stern look. "You worry too much, m'dear. Where's your sense of adventure gone? You havena once asked me to go fishing with you this summer, nor grouse hunting."

"'Tis no' that I havena wanted to."

"I know—the trouble." She sighed and stepped behind him to shed her clothes. "The MacKinnion's ruined all our fun this year. Soon 'twill be too cold to come here. I've only enjoyed my pool four times in these months, instead of twice weekly. Soon I'll be married, and then where'll I be swimming?"

"I doubt The MacDonough will allow you your sport, Sheena," Niall said. One of his moments of maturity was upon him.

"Dinna say that, little brother, or I'll no' agree to the vows," she said sharply.

Sheena dived into the crystal-clear water and came up in time to hear Niall call down to her, "Do you have a choice, Sheena?"

She frowned. Did she? Her father was firmly set on Alasdair MacDonough. He had heartily agreed to the match because MacDonoughs, who lived halfway between the Fergussons and the MacKinnions, were at peace with the MacKinnions and could help Dugald sue for peace.

She had met Sir Alasdair for the first time on the day they were betrothed, so she knew little about him. He was pleasing to look upon and not nearly as old as William, although not as young as she would have liked, either. He was about thirty-three years old. Her father was undoubtedly trying to please her by choosing a young, personable husband. She was sure of that—and just as sure that he hadn't detected the arrogance of The MacDonough. She had seen it, though, and knew he

29

was unbearably self-centered. He would probably put restrictions on her, and his pride would demand she conform.

Sheena bristled. "'Tis no' nice of you to remind me of my plight, Niall Fergusson," she called up to him, piqued. "I dinna see you facing anything so loathsome as marriage to a stranger."

"Nay, but Father has threatened to send me to an English court the next time I get into trouble. He says I'm too old to be pulling pranks and breaking rules."

"Aye, and so you are."

"So what am I doing *here,* I ask you?"

"Protecting me, just as I'll protect you from Father if we're found out. Dinna fash yourself, Niall. He'll no' send you away for something so harmless."

"Risking your life is no' harmless, Sheena," Niall retorted. "Do hurry."

He threw down her soap as a hint, and Sheena saw she wouldn't get a long swim. She began to wash herself, frowning at her own thoughtlessness. Niall really was terrified of being sent away to a court full of strangers, and English strangers at that. She knew it, yet she risked their father's wrath for a few moments of her own pleasure. It wasn't right. Niall came with her to the glen only because he loved her. If she got him in trouble because of it, she'd never forgive herself.

"I'll make it up to you, Niall. The next time you get into trouble, I'll take the blame. I used to, remember."

"Yes, I know you did."

"What can Father do to me when I'm to be married in two months?"

"Give you a taste of the taws."

"Och, he wouldna. I'm too old for the leather strap. Dinna worry about being sent away, Niall. But once I'm married and gone, you're on your own, laddie."

"I'll be raiding then, as Father promised. That'll be enough adventure to keep me out of trouble."

"You sound as if you look forward to raiding," Sheena said, shocked.

"Raiding the MacKinnions, yes. I'd give anything to meet The MacKinnion himself."

Sheena gasped. "Are you daft, Niall? He'd chop off your head. He's a mean one, and no mistake."

"I dinna believe all the stories about him."

"He's a thieving murderer! Have you forgotten six of our clan have died these last months?"

"And a like number of his clan, no doubt, since Father was honor-bound to raid them, as well. But you canna deny he's brave, Sheena, the bravest man we know of."

"I dinna deny he's bold, but you dinna have to be praising him."

"I respect his courage."

"Respect him all you like, just pray you never meet the man, or you'll be respecting him from your place inside a coffin."

Sheena finished her bath, left the pool, and wrung out her hair to braid it. As she donned her clothes, Niall spoiled the pleasant day by

31

announcing, "Cousin William returns today."

Sheena's eyes closed in dread. "Are you sure?"

"Aye."

"You've got to stay close to me, Niall. Please. If he finds me alone, he'll start his threats again."

"You managed to avoid him after he threatened the MacKinnion match."

"Aye. And fortunately Father decided on The MacDonough while Willie was away, and 'twas arranged 'afore he returned."

"You want Sir Alasdair then?"

"Better him than William. But I'm no' married yet," she pointed out. "There's still time for our cousin to cause trouble. I fear he's very bitter and would do it for spite."

"Why don't you just tell Father?"

Sheena shook her head firmly. "William would only deny it. He'd say I wanted revenge for some imagined slight. Father might believe him, for he knows I despise William. And he trusts him. William was Mother's favorite cousin."

Sheena could have bitten her tongue. Why had she mentioned their mother? She had died a few days after Niall's birth, and he foolishly blamed himself. It upset him to talk of her. Sheena had never been close to her mother, being her father's pride and joy, but Niall had never known her at all.

"I'm sorry, Niall. Come on, we'd best be getting home 'afore the sun gets much higher."

They had just safely reentered the tower house and gone around back to the kitchens when the commotion started. The patrol returned at a tearing gallop with an unconscious prisoner. Word spread through the house like quicksilver that the man captured was a MacKinnion.

That night, Dugald Fergusson was in his glory. He had a MacKinnion in his dungeon who could be ransomed for the return of all the Fergusson live-stock taken that summer. Just in time for market, too. It would be a prosperous year after all.

Killing the man was never considered. That would be suicide, bringing the whole MacKinnion clan down on them. To kill a man in a fair fight was one thing. To kill a prisoner was something entirely different.

Sheena slept that night with no thought for the man in the dungeon. William MacAfee was on her mind—and conceiving ways of avoiding him while he was a guest in the tower.

Niall slept not at all, for he could think of nothing else but the man in the dungeon. A MacKinnion, a real live MacKinnion!

Chapter 5

JAMES MacKinnion woke with a terrible ache in his head. There was a bump the size of an egg on the back of his skull. His eyes opened, seeing nothing but blackness. He decided to keep them closed against the pain. It was too much effort just yet to wonder where he was, or even if he might be blind. But the ache throbbed so badly that he couldn't drift back to sleep. Slowly, he became aware of things.

The coldness against his cheek was hard earth. The smell around him was stagnant. The tickling over his bare knees was from bugs, or worse. He sat up to swipe the pests away, but the pain shot through his head, and he lay back down ever so gently.

Where he was was beginning to disturb him. The last thing he could remember was being surrounded by Fergussons who had seemed to come out of thin air. But the truth was he had not been watching his back, but had had his eyes on the pool in the glen

34

where he had once seen that beautiful young girl. If he had not been off his horse, waiting there like a fool for her to appear, he wouldn't have been surrounded and struck over the head before he could even draw his sword.

So. He was captured. The smell and the dampness began to make sense. A dungeon, no doubt in Tower Esk. Jamie almost laughed. There was no fool like a stupid fool, and he was certainly that. He had acted like a lovesick boy, coming to that glen more than a dozen times in the last months, hoping just to see the girl one more time. Yet that wasn't the whole truth. He had hoped also to learn who she was. But she had never appeared. No doubt, as he had once supposed, she was a beggar passing through. He would never see her again.

He had ridden here alone, as he had the other times. Not even his brother knew where he had gone, for he had admitted his obsession with the girl to no one. It would be several days before his brother would begin to worry. Even then, no one would guess he was in a Fergusson dungeon.

How many days would he have to spend here before old Dugald let him go? Oh, Jamie had no doubt that he would be let go. Dugald couldn't afford to keep any MacKinnion prisoner. Even if he found out who Jamie really was, he would have to let him go.

The creaking of wood above alerted Jamie. He was no longer alone. But if he hadn't heard the trapdoor opening, he would have doubted his senses when a pixielike voice whispered, "Are you really a MacKinnion?"

The voice had no body. All was still pitch black. Cold, fresh air poured down on Jamie, and he welcomed it and breathed his fill before he answered, "I dinna talk to a body I canna see."

"I dare no' bring a light. Someone might see."

"Well, you'd best go then," Jamie said with a touch of humor. "It wouldna do for you to be seen talking to a MacKinnion."

"Then you really are?"

Jamie didn't answer. The trapdoor was quickly closed, then opened again a few minutes later. A small round head with a thatch of dark red hair peeked over the narrow opening in the ceiling. Dim light from a candle spilled down into what Jamie could see was a deep pit. The dungeon was about seven feet round, just a pit dug in the earth, its floor packed down hard. The dirt walls might have been climbed, but the trapdoor was in the middle of the ceiling, and, even if reached, it was undoubtedly kept bolted.

Jamie had seen dungeons like it before. They were convenient because no guard was needed. They were impossible to escape from. He would have preferred a stone dungeon. At least the air wouldn't have been as stagnant, and he might have had a little light.

"You didna eat your food."

Jamie sat up slowly and leaned back against the wall, a hand to his head to hold back the pain. "I dinna see any food."

"In the sack, over there by you." The boy

pointed. "They just drop it down. 'Tis bound so the bugs dinna get it 'afore you do."

"How thoughtful," Jamie replied tonelessly as he grabbed the sack and opened it. There was a chunk of oatbread and half of a small heathcock— fine for a peasant, but he was used to better. "If this is all that's allotted a prisoner, it looks as if I'll have to be escaping in order to get a decent meal."

"You're no' a guest, you know," the lad said stiffly.

"But I'll be treated as one if I'm no' to grow bitter over my confinement," Jamie replied casually, as though arrogance came naturally to him. "Old Dugald wouldna care for my anger, I can assure you."

"Och, but you're a bold one to be talking of revenge from where you sit."

"And who is it I'm talking to?"

"Niall Fergusson."

"I've no doubt you're a Fergusson, but which one?"

"I'm Dugald's son."

"The young laird, eh?" Jamie was surprised. "You're a wee one, to be sure."

"I'm thirteen," Niall said indignantly.

"Are you now? Aye, I've heard The Fergusson tried often enough to get you 'afore you finally came along." Jamie chuckled. Then he groaned as his head throbbed again.

"Are you hurt?" Niall asked with genuine concern.

"Just a wee bump."

Niall fell silent as the prisoner tore apart the bird and began to eat. It was a large man he was looking down on, wrapped in a green and gold plaid with two rows of tripled black stripes. His legs were long and hard-muscled, his chest wide. The plaid distorted the rest of his shape, loosely wrapped as it was, but Niall could guess by the size of him that the clothes hid a remarkably strong body. The man was young, his face smooth and boylike despite the hard jaw and firm lips, the narrow, hawklike nose. It was a face of strong character, and disgustingly handsome.

"You've golden hair," Niall said suddenly.

Jamie grinned and looked up at the lad. "You noticed, did you?"

"They say not many have golden hair like The MacKinnion himself."

"Och, well, there are those of us who can thank a Norman ancestor for golden hair."

"A Norman? Really? One of those who came with King Edward?"

"Aye, a few centuries back that was. You know your history."

"My sister and I had a good teacher."

"You mean your sisters. I know. You have four of them."

"Only one studied with me."

Niall paused, angry with himself for mentioning Sheena. It would be almost sacrilegious to talk of her with this Highlander. He shouldn't have come at all. Heaven help him if he were found! But he had been so full of curiosity that he hadn't been able to talk himself out of it.

"Do you know The MacKinnion well?" he asked the prisoner.

Jamie smiled, and his face softened. "You could say I know him better than any other man knows him."

"Are you his brother, then?"

"Nay. Why do you ask about him?"

"He's all anyone talks about. They say there's no man braver."

"He will be glad to hear it."

"Is he as terribly mean as they say?"

"Who says he's mean?" Jamie grunted.

"My sister."

"Your sister doesna know him."

"But she's heard more stories of him than I have," Niall replied.

"And no doubt told you all."

"Nay. She didna want to frighten me."

"Ha! I can see she has a low opinion of me. And which sister is this?"

But Niall didn't answer. He was staring at the man wide-eyed, for he had caught the slip of the tongue, even though the prisoner didn't yet realize it.

"'Tis you!" he gasped. "You're him! *The* Mac-Kinnion. And my father doesna even know!"

Jamie cursed himself silently. "You're daft, lad."

"Nay. I heard you!" he cried excitedly. "You said, 'She has a low opinion of me.' Not *him,* you said '*me.*' You're James MacKinnion!"

"Tell me this, lad," Jamie demanded. "What has

your father planned for me?"

"To ransom you back."

"And what would he be doing then if he thought I was The MacKinnion?"

"I dinna know," Niall said thoughtfully. "He'd probably let you go free without any demands at all. Would you no' prefer that?"

"Nay," Jamie replied, surprisingly. "'Tis no' something I'm proud of, being caught unawares, and I dinna care to hear your father gloat over it. 'Tis bad enough I'll get all the ribbing when I'm home."

"There's no shame in it," Niall insisted. "There were five against you."

"Five I could've taken if I'd been mounted and seen them coming."

"How could you no' see them on the moor?"

"I wasna on the moor. I was in a wooded glen." Nial gasped. There was only one wooded glen on Fergusson land, the glen where Sheena went to swim.

"Why were you there?"

Jamie did not notice the change in the boy's tone. "I'll no' be saying, for it only adds to my shame."

"You'll tell me if . . . if you want me to forget you're *The* MacKinnion."

Jamie wasted no time. "I've your word on it?"

"Aye."

"Very well, though I doubt you'll ken a man's foolishness. I was looking for a wisp of a girl I once saw bathing in the pool there."

Color rushed into Niall's face, turning him bright

40

pink with anger and shame. This man had seen his sister! She would be mortified if she knew. He was in an agony of shame.

"When did you see her?" Niall croaked.

"What?"

"When did you see this girl?"

"In the spring."

"And did you see her this morning?"

"Nay, the pool was empty." Jamie leaned forward hopefully. "Do you know the girl? I thought perhaps she was a beggar girl and was long gone."

"No Fergusson would be foolish enough to bathe in that glen," Niall lied stiffly. "She's likely gone, yes."

"Aye, I didna really believe I would see her again," Jamie agreed wistfully. "She was just passing through this place. Yet . . . I did hope otherwise."

"And what would you have done if you had found her again?"

Jamie grinned. "I dinna think you're old enough to know the answer to that."

"You're the savage my sister says you are, James MacKinnion!" Niall snapped furiously. "I'll no' be talking to you again!"

Jamie shrugged. The boy was innocent still. He didn't have a man's desires yet, so he couldn't understand them.

"Suit yourself, lad," Jamie said shortly. "But you'll be keeping your word?"

"I've given it—I'll keep it!"

When the trapdoor had closed and the bolt had

41

slid into place, Jamie regretted teasing the boy. He had enjoyed the company and doubted he'd get more very soon.

Niall returned to his room, but he got no sleep. After a while, his anger cooled, and he was able to think about the meeting rationally.

The laird of the MacKinnions was in their dungeon! Niall would be hard-pressed to keep that news to himself. And the fact that The MacKinnion had seen his sister in the altogether? It galled him that any man would have spied on her, let alone their enemy. But what was done was done, and he could do nothing about it except see to it that Sheena never swam naked there again.

And the rest of it? Niall was not so young that he hadn't understood Jamie perfectly well. The MacKinnion desired his sister and might have ravished her if he had found her at the pool. Niall would have been no defense against a full-grown man. Fortunately it hadn't come to that. The MacKinnion must have come to the pool only minutes after he and Sheena had left. But the man *had* come looking for her. He must never know that Sheena Fergusson and the girl he lusted after were one and the same.

Chapter 6

S HEENA was in the sewing room, dressed in one of her prettiest frocks, a bright yellow gown that contrasted vividly with the dark burnished red of her loose, flowing hair. She was unhappily working on her wedding gown, two of the household servants helping her. The gown was going to be lovely, two shades of blue, in rich velvet and silk, and the darker blue a near match to her eyes. But Sheena felt no pleasure in it. The wearing of that gown would bind her to a stranger and take her away from her home.

The sewing room was as good a place to hide as any, since her sisters were still abed and she need not be bothered by them yet. Even though her marrying was a certainty, their hostility had not lessened. Margaret's was worst, for she blamed Sheena for making her wait so long to marry Gilbert MacGuire. And all three of her sisters had always resented Sheena's resembling their father, who was quite handsome. While not overly large, he had a strong build, and his hair was the same deep red as hers, though he was nearly fifty. Only at his temples was there a little dusting of white. His eyes were as clear and as blue as hers.

Her mother had, in fact, been rather plain, and her sisters all resembled their mother. Elspeth did have their father's blue eyes and a slight tinge of red in her brown hair, but Margaret and Fiona had their mother's lackluster pale blue eyes and plain brown hair. Sheena had often wished she looked more like her sisters. Being called a beauty could be a cursed nuisance.

The rift between Sheena and her sisters was deep and very close to hatred. It didn't bother Sheena terribly, however. She had never been close to them. As the firstborn, she had learned skills at her father's side that he would not have taught her if Niall had been born sooner. Dugald had taken her fishing and hunting. When Sheena was five, after Fiona was born and Dugald had despaired of having a son, she got her first pony. Her interests did not include her prissy sisters, who flocked about their mother. The breach between them widened as the years passed.

Sheena still could not blame her father for the pain he was putting her through now. The clan came first. She understood that.

She was also in the sewing room because it was the last place William MacAfee would look for her. She still didn't know exactly what it was about William that she so disliked. He had a decidedly mean look about him, a subtle cruelty in his face that she had noticed even as a child.

His interest in her had started when she was only twelve. He was always pulling her aside to talk to her, scolding her for this or that, interrupting her play with Niall. When she was sixteen he had asked her to marry him. She had been as disgusted and as frightened of him then as she was now.

William held too much influence over her father, that was certain. And once her father made a decision about something, he was seldom swayed. That had worked against William when Dugald decided Sheena would marry The MacDonough. But Dugald's mind could be changed if the persuasion was powerful enough. Until she was married to Alasdair MacDonough, hateful though that idea was, she would not be safe from her cousin.

William and her father were, even now, below in the hall discussing how to contact the MacKinnions to demand the prisoner's ransom. She hoped Niall was with them, so that he could tell her what they discussed.

As if her thoughts had summoned him, Niall burst into the room. "So, here you are! I've been looking everywhere for you. I never thought to be finding you in here."

Sheena grinned. "Well, you have. What are you so excited about?"

Niall looked at the two servants, and Sheena dismissed them.

"Well, now, what has you in such a bother?" She patted the chair beside her, but Niall was too agitated to sit.

"I wasna to tell anyone!" he burst out, his light blue eyes aglow. "But I canna keep it in. I have to tell you, Sheena, but only you."

She smiled at his exuberance. Niall could get excited over the smallest thing, and each small thing was of great importance for a while.

"I've been to the dungeon!"

"When?"

"Very late last night."

Sheena was not amused now. "You know you shouldna have, Niall."

"I know, but I couldna help it," he confessed. "I *had* to see him."

"And did you?"

"Aye." Niall grinned now and rushed on. "And you wouldna believe the size of him, Sheena! And he has such a mean look about him. He talked to me like a man—well, most of the time he did."

"You talked to him!" she gasped.

"Aye, I did, and for a long time, too. But that's no' what I have to tell you, Sheena. 'Tis James MacKinnion we have in our dungeon. The Mac-Kinnion, not one of his men, but him! And he's as bold as they say."

Sheena felt cold, and suddenly it was as if she couldn't breathe. But Nial turned even colder and they both started as, behind them, Margaret Fergusson echoed, "*The* MacKinnion!" The door hadn't been shut properly, and Margaret had heard. She ran, then, and Sheena found her voice. "Go after her, Niall! She's surely gone to tell Father."

Nial raced through the doorway, but Margaret

46

was already running down the stairs that led to the hall. He could hear her shouting.

He turned to Sheena. She had never seen her brother look so miserable. "What am I to do?"

Her heart ached for him. "Dinna worry, Niall. You were no' forbidden to go near the dungeon. Father will be angry, but he'll no' punish you."

"It isna that, Sheena. 'Tis *him!* I gave him my word I'd no' tell about him!"

She was a touch angry that Niall should worry about breaking his word to a MacKinnion, even the laird himself. "Then you shouldna have told me," she snapped.

"But you're no' just anyone," he protested. "You wouldna have told."

"Well, but you see what happened?" She loved his devotion to her, but he had to understand.

"I know." Niall was near tears. "He'll hate me for this."

"What's got into you, Niall?" she cried. "You're a Fergusson. He already hates us all." She turned away and lowered her voice. "I just wish you'd kept the secret. What William will make of it with Father is what I fear."

Niall was doubly miserable. "Should I lie to Father? I can say Margaret was mistaken in what she heard, or I was only jesting."

"Nay, you canna lie, for Father will no doubt confront The MacKinnion, and who's to say he willna admit the truth? Why should he want it kept secret?"

"He's ashamed because he was caught."

"Och, men and their strange ideas are beyond me. He'll be released sooner now, so he should be glad. Father wouldna dare keep The MacKinnion."

The Fergusson bailie came to the door to tell Niall he was wanted below.

"You'll come with me, Sheena?" Niall asked, his eyes pleading.

"Aye, if you'll promise no' to leave William alone with Father after I'm gone. Father will send me from the room when they discuss what to do, but I must know what William suggests. So you must stay."

"I'll stay if they let me."

Dugald Fergusson was more upset than Sheena had expected. William's eyes were drawn to her the moment she walked into the hall. There was a smug look about him that boded ill. Niall was standing before their father.

"'Tis true then, you were down to the dungeon?" Dugald demanded.

"Aye."

"You know you had no business there?"

"Aye."

"Is it true what you told your sister? Have we James MacKinnion himself down there?"

Niall hesitated a moment too long before answering, and Dugald backhanded him. Sheena gasped and moved to Niall's side, her eyes furious.

"You didna have to hit him!" she shouted at her father. "He's done naught that was so terrible."

"He knew we had James MacKinnion but he didna tell me so."

"He would have."

"When? After I'd ransomed a man I thought only a crofter? Sweet Mary!" Dugald blustered. "I've a son who keeps secrets from me and a daughter who defends him!"

"What secret?" Sheena snapped. "If you'd gone down and talked to the man yourself, you'd have found out easily enough who he was."

Dugald glared at her, but the truth of that was plain. And he was wasting time bickering. The fact that he had James MacKinnion in his dungeon turned his blood cold. For all he knew, the Mac-Kinnions were planning an attack on the tower at that very moment.

"I've got to let him go," Dugald said wearily. He sounded defeated.

"Dinna be hasty, now," William warned. "The man's been injured by us and shamed. He'll no' take kindly to that. He's probably even now plotting the revenge he'll have as soon as you release him."

"But I canna keep him in the dungeon."

"Aye, you can. A few days will no' hurt, until you devise a means to protect yourself."

"You have something in mind?"

"Aye, a way to end the feud for good."

Sheena stiffened. "Dinna listen to him, Father! Just let the man go. For his release, make him give his word to end the feud."

"The word of a MacKinnion is worthless," William said flatly.

"You dinna know that!" Sheena turned on him

hotly, eyes flashing.

"Enough blathering," Dugald interjected angrily. "This doesna concern you, Sheena, so get you gone."

"But—"

"Go! Your betrothed comes this night to plan the wedding, so prepare yourself." He waited until she had stalked from the hall before he looked at his son. "Off with you, too, Niall. And so there'll be no mistake, if you go near the prisoner again, 'tis the English court for you!"

Sheena waited on the stairs for Niall, but the distance was too great for her to hear what William was telling her father. But she knew.

"God help me, Niall, I dinna know what I'll do if I'm given to The MacKinnion."

"Dinna talk like that," he scolded.

"I hate William!" she hissed furiously. "I swear I'd kill him if I didna think I'd burn in hell for it."

"You're worrying 'afore the fact, Sheena. 'Tis doubtful Father would listen to Willie this time. You're already betrothed. 'Twould mean breaking that and starting a feud with the MacDonoughs."

"You think that would matter if a MacKinnion match were possible?"

Niall frowned. "I know, but you're still worrying 'afore you should. There's naught to say The MacKinnion would accept you. Why should he?"

"I said the same to William, but he claims any man would want me if he saw me," she replied miserably. "Och, why do I have to look like this?"

Niall's heart sank as he remembered. The Mac-

Kinnion *had* seen Sheena. And he *did* want her. She was terrified of him, and Niall could not blame her. Only what could he do to help her?

"He doesna know you're the one he wants, Sheena," Niall tried to reassure her.

Her brow knit in curiosity. "Now what did you mean by that, I'd like to know?"

"I . . . I mean he hasna seen you yet, so he canna know if he would want you or no'."

"Aye, but what if Father shows me to him?"

"I'll hide you if I have to," Niall said impulsively, reminding Sheena that he was, after all, just a child.

"I wish you could, Niall, but I'd like to know where a body could hide on the open moor. There's no crofter would go against their laird to take me in."

"I'll think of something. Dinna fear."

For his sake, she smiled. "I'll hold you to that, little brother. For I swear I'll no' wed James MacKinnion. I'd rather die."

Chapter 7

JAMIE shielded his eyes against the sudden light. And then, just as abruptly, a large bundle was pushed through the trapdoor. Bedding? Even a pillow? Jamie frowned. Why would he be getting special treatment? The light disappeared and then returned as a rope ladder slid through the opening. A man started climbing down the ladder. He had two hefty sacks tied to a rope strung behind his neck. He set them down as soon as he reached the floor and turned to face Jamie.

"Your dinner," he said, indicating the sacks. "There's wine, and a candle, and some other things."

Jamie kept his face blank. "You treat all your prisoners so lavishly?"

"I'll no' be mincing words with you, lad. I know who you are. We've no' met 'afore face to face, but I'm Dugald Fergusson."

Jamie got to his feet. It was only common courtesy.

52

"And who is it I'm supposed to be?" he asked.

Dugald raised a reddish brow. "You deny you're James MacKinnion?"

Jamie sighed. "Nay, I'll no' deny it. So where does that leave us, Fergusson?"

"I dinna like it that you're here any more than you do. But as it is, I have you, and I would be a fool no' to benefit from it."

"Naturally." Jamie sighed. "Have you contacted my clan then?"

"Nay," Dugald replied with a slight hesitancy. "I'll no' deal with them, but with you."

"With me? And how is that?"

"It has been suggested to me that you should marry one of my daughters."

Jamie tensed, trying not to look shocked. It was the last thing he'd expected to hear. "And who hates your daughters so, to make such a suggestion?"

Dugald frowned. He hadn't thought of that. William had suggested Sheena in particular, not just one of his daughters. Did William, in fact, hate Sheena? It bewildered him to think that. He had been aghast at William's suggesting Sheena, but not at the idea itself, for it was something he had long considered. William's thinking was sound.

"I dinna like your tone, MacKinnion."

"And I dinna like your suggestion!" Jamie snapped. "If I ever marry again, and I have no intention of doing so, it certainly wouldna be a Fergusson."

"Dinna think I like giving you one of my

daughters!" Dugald replied sharply.

"Then why are we discussing this?"

"I want peace, lad."

"Do you?" Jamie said dryly. "You should have thought about that 'afore you began the feud again."

Dugald was stunned. "*I* didna break the peace! You did!"

Jamie might have laughed if it weren't so pathetic. He had been right about Dugald Fergusson. The man was insane, and no mistake. He would get nowhere arguing with a man addled in his wits.

He sighed. "If 'tis peace you really want, I'll give it to you. You have my word on it."

"Och, lad, I wish I could accept your word, truly. But I'd be a fool to trust you."

"That leaves you nowhere, then."

"Nay, it leaves you here, permanently, unless you accept one of my daughters and agree to trouble us no more."

"Old man." An iciness crept into Jamie's tone. "You keep me here at great risk, you know."

"I'm no' so sure. I dinna think we'll be attacked if attack would put your life in danger."

Jamie nearly exploded. "You threaten my life, and my men will tear your tower down stone by stone."

"Then you'll die!" Dugald shouted, just as angry. This was not going the way William had said it would. Yet he was committed to this plan, this way of getting a treaty.

"You'll change your mind when you're here long

enough," Dugald said, not all that confidently, however.

The words made Jamie seethe. The man would not tell his clan that he was here. He tried a different tactic.

"Very well, Fergusson. I'll marry one of your daughters, if you'll agree to my terms."

Dugald was surprised, and leery. "You're no' in a position to demand terms."

"Then we've no more to talk about."

Dugald glared at him. "What terms? I'll hear them. I am a reasonable man."

"I was married once 'afore."

"Aye, there's no' many dinna know that."

Jamie shrugged. The tragedy of his marriage was well known, but few knew the truth.

"I dinna know my wife, nor she me, 'afore the wedding," Jamie continued coldly. 'I'll no' go into more of it, for 'tis something I never talk about. Enough to say . . . the marriage was a mistake."

"What has that to do with my daughter?"

"If I had tried the girl I married 'afore the wedding, I'd have known she was so frightened of men she couldna bear a man's touch. I swore I'd never marry again without trying the girl first. Are you willing for me to try all four of your daughters 'afore I choose one?"

Dugald had turned bright red even before Jamie was finished. "There will be no trying of my daughters—nor handfasting, either!" he growled. "And 'tis only three daughters I'm letting you choose from, no' four!"

Jamie's humor returned and he couldn't resist baiting Fergusson. "You've four daughters, Fergusson, and no' one wed yet? What is wrong with the one you're no' offering me?"

"She's betrothed."

"You surprise me, old man. You think I dinna know what goes on here? That I'm no' aware of the three matches you've made in the last months, and with which clans? If 'tis your youngest you're no' offering, why no' say so?"

"You can have my youngest, though if you've any decency, you'll no choose her. She's too young to wed," Dugald retorted. "'Tis my oldest you canna have."

"Why? Has she a love match?"

"Nay, she's the only one who doesna want to marry yet, and if we have peace, she'll no' have to."

"Ahhh . . . now I ken. She's your favorite, eh? Too good for the savage MacKinnion?"

Dugald wouldn't answer. "When you're tired of this hole, lad, I'll let you see my daughters and make a choice." Jamie's humor was gone, and his voice was coldly final. "I wasna jesting when I said I must try my wife 'afore marrying her."

"You'll change your mind after a while in here."

Soon Jamie was alone again and doubly furious. To think he had been fretting about facing the jesting of his kin! There had never been the slightest notion that he wouldn't be released.

There would be no cause for worry, even now, if only his clan knew he was there. Old Dugald had just been bluffing about that. Faced with an actual attack, he would have no choice but to let Jamie go. But who was to tell his clan he was there?

For hours he contemplated revenge, and soon the empty wine flask lay in his lap. But his anger kept him sober. He devised countless ways to make an unwanted wife suffer. And—sweetest revenge—he would not kill Dugald Fergusson, but take him prisoner and daily report to him the abuse of his daughter. Too bad it could not be the favorite daughter.

Jamie's anger buzzed around him. He could not remember ever feeling so frustrated. Even when his first marriage was arranged for him, he had not really felt trapped. He had not wanted the Mackintosh girl. She had been a bonny lass, but a stranger. His father had wanted the match, and so it was done. He would not even have considered disobeying his father's wish. Afterward, both father and son greatly regretted the marriage. Instead of an alliance, they made fresh enemies, for the Mackintosh laird blamed them for his daughter's death.

The creaking of the trapdoor signaled that Jamie was to have more company. He was too incensed to speak to the laird again. "If that's you, Fergusson, I'll thank you to leave me be. I'm no' finished yet devising all the ways I'll be making your daughter suffer when she's my wife."

Jamie heard a gasp and leaned forward to try to see into the opening. "If that's no' you, old man, then who?"

"'Tis me."

"Who is me?" Jamie growled.

"Niall Fergusson."

"Is it now?" Jamie sneered, leaning back against the hard wall. "The very lad who keeps his word for but a few hours? Come to gloat, have you, over your fooling The MacKinnion into believing there was honor in your oath?"

"I didna mean to betray you," Niall said in a weak, frightened voice.

"Now you insult me with lies. There is no half measure in a betrayal."

"But I told only my sister," Niall protested. "She would have kept the secret."

"Then the bitch—"

"Dinna call her that!" Niall cut him off with such fury that he surprised both of them. After a moment, with more control, he said, "She told no one. 'Twas another sister who overheard me in the telling and ran to my father. I couldna stop her. But I dinna disclaim the responsibility. The fault was mine. 'Tis why I risked coming here again—to tell you how sorry I am."

"You canna be as sorry as I, lad," Jamie said bitterly. "And I swear if I had my hands around your neck at this moment, you'd see how I repay those who betray me."

Niall's breath came with difficulty, as if those very hands were indeed about his neck. "What did my father say to make you so angry?"

"Dinna jabber now and pretend you've no idea!" Jamie hissed.

"But he didna tell me. He's no' happy that I kept your identity from him."

"Then let me have the honor of telling you we'll be brothers-in-law 'afore long," Jamie said with heavy sarcasm.

"I dinna believe you!" Niall replied raggedly. "He wouldna give her to you. She's his favorite."

Jamie's brows narrowed thoughtfully. "You dinna like the idea of my marrying your sister?"

"Why should you?"

"Because your father willna let me out of this hole until I do."

Niall sucked in his breath. "But your clan will come."

"He intends to hold them off by threatening my life. He has it all planned. Your father has made certain I will marry your sister."

"But she'd rather die than marry you," Niall groaned.

Jamie laughed. It was obvious that the father's favorite was also the son's. Let him think his beloved sister was the one Jamie was to marry. He deserved to suffer, if only for a short while.

"She will indeed wish for death once she is mine . . . but I'll make sure she lives," Jamie said ominously.

"You wouldna really hurt her, would you?"

"Aye, I would. For 'tis forced I am to marry her, and I dinna like being forced."

"But 'tis no' *her* fault," Niall insisted. "She has no say in this, either!"

"Your father is no' considering that, so I willna,

either," Jamie said darkly.

Such vindictiveness was beyond Niall, and he was getting more and more frightened. "You have no' seen my sister, MacKinnion. She is a rare beauty. Truly, you would be pleased to have her for your wife."

"Lad, you dinna ken," Jamie replied coldly. "It doesna matter if she is the most bonny lass in all of Scotland, she's her father's daughter, and I'll make her suffer for being that. After I wed her and take her home with me, she'll never leave my castle. She'll be locked in a tower forever. I'll visit her twice a day, once to beat her and once to rape her. That is the life she will live."

There was only silence, and after a while Jamie said, "You've naught to say, Niall Fergusson?"

"If I thought you'd really treat my sister so, I'd have to kill you."

Jamie laughed. "You're welcome to try, if you like. But you ken you'll be cutting your own throat and your sister's and even your whole family's. You won't kill The MacKinnion and live long enough to tell about it."

The trapdoor slammed shut. Jamie's mouth tightened in a snarl. Taunting the boy had not relieved his smoldering rage.

Before an hour had passed, the trapdoor opened again, and Niall poked his head over the opening. Jamie shrugged. He had known the boy wouldn't keep the story to himself. He was too frightened.

"So you've confronted your father, have you?"

"Nay. 'Twill do no good to try to change his

mind. And I told you, he's no' happy with me right now. He'd no' listen to me one way or the other."

Jamie relaxed. The boy had not come back to call him a liar. He still didn't know the sister he feared for was safe from Jamie.

"So what has brought you here again, lad?" he asked.

"I canna face my sister tomorrow, knowing what I know," Niall said miserably. "I canna bear it that she'll be suffering. You've confirmed what she already believed about you. 'Tis why she'd rather die than go to you."

"You think I'll let another wife of mine kill herself?" Jamie snapped. "She'll no' die. I'll see to that!"

"I wonder which is better," Niall responded brokenly.

"You've a lot to learn, lad," Jamie sneered. "Where there's life, there's hope."

"You dinna give *me* much hope," Niall said, but plunged ahead anyway. "I've come to plead with you no' to hurt my sister for what was none of her doing. Please."

Jamie was touched. The boy had courage. And he loved his sister.

"You listen to me, lad, and listen well. I've no sympathy for this sister of yours. 'Tis your father you'll have to plead with. I've no choice in this matter, not really."

"You're wrong. You could treat her fairly if you wanted to."

"But I don't want to. Why should I? I'm naught

but a savage, remember?"

"Then I canna let you wed her."

"If you've a way to stop it, lad, you have my gratitude." Jamie gave the promise lightly, for he was past hope, and he couldn't take the boy very seriously.

"I'll let you go," Niall stated after a pause.

"What's that?"

"I'll let you go," Niall said firmly. "'Tis the only way. You'll be gone, and she'll be safe from you."

Jamie jumped up. He could hardly contain his sudden excitement. "Are you serious, lad?"

"Did I no' say it?"

"When?"

"Now, while the tower sleeps."

Without further ado, the ladder came sliding through the opening. But it stopped just short of Jamie's outstretched hand, then snapped back several feet.

Jamie was beside himself with disappointment. "'Tis a cruel game you're playing, lad?"

"Nay," Niall assured him. "But I'm remembering what you said about getting your hands around my neck. You'll no' kill me when you're free, will you?"

Jamie laughed. "You're no' to fear, lad. If you get me out of this tower, you'll have my friendship for life."

The ladder slid all the way down, and Jamie climbed it quickly, stiff though he was. The boy was gullible to believe him, yet Jamie had meant what he said. If he could safely escape Tower Esk, he'd owe the lad, and he wouldn't forget that.

"Och, but you're bigger than you seemed," Niall said, awed when The MacKinnion was standing next to him.

"And you're as wee as I supposed," Jamie grunted. Now that he was out of the dungeon, he wanted to get away. "If you'll just show me where the stable is—"

"Nay, you canna go there!" Niall gasped, already regretting his decision. "Men sleep in there. You'll be discovered, and I will have risked all for naught."

"I'll no' be leaving without my horse, lad. But dinna fear. I'll kill no one unless I have to. I'm out of that hole, and I'll no' be put back in it."

"But the alarm will be given."

"It doesna matter, lad. Once on my horse, they'll never catch me. Ah, lad, you worry over minor things," Jamie said as he started moving through the storage area toward the stable. "I've told you I'll no be caught."

Niall was right behind him. "'Tis myself I fear for, MacKinnion," he admitted reluctantly. "You'll be gone—but I'll be left here to take the blame."

Jamie turned around sharply, and Niall nearly ran into him. "You're welcome to come with me, lad."

"I'm no' a traitor!" Niall said, aghast. "What I did I did for my sister's safety. Otherwise, I'd no' have let you go."

'I know that," Jamie said softly. "And, in fairness, there's something I must tell you. Your oldest

63

sister, she wasna—"

Jamie didn't have a chance to finish his confession because light appeared on the stairs nearby, and Niall pulled him back between two large casks of meal.

"Niall," a girl's voice called out, "Niall, if you're down there, answer me. Niall!"

"Who is it?" Jamie whispered.

"My sister. She probably went to my room and found me gone, so she's looking for me."

Jamie straightened from his crouched position. "I think I'd like to see the lass who warrants such devotion."

"Nay!" Niall panicked and held on to Jamie's arm for dear life. "She'll scream if she sees you. She'll give you away 'afore you even reach the courtyard. You'll be trapped down here, and without a weapon."

"I suppose," Jamie relented. "And now that you mention a weapon, I'll be needing one."

"I'll no' help you there, MacKinnion. 'Twould be helping you kill my kin. That I canna do."

"Aye, you've done enough. I'll make do." Jamie had seen a board he could make use of once the way was clear to mount the stairs.

But the light on the stairs was still there. The girl didn't call again, however, and after several moments, the light dimmed, but only a little. Then there was another voice at the top of the stairs, and Jamie steeled himself.

"What do you here at this hour?"

Jamie heard Niall groan.

"And who is that?"

"My cousin William."

"Will he come down here?"

"I dinna know. Shh!"

"Well cousin?" The man spoke again.

"I was . . . 'tis none of your affair, Willie!" the girl snapped.

"Gone down for a peek at your future husband, eh?" William chuckled.

"I'd no' go near him, and you know it well."

"No," William conceded, but added spitefully, "you'll be seeing him soon enough—when you wed him."

"You're a bastard, and no mistake, William MacAfee!" the girl hissed. "Let me pass."

"You still didna answer. What were you doing out here?" William's tone was sharp.

"I couldna sleep. I went for a walk."

"Sure you werena trysting with MacDonough 'afore the betrothal's broken?"

"If I was, that is none of your affair! Many things are none of your affair!"

The light moved away, but it was several minutes before the man's footsteps moved away, as well. "Your sister doesna like her cousin, eh?"

"Nor do I," Niall replied bitterly. "'Twas his idea she be given to you, and for *spite*. He wanted her for himself, you see, but she wouldna have him. The arrangement with you was only for spite."

"And The MacDonough's here? Your cousin said she might be trysting with him. Would she?"

"She wouldna do that!" Niall replied indignantly.

"She doesna even know her betrothed. But aye, he's here. He came this evening."

"You know I have a treaty with Sir Alasdair," Jamie chuckled. "If he's here, he'll no doubt be blamed for setting me free."

"You think so?" Niall asked, hopeful for the first time.

"Aye. Your father would naturally suspect a MacDonough 'afore a Fergusson."

"But The MacDonough doesna know you're here."

"He could have overheard talk. Cheer up, lad. And dinna take the blame unless you have to."

Jamie picked up the board, and Niall led the way to the courtyard and pointed out the stable and gate house. "They should all be asleep," Niall whispered.

"You'd best be off to bed yourself, lad. If the alarm is given, you dinna want to be found outside your own room. I just hope they won't know I'm missing till morning."

"I'll no' see you again then, will I?" Niall said regretfully.

"Nay, lad, 'tis doubtful we'll meet again. You're a brave one, Niall Fergusson, and no mistake. I won't forget you."

"And you're a mean one, James MacKinnion," Niall returned with a grin. "I won't forget you, either. You wouldna have made me a good brother-in-law, but you're a fine enemy."

"Or perhaps a friend," Jamie said, and tousled the boy's dark red hair. "I meant what I said about that. But I'm off now. Truly, I hope you dinna suffer for my freedom."

"Maybe I willna have to. As you said, The MacDonough is here and will be suspected. My sister doesna want to marry him anyway, so I'll no' mind if he takes the blame."

Jamie laughed. "Always you have your sister in your thoughts. And I never even learned her name."

"If my father didna tell you, I'll no' do so. Goodbye to you, and Godspeed, MacKinnion."

Chapter 8

SHEENA woke later than usual, for which she blamed her midnight search for her brother. The sun was already peeking through her tiny window as she dressed and hurried to Niall's room. He was still abed.

It took several hard shakes to stir him, and even then he groaned but wouldn't open his eyes. Sheena was not daunted.

"Come on now, little brother." She shook him again.

"Och, Sheena, leave me be," he grumbled. "I didna get much sleep."

"I want to know why," she said sharply, remembering her fear when she couldn't find him in the middle of the night. "I came here last night to talk to you, but you were gone. Where were you, Niall?"

He didn't answer. He had fallen back to sleep. Impatient, she slapped his backside, none too gently.

"Where were you, Niall?"

"I canna tell you, Sheena," he mumbled. "Truly, you dinna want to know."

She frowned. And then a chill raced through her. Where else would he have been that she wouldn't want to know about but with The MacKinnion?

"Och, Niall, I pray you're no' found out," she whispered, but he wasn't listening.

She left him to his sleep. The hall was nearly empty. Only one servant was there, looking at the half-eaten breakfasts scattered over the tables. Sheena viewed the cold bannocks and barely touched bowls of porridge and cream, and her uneasy feeling deepened.

"What is going on, Alice?" she asked the servant. "Where are my father and his men?"

"'Tis what I'd like to be knowing, lass," Alice replied testily. "There was a to-do in the courtyard, and the bailie came running in to see your father. Then everyone ran out of here."

Sheena headed for the small courtyard, but before she reached the doors, Margaret and Elspeth stepped through them, blocking her way.

"So there you are." Margaret took her usual disagreeable tone. "Where were you during all the fuss?"

"I only just came down," said Sheena. "What has happened?"

"You havena heard?" Elspeth gasped. "The MacKinnion escaped. Father's no' said so yet, but of course The MacDonough helped him. Who else?"

69

"This better no' break your betrothal, Sheena," Margaret added coldly. "I'll no' stand to have my wedding delayed any longer. Nor will Gilbert."

They left Sheena without noticing her reaction. She was standing stock-still, and her whole body tingled from a rushing of blood, as if it were flowing right out of her. Alasdair hadn't known The MacKinnion was there, so Alasdair couldn't have released him. *Oh, Niall, Niall,* what have you done? Sheena cried silently.

She didn't have to ask him. Somehow, she knew her brother had let The MacKinnion go. But why? She took a deep breath, steadying herself against the doorway. She knew the answer. It was William's threat and her father's decision. Rather than let her wed the cruel enemy, Niall had released him.

Astonishment and fear turned to relief, and Sheena wanted to rush upstairs and shower her brother with grateful kisses. She need no longer fear the savage Highlander! Just possibly, The MacDonough would be blamed, and she wouldn't have to wed him, either.

She was smiling happily when the hall began to crowd and she met her father's frowning countenance.

"Why are you so happy? There's naught to be cheerful about," Dugald said coldly.

"I'm glad he's gone." Sheena wasn't afraid to admit that much. "You would have wed me to him, and I'd never have forgiven you for it.

Sheena hadn't seen William's tall frame because

70

her back was to him, but he moved to stand beside her father. "You wanted a reason, Dugald. Now you have it."

Sheena looked from her father's stern face to William's accusing expression. "What do you mean?"

"Do you deny you were in the courtyard late last night?" Dugald asked silkily.

"I couldna sleep, Father, so I went for a walk. Where is the harm in that?"

"An easy excuse," William replied, his tone deliberately dry.

"And what was your excuse for being there, cousin?" Her eyes shot sparks at him. "You were up and about at the same time. You failed to mention that."

"I dinna need an excuse." He glowered at her. "'Twas no' *I* who wanted The MacKinnion gone. You've already admitted that you did."

Sheena gasped, his intention clear. "So you think *I* let him go?"

"Either you or your brother did," William said sharply.

Outraged, Sheena demanded, "How dare you accuse Niall? He was forbidden to go near the dungeon, and he wouldna have disobeyed."

"She's right," Dugald said gravely. "The lad is no' in question."

"But I am?" Sheena turned to her father, incredulous. That he could even consider such a thing!

When he didn't answer, Sheena began to panic. His silence accused her. But how could he?

71

Others had gathered around to hear the exchange, and Sheena could see herself being condemned. Even her betrothed had appeared, looking thoroughly appalled. How dare he? And why had her father not accused him?

Sheena's temper had ignited. She pointed at her betrothed. "I want to know why I am accused 'afore *him?* He had more reason than I!"

Alasdair's gray eyes stabbed Sheena with their sudden intensity. "I'll no' answer that charge," he said stiffly. "Nor will I marry a wench who turns on her betrothed and betrays her own family, as well!"

As he stalked from the hall, Margaret screeched, "He's broken the betrothal! 'Tis certain she planned this!"

The faintest satisfaction reflected in Sheena's darkly glowing eyes, but her father mistook it and growled, "Is that true, Sheena?"

She stiffened. "I didna want to marry him, as you well know, but I wouldna go to such lengths to prevent it. Now tell me why you've let him go without questioning him about this?"

"With such an important prisoner below, do you think I'd let an ally of his roam about freely?" Dugald's reply was sharp. "MacDonough's room was watched, and I am assured he didna leave it once all night."

That left only her with reason enough to free the Highlander—her and Niall. But Niall wasn't suspected, and she would keep it that way. He had done it for her. She wouldn't let him suffer for that.

She thanked heaven he was not there, for he would have spoken up. It hurt that her father was so quick to believe her guilty.

"Have you done this thing, Sheena?"

"'Tis too late to be asking me that, Father," she said, her voice choked. "You've already found me guilty. I see it in your eyes. How can you believe this of me?"

"There, she canna deny it," William said quickly. "She deserves hanging for the traitor she is." He was thinking fast, knowing he mustn't give Dugald time to consider.

"I'll no' be hanging my daughter for something she did in desperation," Dugald growled. "She thought she was to marry The MacKinnion, and since I didna tell her so, only you could have told her. You're as much to blame as she is, so I'll thank you to stay out of this from here on."

William had the sense to remain silent.

"You canna mean to just forget this, Father!" cried Margaret. "You've always favored her over the rest of us, and look how she's repaid you."

"That's enough, lassie."

"Nay! I'll have my say," Margaret insisted. "I'll no' have my wedding delayed more because of her. You've made me wait because you didna want to shame her, but now she's shamed us all. Her betrothal's broken, and no other man will ever have her, for if she'll betray her own family, she'll betray her husband. She canna be trusted ever again."

"You'll have your wedding as planned, Margaret," Dugald said in a tired, saddened voice.

Perhaps he knew he'd been too hasty in blaming Sheena. But it was too late to reconsider.

"She'll be leaving Tower Esk," he said, resigned.

Sheena stared at her father, disbelieving and horrified. Banishment? To be sent away from her home and family?

"Dinna look at me like that, Sheena," Dugald said in a ragged voice. "'Tis no more than you deserve."

"Where am I to go?" she asked, her throat constricting.

"You'll go to your aunt in Aberdeen. A nunnery's a good place for you to contemplate the wrong you've done your family. To your room, now. You'll stay there until tomorrow, when you'll be taken north."

Sheena ran from the hall, refusing to let anyone see her tears. Fortunately, no one followed, and she dried her eyes before she reached Niall's door. He was still asleep, and she stood quietly for a moment, trying to compose her thoughts before she woke him.

At last she sat on the bed and said, "Niall, you have to wake and listen to me 'afore someone comes."

The seriousness in her voice alerted him, and he sat right up. He took in her expression, and, all at once, he knew what was wrong.

"The alarm's been given?" he began. "They know he's gone?"

"Aye, they know," she said miserably.

He mistook her tone for disapproval and blurted, "I had to do it, Sheena! The MacKinnion said he'd beat you and rape you and make you suffer all your life if he was forced to marry you!"

"My God!" Sheena gasped. It was worse than she had known.

"You see, I had to let him go, for he wouldna listen to reason. He was furious, and no mistake. He said you dinna force a MacKinnion against his will and no' suffer for it. It didna matter to him that you were no' to blame. He swore he'd make you suffer and suffer, Sheena."

"Then I'm doubly grateful to you, Niall," Sheena said, her voice soft.

"Grateful? You're no' angry?"

"I knew you did it for me. 'Tis thankful I am, and no mistake. And you're no' to feel bad when I tell you . . . I've accepted the blame."

"You? But The MacDonough—"

"He was watched, Niall," Sheena explained. "They know he didna do it, and William managed to make our father blame me."

"But Sheena—"

She held up her hand. "Listen to me. I've come out of this better than you think. The MacDonough broke the betrothal, so I dinna have to marry him. And thanks to you, I'll no' be given to The MacKinnion." She grinned. She really was better off than she had been. "I'm being sent away as punishment, Niall, but to Aunt Erminia in Aberdeen. 'Tis not so bad. I'd rather that than marry!"

"You'll become a nun?" he gasped.

"Father didna say that, so dinna worry. And I havena seen our aunt for years. 'Twill be a pleasant change, and I'll no' have to worry about a husband being forced on me, at least not for a while. Truly, Niall, I'm no' unhappy."

"But you'll come back?"

"Father was very angry, so I canna say. But even if I am forced to become a nun, I think I would prefer that to a loveless marriage."

"You dinna mean that, Sheena."

"Yes, I do. Our parents didna love each other, Niall. You never saw them together, but I remember well enough. Without love, I'd rather never marry."

"I'll talk to Father."

"You willna!" she said sharply. "If I stay here, he'll only find another man for me. I'm going, Niall, and you're no' to try and prevent it. And you're never to confess what you did, you understand? You promise me?"

He nodded, but reluctantly. This was not the way it was supposed to come out. But he no longer had any control over events. Everything had been decided. He had acted on impulse, because of his love for his sister. But the outcome was not his to determine after all.

"I'll come and visit you soon," he said.

"If Father lets you, I'll be glad of it." She smiled.

Suddenly Niall threw his arms around her, tears coursing down his face. "Och, Sheena, I'm so sorry!"

"Hush now, m'dear. This is no' your fault. And

you're no' to fret for me. I'll be fine in Aberdeen. I've never been so far north 'afore. I'm actually looking forward to going. 'Tis better Father and I part, at least for a while. I couldna live here with him now."

Chapter 9

IN the weeks that followed, Sheena was often to remember that last intimate talk with Niall. Aberdeen, nearly fifty miles from home, was like a foreign land. It was crowded and filthy, and you couldn't walk through the town without fear of having someone's chamber pot or garbage dumped on your head. But it was a thriving market center, and exciting, with a crowded harbor and every kind of craftsman working in the town.

Sheena spent her first days exploring, but soon gave that up. Oh, the sights were grand—the abbeys, the university, all the shops—but there were too many Highlanders. They were easy enough to spot, their legs bare between plaid and boots. Lowlanders wore tights or combinations of hose and puffed breeches. Lowlander peasants wore trousers.

If the intimidating Highlanders were not enough to make her shun the town, there was a continual stream of beggars accosting her on every corner.

Aberdeen was overrun with poor people, poor seeking work or professional beggars.

Every morning Sheena left her aunt's austere rooms at the nunnery and walked to the poorhouse, a stone building in a terrible state of ruin. Given over as a house of charity, it was a few blocks from the nunnery. The house had been intended as a resting place for weary travelers, where they could get a hot meal and a clean bed for a night or two while looking for work. But it had deteriorated into a slum for beggars and vagrants. A small house, it contained only ten beds. The rule of one or two nights' stay only still applied, and there were always new faces at the door.

Sheena's aunt was not obliged to go there every day, but she never failed. A priest lived there, seeing to the distribution of meals, but he was too old for all the work the place required. Those who slept there were asked to wash their bedding and clean their eating utensils for the next guest, but the rule was never obeyed, and only the nuns' daily care kept the place from becoming a pesthole.

When Sheena saw how tired her Aunt Erminia was, she insisted on helping. Her aunt's day usually consisted of spending the morning at the poorhouse washing and cleaning, then working at the hospital for several hours, then returning to the poorhouse before going home.

Sheena was appalled. All that work, and Aunt Erminia was nearly fifty! There was no reason she couldn't help at the poorhouse and make her aunt's day that much shorter.

It worked out well. Sheena was young and energetic and could do the work in half the time it took Aunt Erminia. The poorhouse was empty by the time she got there every day, so no one bothered her. She and her aunt were able to spend afternoons in the quiet of the nunnery, talking or sewing together. If Sheena missed her home and the activities she was accustomed to, she didn't show it yet. She did achingly miss her brother, however. There was no one young and lively at the nunnery, and she felt so alone.

After a month, Sheena had not heard from home, from Niall or her father. She had repaired the jerkins and plaids of the poor, learned countless new stitches from her aunt, and refurbished and mended her own wardrobe . . . and was deathly sick of sewing. She wanted to ride, hunt, and swim before the first snows. She needed adventure, or at least some mischief, and, oh, how she missed Niall!

For the first time, Niall would be raiding. Autumn was the traditional time for lifting, as the stealing of livestock was termed. Whatever the Fergussons lifted that year would be kept, not sold, for they had lost too much to the MacKinnions to be able to sell any.

The morning in late September when Sheena pulled her cart of bedding along to the river was dismally gloomy. Not just the usual Scottish gloom, either, but a full mass of dark clouds that signaled a storm. She worried about her wash. She was in the habit of hanging the bedding by the river to dry in the brisk breeze, rather than at the parish yard, where surrouding buildngs blocked the wind. If it rained, the wash would have to be hung inside the poorhouse, and it would take all day to dry.

That had happened before, so Sheena had been there in the late afternoon when the poorhouse started to fill. She didn't want to be there again, to see the thin, sunken faces, the ragged, filthy clothes. She hoped it wouldn't rain.

She hurried, rubbing her hands before she was finished. Her poor hands. How white and smooth they'd once been. Now they were red and sore and cracked.

"Need some help, lassie?"

Sheena gasped and turned around quickly. She had not heard the young man on his horse approach, for the wind was whipping hard. It flapped his plaid around him and played havoc with her green skirt.

He was a Highlander, his plaid very close to her own colors. He was young, too, about her age. There was something about his face that put her at ease. True, it was a very handsome face, but that wasn't the reason. There was just something about him.

"'Tis kind of you to offer." Sheena grinned, amused. "But I canna imagine a Highland warrior doing the poorhouse wash."

"You're a beggar?" He was shocked, and the surprise in his voice made her laugh outright. "Of course I am. Do you think I'd be washing this bedding unless I had to?"

"But . . . you dinna look like a beggar."

"Well, I'm new at this. I mean, I have only recently fallen on hard times."

"You've no family?"

"Och, but you're full of questions, and you're wasting my time, you are." Her voice was stern, but her eyes twinkled.

It had been so long since she had spoken to anyone near her age, and a handsome man at that. How she wanted him to stay. But, of course, he wouldn't.

"'Twill rain soon, and I'll have a wet wash," she sighed.

She bent to wring out the last sheet and hang it with the rest on the trees by the river's edge. When she turned around again, he was right behind her, having left his horse. He was much taller than she was, and she had to look up to see his face.

"You're so pretty—a rare beauty," he said, wonder in his voice. "I saw you passing the cattle yard."

"And decided to follow me?"

"Aye."

"Is that a habit of yours then, following girls?" Sheena bantered.

But he remained serious. "Can I kiss you, lass?"

The sudden request shocked her. "I'll box your ears," she replied tartly.

He laughed, relaxing a little. "You're a saucy wench. 'Tis plain to see you've no man to answer to."

"And you're much too bold for my liking," she returned, uneasy now. His eyes were devouring her, no longer simply appreciative.

She tried to move past him, but he put out his arms to stop her. "You'll no' be running off when I've only just found you. You may be a vision, but I won't let you dissolve."

His arms were stretched wide, and Sheena suspected he would grab her if she dared move. She didn't like this one bit. He was young, but he was big. And a Highlander, too.

"What is it you want then?" She glared at him.

"You're much too bonny to be begging for your keep. I'd like to be your man and take care of you."

By then, Sheena was completely unnerved. But wasn't it just like a Highlander to be insanely impulsive?

"You've no' much sense, lad," she scoffed. "You're barely more than a boy yourself, so how can you take care of me?"

He scowled, and Sheena had a glimpse of the man he would be one day, fierce and temperamental. She shouldn't have laughed, she realized too late. Highlanders didn't take lightly to being ridiculed, and this one was very proud.

"I shouldna have asked you, lass," he said stiffly, but she felt no less on guard.

"I'm glad you understand that."

"Nay. I should have done what my brother would do."

Sheena felt her heart constrict at the ominous tone.

"He'd have taken you . . . and so shall I."

His hand gripped her arm, and Sheena

screamed. She was lifted in his arms, screaming. Neither her screaming nor her struggles bothered him at all. There was even a glint of amusement in his eyes.

The Highlander wasted no time. She was thrown atop his horse, and he was behind her in an instant, his arms circling her so she couldn't move. His arms bound her firmly in front of him as the horse charged into the shallow river, crossing to the south side. Sheena's boots and long skirt were soaked, but she wasn't thinking of anything except how distraught her aunt would be. What would she make of Sheena's disappearance? She would send word home, of course. Poor Niall. Would he think she had run away? And her father? He had denied her his protection, and this had happened because of his decision. He would be so upset! She could find nothing soothing in that thought, however.

"Where are you taking me?" Sheena shouted over the wind.

"To my home."

"For how long?"

"Why, forever."

Absurd! The Highlander couldn't just keep her like a stray dog. Was he insane? Keep her forever? Nonsense! It was just boasting. She would find her way back to Aberdeen, or her family would find her. The Highlander couldn't get away with this. He couldn't.

Chapter 10

THEY had traveled less than a mile when the rain descended, finally, in a fury. The storm felt ominous to Sheena, as if it portended her destiny. As one mile turned into many, that thought haunted her.

The Highlander unwrapped his plaid as the storm began and gave it to her. She took it gladly, and used it to cover her head.

After that, she couldn't see where they were going. The lad was in a hurry, appearing to race the storm. The miles melted away, and more than twenty were gained before the rain stopped and he slowed down.

Sheena threw off the wet plaid. It had rained so hard that she was soaked clear through despite its protection. It was undoubtedly afternoon, but so gloomy she couldn't be sure just what hour. On either side of them were mountains, big gray masses with dark clouds surrounding them. They were in a deep valley between two mountain ranges, riding along the river's edge. Sheena shivered as she began to understand that they were in the Highlands, going deeper into them. She wanted to cry. Tears stung her eyes, but she held them back fiercely. She wouldn't show her young captor how helpless she felt.

They were moving along slowly, for the horse was winded from his long journey. Sheena turned around to face her abductor, then turned back to stare straight ahead.

"You've no right to keep me. My family will be very angry about this."

"You've already admitted you've no one," he said smoothly.

"I dinna say that! You did!"

"Well, no matter," he said cheerfully. "A beggar's family can have no power. You're mine to keep—and lucky you are I'm having you."

"Lucky?"

"Aye," he boasted. "'Tis fine clothes I'll be giving you, and jewels to match your deep blue eyes. You'll never have to beg again. Can't you see how glad you should be?"

Sheena felt her frustration mounting. "Does it no' occur to you that you have *stolen* me?"

"When we're wed, you'll be glad of it," he laughed.

"Wed?" she gasped, turning again to look at him.

"Of course, wed," he replied. "You dinna think I'll shame you with less than marriage?"

"You dinna know me! You canna want to wed me!"

"But I do. You're special, and no mistake. I know that well enough."

"Well, I'll no' wed you, and that's that!" Sheena said, furious and helpless to do anything about it.

"You're stubborn now, but you'll change your mind," he said confidently.

Her fear had been overcome by anger, but fear returned as she saw a great stone castle appear ahead, dark clouds floating around its tall towers. They had traveled fifteen to twenty miles since midday, but at a much slower pace. The last mile or so before they reached the castle was straight up into the mountains. It was now nearing night, and the Highland fortress ahead was a gloomy place indeed.

"Your home?" Sheena asked, her voice tremulous.

"Aye," he declared proudly. "It looks cold, I know, but 'tis pleasant enough inside."

"But such a big castle," she said, awed. "Are you related to the laird here?"

"I'm his brother."

Sheena didn't know whether to take hope or not. Surely the laird could see that she was returned to Aberdeen. But perhaps the laird indulged his younger brother.

"I'll have to hide you for a while," the boy said, sounding uneasy for the first time as they approached the large gatehouse in the center of a long wall. The wall was flanked by round towers.

"I'll need to get my brother's approval 'afore he knows I have you," he explained.

"Are you afeared of your brother?"

"Afeared?" He laughed, but she was not convinced.

"But you need his permission to marry me, don't you?"

"Aye."

"And what makes you think he'll let you wed a beggar?" Hope was growing.

"When he knows how much I want you, he'll agree."

But the lad now lacked his earlier self-assurance, and Sheena began to get some of her confidence back.

The gate was opened, and they rode into a large inner courtyard. Ahead was a great hall with a tower at each end. Connected to it on the left was a square building three stories high, with two outside stairs leading up to the second floor. There were many arched windows. There were other round towers, as well, and a stable to the right, as well as smaller buildings near the walls.

"I bid you welcome," the lad said congenially. Sheena said nothing.

A ginger-haired youth came for the horse. "You're back so soon, Colen."

"Aye. Is my brother about?"

"He's in the hall," the lad answered. "And where are the others?"

"I left them to their sport. I was in a hurry to be home, so I didna wait for them."

"And what have you there, Colen?"

This was a new, deeper voice. Sheena tried to

turn to see who it was, but her abductor shielded her. She felt his nervousness.

"'Tis none of your concern, Black Gawain," the young man said testily.

"A secret, eh?" The man chuckled. "Does your brother know you've brought someone back with you?"

"Nay, and I'll thank you no' to tell him. I'll tell him myself when I'm ready."

He swept Sheena off the horse and carried her away from Black Gawain before she could see the man. She did not like this furtiveness of Colen's.

"Colen, is it?" she said, wishing he would put her down. But she knew how difficult walking would be after the long ride.

"Aye."

"Where are you taking me?" she asked.

"To my room. You'll stay there."

"I'll no' stay in the same room with you," she said firmly.

"You've naught to fear. Dinna fash yourself. I'll no' touch you 'afore we're wed."

She wasn't convinced. "I'll no' stay with you. 'Tis no' proper."

"There's nowhere else you can stay," he said in exasperation. "I canna give you a room to yourself without my brother learning of it."

"Then let him learn of it!"

She struggled, and he put her down on her feet, one arm around her neck and a hand covering her mouth, for she had tried to scream. He dragged her along with him up the outer stairs of the large square building.

Black Gawain watched until they were out of sight, then shook his head as he moved off toward the hall. It was not his concern if young Colen wanted to keep a mistress, even an unwilling one. But he couldn't see why he should keep it a secret from his brother. The laird wouldn't mind. He had enough women of his own. Gawain chuckled, wondering how long a secret like that could be kept from the leader of the clan.

Chapter 11

IT was not until six days later that Sheena discovered just where she was. Six days, locked in
Colen's room. He had managed to learn her first
name, but no more than that. Sheena was a stubborn woman, and no mistake.

"Are you serious, Colen? Do you mean to tell
me your brother spent the entire day locked in his
room with his mistress? He didna even come out
for food?"

"She's a new one," Colen tried to explain. "He
often does that with a new one."

"How much more of this am I to take? First he's
busy, then he's no' to be found, then he's angry,
then something else. And all the while you keep me
locked up. Well, I'll no' stand for it anymore!"

"Sheena, please—"

"Nay, no more excuses. I agreed to give you
time because I wanted to leave here peaceably,
without making a fuss. Yet you put it off and put it
off. It's been six days!"

"I did tell him I was ready to marry," Colen defended himself.

"But you didna tell him about me, about my being here. As soon as he asked what settlement was expected, you said no more."

"He was no' ready to hear that there would be no settlement. He must be in a good mood to be hearing that."

"So I must wait for the mood of your brother to change? The truth is, you're afraid of his answer. You've made too much of this, Colen. It has become too important to you. Do you no' see that?"

"But it *is* important."

"Aye. So important you'll jump at any excuse no' to talk to your brother."

"I couldna bear it if he said I couldna marry you," he replied, downhearted.

"How will you bear it when you can't change *my* mind?" she asked, not unkindly.

"Women are fickle," he returned. "They're known to change their minds. It's no' you I'm worried about, it's my brother."

"Fickle! Who told you that nonsense? Nay, dinna answer," she said dryly. "Your dear, sweet brother."

Colen laughed. "I've never heard him called that 'afore."

"Is he so terrible?"

"At times. MacKinnions are known for their fierce tempers, but Jamie can be the worst."

"*MacKinnion?!*"

"What's the matter?"

She had gone deathly pale.

"*You're* a MacKinnion? James—he's *The* Mac-Kinnion!"

Colen became quite alarmed by her appearance. "What's wrong, Sheena? I told you who I was, so that's not it."

"You never!"

"But I did. I must have. What's wrong?"

"'Tis no' possible!" She started to laugh hysterically.

Poor Colen didn't know what to make of her behavior, but when she flew toward the door, he was right behind her. He caught her arm, and she shrieked wildly. "Dinna you touch me!"

He slapped her, and the sound was as loud as a whipcrack. She was stunned for a moment, and then her eyes flashed and she slapped him back just as hard.

Colen was shocked. He stepped back, a hand to his cheek.

"You *hit* me!"

Sheena might have laughed. "You slapped me first. I'll no' take that from you or anyone."

"But you . . . hit me!"

"Aye, I did, and with good reason," she replied. "What reason did you have for hitting me?"

"You were acting crazy. I was trying to calm you."

"Maybe I was," she sighed. Her mind was clearer, the panic ebbing. "But you're twice the size I am and had no business laying a hand on me." Her voice rose again. "And I *willna* stay here any longer!"

"Aye, you're right," he admitted sheepishly, surprising her. "'Twas wrong of me to put it off so long and keep you a prisoner here. I'm sorry. I'll settle it tonight, I promise."

"Why no' now?"

"I'm to leave shortly, to get back the horses that were lifted the other night."

"You mean you've a raid to do? Today?"

"Aye. But as soon as I return, I'll settle it."

"You swear, Colen?"

He nodded and turned to leave. At the door he stopped, absently rubbing his cheek. "I've never been slapped by a girl 'afore."

"Then 'twas high time, for you're a stubborn brute if I've ever met one."

"And you're a spunky lass," he chuckled. "You wouldna catch a MacKinnion woman slapping back. She'd get a fair beating if she did."

"Is that what your wife should expect?"

"Och, Sheena, I wouldna hurt you."

"Of course not," she replied sarcastically. "You'd only have to have everything *your* way *all* the time, as you have so far."

"Will you give me this one last day without making a fuss?" Colen asked in parting.

Sheena hesitated, but only to make Colen nervous. There was no question anymore about her causing a stir. She couldn't risk it, not when a MacKinnion might come to investigate. Maybe even The MacKinnion himself!

"This one day and no more, Colen,"

she said at last.

He grinned. "If I'm no' back by dark, a girl will bring you food. And dinna fret, lass."

He left, and she was free to take in fully what she had just learned. For six days, she'd been living in the midst of Clan Kinnion! Her family's great enemies were outside that door . . . in the next room . . . all around her. And The MacKinnion was among them. She sat down on the bed and let the realization take hold of her. She was living a nightmare.

Chapter 12

C OLEN'S brother had returned to the hall after speaking to the gatekeeper and learning there was no sign of Colen yet. He was not worrying over the men, just the success of the raid. One of his prize stallions had been lifted, and the laird wanted it back. He ought to have gone himself, he knew that, but Colen had been so nervous all week, his brother felt he needed the diversion.

It was a quiet night. There were no guests, so only one long table was filled. These were castle retainers. Servants bustled about, refilling trenchers, pouring ale.

The laird's own table had yet to be served. It was considered a crime to serve the laird's food before he was ready for it, for if there was anything that could turn James MacKinnion sour, it was a cold meal. New servants learned this the hard way. Jamie's wrath could be quite entertaining—as long as one wasn't the recipient of it—and no one volunteered the rules to newcomers.

Right then, Jamie's table was empty except for Jessie, who sat looking sullen. Jamie had kept her waiting, and she didn't like that one bit. Jessie Martin was first cousin to Jamie's brother-in-law, Dobbin, and she had come to Castle Kinnion with Dobbin and Jamie's sister Daphne when they visited, three weeks past. But she had not left with them. During those three weeks she had made it known that she was available to Jamie, and he had finally taken her up on her offer.

He had had his fill of her by yesterday—or so he thought. But seeing her now in a low-cut burgundy velvet gown, he admitted he'd never found a better mistress. If only his Aunt Lydia hadn't taken such a dislike to Jessie. But she had, staying in her room in the north tower and almost never coming out. Aunt Lydia couldn't tolerate a forward, brazen woman.

But sometimes a man needed such a woman in his life, especially a man who was not looking for a wife. She was experienced in ways of pleasing a man, Jessie was. After four unsuccessful handfastings, she claimed she had given up on marriage. Jamie wasn't sure about that. He'd never yet met a woman who didn't pine for marriage. But Jessie would be disappointed if that was what she was after.

"Can we begin now?" Jessie said petulantly as soon as Jamie took his chair.

He didn't care for her tone and replied, "They'll serve, now I'm here. But you didna have to wait for me, lass."

"They'll no' serve this table until you're seated," she reminded him tartly, regretting it when she heard his reply.

"There's ample room at the lower table, and plenty of food."

It was a privilege to eat at the laird's table, and Jessie knew she was being reminded of that. Jamie could be very hard. But she wanted James Mac-Kinnion. She wanted him badly. She had never known such a handsome man. Handsome and rich, a laird, he was everything she desired. She had realized that when she first saw him at her cousin's wedding, and from that time she had nagged and begged and cajoled Dobbin to bring her with him to Castle Kinnion. It had taken three years for him to agree, and now that she was finally here, she had no intention of ever leaving.

"Och, Jamie, dinna mind me." She smiled sweetly. "'Tis a sour nature I have when I'm hungry. But I'll no' take it out on you again."

Jamie was not fooled. "I hope I can count on that, Jessie, for I'll tell you now, I've no liking for a bitchy woman, nor one who argues and nags. I dinna have to put up with that sort of nonsense, nor will I. You're a bonny lass to be sure, and I'll take care of you as long as you share my bed. But you've no other hold on me, Jessie."

"I know. And I didna mean to anger you," she quickly assured him, desperate to drop the subject. "Look. The girl comes with our . . ."

Jessie didn't finish, for the girl who came in from the kitchen with a platter of food walked toward the end of the hall and the bedchambers. The laird's table was not her destination. When the girl, Doris, went through the archway at the end of the hall, Jamie's curiosity was aroused.

"And where are you off to now?" Jessie demanded, already forgetting her apology.

Jamie didn't answer. As he left the table, another servant came from the kitchen tower with his food.

"Gertie." He stopped her with a grin. "Go on and serve Mistress Martin, even though I'm not there. She's nigh to fainting from what I've been hearing."

The old servant looked up at him and said solemnly, her eyes twinkling, "Aye, Sir Jamie, we wouldna be wanting that."

"And where is young Doris off to?"

"Doris? I dinna know. She said your brother set her to some task if he wasna back 'afore dark."

"Did he now?"

Jamie followed Doris up the stone steps to the second floor. His own bedchamber ran along one side of the building, and there were two smaller guest chambers opposite. But Doris had not stopped there. He caught sight of her at the end of the corridor, turning up the stairs leading to the top floor, where Colen had one of the four rooms.

"Doris!"

She poked her head back around the corner and then came into full view under a torch set by the entrance to the third floor.

"Where are you off to with that?" he asked when he reached her. "We've no one ill up there that I've no' been told about, have we?"

"Nay, I dinna think she's ill."

"She?"

"The lass young Colen's keeping in his room," Doris explained. She was wary, but she couldn't keep anything from the laird.

"He's keeping a lass there? Who?"

"I dinna know, Sir Jamie, I've no' seen her. But 'tis strange. He told me to be sure and lock the lock after I left the food in there. Now why would he be locking the poor lass up? It dinna seem right."

"Why indeed?" Jamie laughed. "Here, give me that. I'll see she gets fed, and I'll find out what I can."

Jamie chuckled as he carried the tray up to the third floor. So his brother had found himself a mistress! One he wanted all for himself. No wonder he had been acting so strangely. The lad was probably having his first love. Jamie had gone through the same infatuation at Colen's age and could remember it well. But it had passed, and he'd never felt that way again. He could almost envy Colen the heart-throbbing experience. Time enough for the boy to learn it wasn't true love. Time enough for disillusionment later.

The door to Colen's bedchamber was indeed locked, and Jamie grinned as he pulled the wooden peg from the latch and pushed the door open. It was dark. Torch light from the corridor fell only a few feet into the room.

Jamie squinted. "Where are you, lass?"

"Here." There was spirit in her voice.

100

He followed the voice, but he still couldn't see her. "We've candles aplenty in this castle." Jamie scowled. "Are you so ugly Colen must keep you in the dark?"

"There's a candle on the table."

"Then why do you no' use it?"

"For what?" the girl asked tonelessly. "There's naught for me to do in this room that I'd be needing a candle for."

Jamie chuckled. Colen had found himself a rare female, one willing to await his beck and call.

Jamie saw the bed and moved toward it, his eyes now able to make out the girl sitting on the edge of it. He put the try of food on the table.

"You're no' the girl who was supposed to bring this," she mentioned warily.

Jamie didn't reply. He found the candle and, after several seconds, had a fair light illuminating the room.

"Now then, lass, who . . ."

The words died as Jamie turned and faced the girl. He caught his breath. The vision before him was not real, it couldn't be. The delicate oval face, the large eyes of a remarkable bright blue, the mass of red hair so dark as to be magenta. Now when had he dreamed of this before?

She was staring at him with open curiosity. Under her perusal, Jamie stood tall. He could not speak. If he spoke, she might disappear. With a sudden jolt he realized why he felt that way. It was the vision! The water sprite from the pool in the glen! Her image had dimmed with the passing of time, but his vivid feelings has not.

She smiled as the silence lengthened, and Jamie thought his heart would stop at the brilliance of that smile. Then she giggled, a bubbling sound.

"I've been known to turn the heads of men," she said in amusement, a mischievous gleam in her eyes. "But I've never struck one speechless 'afore. I think I like it."

Jamie would have taken offense if anyone but this vision had teased him so. He delighted in her laughter and didn't mind at all.

"I . . . I've never lost my tongue so completely 'afore. But now I've found it, you'll be telling me who you are."

"I dinna think I will," she said.

"Why?"

She shrugged prettily and looked away. "I've no' told Colen, so why should I be telling you?" she answered pertly, reaching for the tray and picking up a sugar roll.

"You're no' a MacKinnion?" he asked.

"Heaven forbid."

Jamie frowned. "From where do you come then?"

"The lad found me in Aberdeen" was Sheena's evasive reply.

"Your home is there?"

Her gaze narrowed. "I've no home to speak of, not anymore. But who are you to be asking me so many questions?"

"Colen didna tell you of me?"

"He told me of a brother, nobody else."

"I am his brother," Jamie replied simply.

Then it was her turn to stammer. "Then . . . you're . . ."

Jamie watched in amazement as she scrambled across the bed and backed up against the wall beside it. She cowered, as if trying to disappear into the stone wall.

"What nonsense is this?" Jamie demanded.

There was terror in her eyes.

"Will you answer me?" he said sternly.

"What are you doing here?" said a voice behind him.

Jamie turned to see Colen enter the chamber, and then the girl dashed across the room and flew into Colen's arms.

An unexpected jealousy took hold of Jamie. Here was a vision he had searched for, had dreamed of countless times. And she was in his brother's arms. Colen had found her before Jamie did.

"Tell me what you've done to the lass," Colen said angrily.

"Done!" Jamie exploded. "I've done naught but stand here and talk with her. But the moment she learned who I was, she acted as if I were the devil himself. I want to know why."

Colen's brows knit in confusion. "Sheena?" he tried to question her, but she clung to him and wouldn't speak.

"Well?" Jamie demanded.

"Stop it, Jamie," Colen replied. "Can you no' see she's upset?"

"I'm no' too happy myself," Jamie growled. "I want to know who she is and why you felt the need to lock her in your room."

"She's just a poor lass, Jamie, with no home or family to speak of. She was staying at the poorhouse in Aberdeen."

"A beggar. I see. And the rest of it?"

"This is no' the time—ouch!"

Sheena pinched Colen and shoved him away. "You'll tell him *all* of it, Colen. Now."

"So the lass has found her tongue."

Sheena swung around to face Jamie but then backed away. She still couldn't bring herself to speak to James MacKinnion, not after all she had heard about him.

If she had not been so frightened, she would have seen his resemblance to his brother, though Colen's hair was reddish-orange and Jamie's was yellow-gold. But The MacKinnion was so young looking and so handsome. There was not a mean line in his face! Was this really her dreaded enemy? He was certainly not what she'd imagined the savage MacKinnion looked like.

Jamie sighed and sat down on the bed. "Colen, lad, I'm close to losing my patience with the both of you. I'm asking you for the last time to tell me what goes on here."

Colen swallowed hard, then blurted, "I want to marry her."

"Marry?" Jamie laughed. "You've already got her, so why bother?"

Sheena flushed bright red at the assumption

being made. It was so typically arrogant, exactly what she could have expected of a Highlander—this one in particular.

Colen frowned darkly. "You're no' to insult her, Jamie. 'Tis no' what you think."

"Marriage was her idea, no doubt?"

"She's no' made up her mind yet. It is I who want to wed."

"Colen!" Sheena warned.

"All right!" Colen snapped, furious. "She says she willna marry me."

"But she came here with you?"

Colen lowered his gaze. "I . . . I took her."

Jamie fell back on the bed and laughed heartily. "Och, Colen, what am I to do with you? Have you no' learned there are enough girls for the asking? You dinna have to take one who's no' willing."

"There's no other like Sheena."

Jamie sobered at that. Indeed, there wasn't another like this lass. That she did not want to marry Colen brought Jamie a great measure of relief.

"'Tis a fine mess we have here, and no mistake," Jamie said thoughtfully. "'Tis plain you're serious, Colen, but I canna consider only your wishes. You've kidnapped the lass."

"But if she *were* willing, would you give your blessing on the match?" Colen persisted.

Jamie stared hard at the girl. How could he bear to see this particular girl wed to his brother? She was his vision made flesh. Yet how could he put his own desires above theirs?

With the greatest reluctance, Jamie was forced

to say, "You would have my blessing on the match if she desired it. But I'll hear what the lass has to say. Sheena is it?" She nodded, and he asked, "Do you want to marry my brother?"

Sheena shook her head adamantly. She knew her silence angered him, but she couldn't help it. She just couldn't bring herself to talk to the man.

"I know you've a voice, lass," Jamie said, surprising himself with his own degree of patience. "If you dinna want to marry my brother, you'll have to be telling me what it is you do want. I canna help you otherwise."

There was no way out of it now. Sheena cleared her throat, but her voice came out in a mere whisper. "I . . . I want to leave here."

"To go where?"

"Back to Aberdeen."

"Dinna listen to her, Jamie." Colen spoke up quickly. "She has no one there. She'd only have to fend for herself again, to beg."

"So what are you suggesting, brother? You canna force the lass to marry you."

"Och, I know. But she can live here. She'll be better off."

"Mayhap," Jamie replied carefully.

Sheena gasped. So Colen's plan was to keep her so that he would have time to win her. But could they really keep her when she was determined to leave?

Sheena's fear made her bold. "Tell him why you really want me to stay, Colen. And tell him the truth."

Colen turned around to face her. "I canna bear the thought of you alone in that crowded place, with no one to protect you. There's no telling what would happen to you in Aberdeen."

"What becomes of me is my affair, no' yours," she reminded him. Jamie's direct gaze flustered her, and she stammered, "He is sure I'll change my mind about him if I stay. That's the *real* reason he wants me here."

"That is possible," Jamie said.

"Nay, 'twill no' happen," Sheena insisted firmly. "I'll no' wed a lad younger than me, and I'll certainly no' marry a Highlander."

Too late Sheena realized she had insulted them both.

But Jamie laughed. "'Tis a Lowlander you've brought here, Colen, lad." He grinned.

"That doesna matter," Colen replied.

"It does to her." Jamie chuckled. "They're no' like us, lad. Did you not know we're all savages to them?"

"She'll find out differently if she stays here."

"Aye. She will."

Sheena bristled. "I'll no' stay here, and you canna make me," she said, hands going to her hips in a rebellious stance.

Jamie didn't like being told what he could or couldn't do, even by this girl who fascinated him so. "I'll no' argue with you, lass!" he said sharply. He watched with irritation as she backed away from him with wide, frightened eyes. He turned on his brother angrily. "I've no patience for this,

Colen. When she's ready to talk to me without shrinking, I'll settle the matter."

Jamie stalked from the room. Sheena collapsed into a chair and asked, "What did he mean?"

Colen grinned, for he had got what he wanted. "You'll be staying, lass."

"I'll be doing no such thing!"

"Aye, you will. There'll be no one taking you back until he says so. And he'll no' be doing that until you give him a good reason why he should."

"I'll leave by myself then."

Colen shook his head, still grinning. "I'll only bring you back, lass, and that's a promise." And he chuckled at the withering look she gave him. "Och, Sheena, you brought this on yourself. Why were you so afeared of him? He didna like that one bit."

"You heard him shout at me."

"Aye, and no wonder he did," he replied. "You dinna tell Jamie what he can or canna do, Sheena. He's laird here. He can do as he pleases."

"No' where I am concerned," she said.

"You're welcome to tell him that . . . if you dare. But I'll no' be able to help you when he turns his fury on you."

She had to get away from there. But she would have to face The MacKinnion again in order to do so. To face the devil in order to escape the devil. Och, God, give her the courage, she prayed.

"I'll see your brother again—now."

He hesited, then lowered his gaze. " 'Tis only fair I tell you. Jamie wouldna have left the matter unsettled if he wasna so angered that he couldna trust

108

himself to give a fair decision. That's the way he is. For some reason, your fear of him has raised his ire. If you force the matter now, you'll no' be happy with his decision."

"You mean he would keep me here for spite? Or out of anger?"

"'Tis more than likely. But if you want to try your luck anyway, I'll no' be stopping you."

"You'd like that!" she snapped. "Och, what am I to do then?"

"Dinna take it so hard, Sheena. No harm will come to you here. And now I've no need to hide you anymore, so tomorrow I'll be showing you your new home."

Chapter 13

THE morning was passing quickly, but still Jamie tarried in the hall. Most of his retainers had come and gone about their business. The few remaining were those who would ride with Jamie when he left the castle. They lounged, waiting for Jamie, jesting with the servants eating their breakfasts at the lower tables. The unexpected lull was welcome, and they did not question their laird's delay in leaving.

Jamie questioned himself, however. It was unusual for him to be found in the hall so late, even when he had no pressing demands. The day was wasting away, but there he sat, waiting. He should have been out on his land. Though the rents had all been collected by his tacksmen, it was Jamie's custom to visit all his crofters, cotters, and grassmen at that time of year to ascertain if anyone had been unduly pressed to meet the rents. But he was doing none of what he ought to be doing.

On the chance of seeing the lovely Sheena this

morning, Jamie sat at his table and waited. He admitted the truth to himself but would never tell anyone else why he was sitting there. Luckily, Jessie wasn't there. She did not make an appearance until midday.

Jamie gave Jessie little thought, anyway. The other lass occupied his mind and had done so since he'd left her the previous evening. Because of her, he had had no desire for Jessie the night before. Because of her, he had lain awake many hours, feeling utterly alone, wondering what the devil he had done to frighten the lass so badly. He couldn't stand her fear of him.

He wanted the exact thing his brother wanted— for the girl to stay with them. How to make her stay was the problem. It would be easy to force her. He had that power. But she would hate him for it, and he was surprised to find that he valued her good opinion.

Just then, all he wanted was to see her. He kept his eyes riveted to the far end of the hall and the arched entrance. What could be delaying her? He had thought surely the girl would want to speak to him, to find out what he wanted to do about her. He sighed. She had every right, after what Colen had done, to demand to be returned to Aberdeen.

Jamie was beginning to feel quite ridiculous, sitting there knowing his men and servants were wondering what he was doing. At last, his vigil paid off. Colen appeared at the end of the hall. Behind him there was a swish of green skirt, and then the lovely Sheena came into view. Jamie's pulse picked up at the sight of her. Colen was holding her hand and seemed to be dragging her forward, though gently. She was looking all around her, and Jamie was suddenly proud of the richness of his hall, seeing it through a stranger's eyes. The wainscot-paneled walls, the painted deal ceilings were the luxuries of a tower house, not a castle. The lower tables had padded benches. The laird's table had English chairs covered in damask, plates of silver and pewter, and Dutch linen to cover the rough wood. There was even a thick Persian rug, and there were several chairs before the great hearth, where Jamie liked to spend evenings. All in all the place was impressive, and that pleased him very much.

But his pleasure quickly turned sour when Sheena spotted him, stopped dead in her tracks, jerked her hand away from Colen, and ran back the way she had come. Colen was after her instantly, stopping her. He swung her back around, and they argued, though in hushed voices. Colen tried to catch her hand again, but she pushed him away and cried *"Nay"* loud enough for everyone to hear.

Jamie could well imagine his brother's embarrassment, for he and the girl had suddenly gained everyone's attention, and the silence that followed was complete. Jamie knew the reason for the long silence. Sheena's extraordinary beauty was spellbinding.

But she seemed not to notice the attention. She took advantage of Colen's discomfort and left him, moving to the far end of the nearest trestle table. She sat down, ignoring one and all, and began to partake of the food left there.

Colen stomped angrily up to the raised dais and the laird's table. Jamie said nothing for several moments after his brother had sat down next to him, glowering across the room. There was ample food left on the table, but Colen didn't move to help himself. Conversations slowly began to resume below, but Colen fumed silently.

Finally, Jamie sighed. "Will you be telling me what that was all about, lad?"

"She thinks I lied to her," Colen answered, his words sharp.

He wouldn't meet Jamie's eyes, so Jamie followed Colen's gaze to what he preferred looking at anyway. "Did you?"

"Nay."

"But she didna believe you?"

"How could she when here you are?"

Jamie turned his attention back to his brother. "And what have I to do with it?"

Colen squirmed. He still wouldn't meet Jamie's gaze. Jamie's curiosity grew.

"Well?"

"Och, Jamie, she wouldna come down here until I convinced her you wouldna be around. She had locked herself in the south tower and wouldna open the door to me until—"

Jamie was frowning. "You put her in the south tower?"

"Aye."

"Why?"

Colen finally turned to his brother, and his eyes,

so like Jamie's, darkened. "I dinna like the drift of your thoughts, Jamie. I've told you I've no' touched the lass. Nor will I till she's my wife. I dinna know if she's a maiden. I didna ask. But it doesna matter to me if she is or no'."

Jamie didn't apologize. He was simply relieved. "What else was I to think, lad, when you kept her locked in your room?"

"But I slept elsewhere."

"Very well. Why did you move her?"

"She didna like staying in my room. She felt 'twas no' proper, and she was right."

"But why the tower? There were plenty of other rooms you could have put her in."

"She wanted a room with a lock on the inside. Mother's tower room is the only one."

Jamie was amused but warned himself not to show it. The room high in the south tower was indeed the only one that could be locked from the inside. Their mother had gone there often, whenever she and Robbie argued, and she had ordered the lock just so she could annoy their father by locking him out. It was ever a source of amusement throughout the castle when it was known the south tower was occupied. Here was another woman locking herself in.

"You say the lass wouldna open the door to you. Now why is that? She may no' want to marry you, but she seemed to like you well enough."

Once again Colen looked away. "I came to escort her to the hall. She didna want to come. She . . . she was afeared of seeing you."

Jamie's scowl darkened. "Why?"

"Och, Jamie, I dinna ken her fear. She has more spunk at times than any lass I know. Then, of a sudden, this crazy fear takes hold of her—like last night. It took me hours to coax her to leave the tower this morning. And she only consented when I swore she wouldna be seeing you. Yet here you are. Why?"

"Never mind why," Jamie replied curtly, his anger mounting. "Does the lass want to leave here or no'?"

"She does."

"So I thought. Then her avoiding me doesna make sense. She needs to talk with me if she wants the matter settled."

"She knows that," Colen replied. "Have you made a decision?"

"Bring her here."

"Now?" Colen frowned.

"Aye, now."

"But you're riled, Jamie," Colen protested. "Dinna send her away just because she displeases you."

Jamie leaned back and sighed. "She angers me with her fear of me, 'tis true, for I did naught to cause it. But I'll no' send her away for that. I've heard your arguments, Colen. Now I'll hear hers."

"But she has none, none that makes any sense." Colen pressed his cause. "In good conscience, Jamie, you canna send her back to a beggar's life."

"If she stays, lad, there's no guarantee she'll marry you," Jamie pointed out.

"I know. But I'd rather see her settled here, even married to another, than prey to scoundrels on the streets of Aberdeen. She's too lovely for that."

"'Tis glad I am to hear you say that, for I dinna want to see you hurt," Jamie replied thoughtfully. "'Tis well you realize now that, if she stays, you'll no' be the only one trying to win her. Many will fall under the spell of her beauty, just as you have."

"I've no doubt of that." Colen grinned, apparently unconcerned.

Jamie was reflective for a moment, then decided to admit, "'Tis only fair I warn you, lad—she has an effect on me, as well."

Colen raised a brow, then chuckled. "I dinna know why that should surprise me. So! No wonder her fear of you riles you."

"That we should both desire the same woman is no' a laughing matter," Jamie said gruffly.

"I know. But there's humor in it, since it has no' happened 'afore."

Jamie was incensed, for he found the situation highly disconcerting. After all, they were brothers. "And if I should set out to win her? You'll no' be thinking that so amusing, will you?"

"You're welcome to try, brother, if 'tis marriage you have in mind," Colen said seriously. "But if 'tis only another mistress you're wanting, I'd no' take kindly to that. The lass says she'll marry only for love. I'll no' stand in the way if she chooses you freely. And you've already given your blessing if she chooses me. What could be fairer than that, eh?"

"You surprise me, lad."

Colen grinned. "And you're forgetting something, brother. Sheena trembles at the mere sight of you. I dinna think you'll have much luck winning her. You frighten her so."

If Colen had desired to bring Jamie's anger over the boiling point, he had succeeded. "Fetch the lass!" he snapped. "It could well be she'll find herself back in Aberdeen tomorrow and no' have to contend with either MacKinnion brother!"

"Now, Jamie, dinna be rash."

"Rash? Sweet Mary!" Jamie swore. "Fair is what I'll be. Now bring her!"

Colen shook his head. "She'll no' come near you if you're scowling like black thunder."

Jamie managed a smile, though it was a dark smile. "Is this better?" he asked sarcastically.

"Ha! Not by much," Colen grunted. "If the lass looks at you and flees, you'll know why."

Movement caught her eye, and Sheena turned to see Colen leaving the laird's table. She knew his path would lead to her, and she wanted to get up and run away. She had already made one scene, and in front of *him*. She was determined not to do so again.

But when Colen spoke behind her, Sheena's nerves shattered. "Lass, my brother wishes a word with you."

"I'm no' ready," she whispered.

"He is."

She turned around to look at Colen. His expression was unreadable. She couldn't look up at the laird's table though, to see what awaited her there. She had spent a miserable night alone, remembering every terrible story she had ever heard about James MacKinnion.

"I . . . I think I would rather wait, Colen," Sheena said nervously. "Truly, I—"

"Sheena." He cut her off. "The time has come."

Knowing there was no choice, she rose and let Colen lead her to the raised dais, his hand firmly on her elbow. The closer she got, seeing James MacKinnion watching her every move with dark, hardened eyes, the more Colen had to force her along. When she came around the table, Jamie stood up, so his eyes didn't leave her.

Standing before him, forcing herself to meet his gaze, she watched his jaw clamp down and wondered what *he* had to be nervous about. She didn't know that she caused it, that her eyes were wide and frightened. She didn't even realize she was pulling back so hard that if Colen had let go of her arm she would have fallen backward.

"By the fire, Colen," Jamie ordered, and a moment later Colen was pushing her down into one of the cushioned chairs, the laird of Castle Kinnion standing in front of the hearth, his back to her. Colen sat down on a bench beside Sheena and gave her a reassuring smile. Then The MacKinnion turned around and pierced her with those brooding hazel eyes.

"Well, Sheena, how do you like Castle Kinnion?"

The question eased her, as he had meant it to.

Whatever she had expected from this harsh laird, it wasn't such a casual, hospitable question.

"'Tis a fine castle, to be sure."

"One you wouldna mind living in?"

She should have known better than to relax her guard so easily. Was he already deciding to make her stay, without even hearing her wishes?

"I would mind," she said firmly.

Jamie chuckled and sat down opposite her. "Well then, we had best settle this. First, I'm sure you know my brother's no' sorry he brought you here. You'll be getting no apology from him."

"I dinna expect one. I just want to leave."

"So you have said. But I hope you will understand my position. You are here, no' of your own design, but here nonetheless. And being here, you are my responsibility."

"But I dinna hold you responsible," she assured him quickly.

"I do." His tone was inflexible. "But that is no' the issue. The fact is, my brother has given sound reasons why you should settle here and make your home with us."

"To marry him!" Sheena gasped, suddenly furious over the way the interview was progressing.

"His reason has naught to do with that. He is concerned with your welfare, lass."

"I didna ask for his concern—or yours."

"Your attitude is unusual," Jamie said thoughtfully. "Another in your position, alone and penniless, wouldna hesitate to accept the security offered here. Why do you refuse?"

"I'll no' be forced into marrying."

"You misunderstand, Sheena," Jamie replied patiently. "'Tis a home, a clan to belong to I am offering you, whether you marry my brother or no'."

Sheena grew uncomfortable. From what he believed of her, thinking her a homeless beggar, what he offered was very generous. But if he knew the truth, he would not wonder at her refusal. To settle among her clan's enemies was unthinkable. But he was being kind, the last thing she would have expected. And that made her seem so ungrateful.

"I . . . I'm a Lowlander," she said at last, jumping to any reasonable excuse. "Though I thank you for your offer, which is very kind, I canna settle here."

"Are we such a terrible lot as you've been raised to believe?" Jamie asked with a smile. "Is it savages you see in this hall?"

"I've no' seen much of your people here, so I canna judge," she returned evasively.

"You disappoint me, lass. Will you no' think about my offer for a time?"

"Nay," she said firmly. "I canna fit in here. 'Tis better I leave now."

Jamie was vexed, and he couldn't keep it from her. "To return to what? The streets? Begging? You'll be giving me a valid reason, lass, 'afore I'll relinquish my responsibility."

Sheena stiffened. He was growing angry again. But then, so was she. By what right did he demand a reason? By what right did he take away her freedom?

"I wish to return to what I know. That is enough reason," she said coldly.

"That is a beggar's life. It appears you dinna know what is good for you."

"So you think!" she snapped, losing her temper under that hard gaze. "The fact is, I'm no' a beggar, nor have I ever been. 'Tis only what Colen assumed."

"Is it now?" Jamie asked smoothly. "Then why have you waited till now to say so?"

"I didna feel the need to tell you."

"You'll be telling me now, though," Jamie said coldly, his eyes narrowed. "From what clan do you come?"

Sheena paled, searching frantically through her mind for a name, a name he could not easily dismiss. "I . . . I am a MacEwen."

"From the landless MacEwens?" he asked scornfully.

She flinched, but answered, "Aye."

Jamie laughed. "And you say you're no' a beggar? 'Tis what the MacEwens are now they're dispossessed, beggars and thieves. No wonder you were reluctant to admit who you are."

Sheena had had enough. She took the ridicule to heart and jumped to her feet, her temper soaring. "The MacKinnions are thieves, as well, and murderers!" she said heatedly. "I dinna see anything so proud in that!"

Jamie came to his feet, and Sheena panicked. His eyes smoldered, and his fists were clenched. She expected him to throttle her. Colen had risen, too, confirming that she was in deep trouble.

"What do you know of the MacKinnions that you can make such a charge?" Jamie demanded furiously.

Choked by fear, she tried to speak but couldn't. Her eyes grew wider until, finally, she fled the hall.

She was mindless of pursuit. She just had to get away. She ran through the nearest doorway, which brought her into the courtyard outside. In the bright light of day came the thought of complete escape, of never having to see that man again. She ran toward the gatehouse.

The portcullis was raised, and Sheena had only a moment to be grateful before the shouts of the gatekeeper came to her. She ignored him and ran on, but she couldn't ignore the other voice, the one she was running from. It was shouting her name, close behind her, so close, too close. . . .

A hand gripped her arm like a steel manacle, pulling her back, and she felt her heart stop beating. So overwhelming was her fright, she fell into a black void, doing what she had never done before. She fainted.

Chapter 14

"SHE'S coming around, I think."

The female voice drew Sheena back. The voice held a measure of kindness, and she opened her eyes quickly to find the speaker. The woman was sitting on the bed beside her. Her face matched her voice—the warm smile, the concern in her hazel eyes. Hazel—like his.

"You'll be fine, lass. You gave my nephews quite a scare."

Sheena didn't answer. The woman continued to smile as she removed a wet cloth from Sheena's brow. She was an older woman, with hair more orange than red.

"Who are you?" Sheena asked.

"Lydia MacKinnion. And the lads tell me you're Sheena MacEwen. Och, and such a bonny lass you are, Sheena. I hope our Jamie wasna too rough in bringing you here. You fainted, you see."

The thought of being in his arms, even unconscious, sent a chill through Sheena. "He . . . he

123

carried me here?"

"That he did, and sent for me in a hurry." Lydia chuckled. "The laddie's never had a woman faint on him 'afore."

"Nor have I ever done so 'afore," Sheena tried to explain. "I . . . I dinna know what came over me."

"No matter, as long as you're all right."

"James MacKinnion is your nephew?"

"Aye, I'm sister to his father, Robbie. Or I was," she corrected, and her eyes suddenly took on a far-away look. "My dear brother is gone from us now. He was a good laird, Red Robbie was, no' like our father who . . . who . . ."

"Take my aunt back to the north tower, Gertie."

Sheena stiffened at the sound of that voice. She had believed she was alone with the old woman. But James MacKinnion and Colen both moved forward as a servant helped Lydia to her feet and escorted her from the room. Seeing the vacant look that had overtaken the older woman, Sheena forgot her own predicament for the moment.

"What is wrong with your aunt?" she asked Colen.

But it was Jamie who answered. "She has spells that come on her suddenly. It happens whenever she thinks of her father. She was witness to his murder, you see, his and her mother's."

"How awful!" Sheena gasped.

"Aye. Lydia was only a child when my grandparents were killed. She has had spells like this ever since it happened."

"She was the only witness," Colen added. "The only one who could tell what happened or why. But she's never told. Whenever anybody asks, she gets that faraway look and retreats into her mind."

"Then the murderers were never caught?"

"Only one man did the killing, lass—the old laird of Clan Fergusson. My great uncle meted out justice to him. You're a Lowlander. Do you know Clan Fergusson of Angusshire?"

Sheena choked, and the fit of coughing saved her from answering. Colen came forward quickly to pat her back, and she fell back onto her pillow.

She couldn't meet either man's eyes for if she did, she would deny it all and call them liars. Her grandfather was not a murderer. It was a Mac-Kinnion—whom she now knew to be this great uncle of theirs—who brought Niall Fergusson before Tower Esk, bound and gagged, and killed him mercilessly where all could see. So the story went. She had heard it all her life. This was the first she had heard of any other killings. It was a MacKinnion who started the feud, everyone knew that. Yet they were saying it was a Fergusson. She couldn't accept that, but . . . it had happened so long ago, long before she was born. Who was she to say what was right? She hadn't been there. Neither had they. Lydia had been there, though.

"Are you all right now, Sheena?" Colen asked, watching her closely.

"Aye."

"Then you'll be telling me why you ran out of the hall," Jamie demanded.

125

With one of them on either side of the bed, Sheena found it easier to stare at the ceiling. "You were about to strike me," she stated flatly.

"Sweet Mary!" Jamie swore. "'Twas nowhere in my thoughts to strike you!"

Sheena looked at him, her eyes reflecting doubt. "You were shouting at me then, just as you are now."

"And with reason!" Jamie replied sharply. "'Twas a serious charge you made against my clan. I would know why."

"Are you no' a reifer?" she asked cuttingly.

"Tell me who *is* no' a reifer? But murderers? We dinna kill for the sake of it."

She knew better, but she wasn't going to argue about it, not when she was surrounded.

"I'm sorry," she said softly. "'Twould seem I spoke in haste, from assumption. But you did, as well. You assume all MacEwens are beggars and thieves, but my family isna."

"You have family then?" Jamie raised a brow. "Your parents are living?"

"My father is."

"Where is he?"

Sheena was heading for dangerous territory again. If this man found out she was a Fergusson, he would undoubtedly kill her, just as his great uncle had killed her grandfather.

"I . . . I dinna know my father's whereabouts," she lied, thinking quickly. "He doesna stay in one place for long."

"Then how can I return you to Aberdeen, where

you've no one to protect you?"

She began to panic again, and couldn't think clearly.

"I've an aunt in Aberdeen. 'Twas with her I was staying."

"In the poorhouse?" Colen scoffed, not believing any of this, not wanting to.

Sheena glared at him. "My Aunt Erminia is a nun, Colen. She doesna live at the poorhouse, but gives her time there, as others like her do. The place would fall to ruin if the nuns didna see to the cleaning of it. I was only helping Aunt Erminia, to make her day easier."

A long sigh escaped Jamie. "'Twould seem you've made a mistake, Colen."

"'Tis you who are mistaken, Jamie, if you believe nonsense!" Colen replied stiffly. "If that's the truth, then why didn't she say so in the beginning?"

"I was too frightened," Sheena said but they were too intent on each other to hear her.

"Nay, it makes sense, lad," Jamie said reluctantly. "Look at her. She doesna show signs of hunger. Her cheeks are full, her body sturdy. She's too healthy to be a beggar."

"Aye, and no wonder. If she pleaded with you for alms, would you deny her? If you saw her on the street and she begged for a coin, who would give her only one? Who could ignore her? With such a face, she could become rich leading the beggar's life! 'Tis no doubt why she wants to return to it."

"'Tis no' so!" she cried. "I've never gone

without, because I've no' had to. My family provides well. They're no' paupers."

"If they provide for you, then why have they no' found you a husband?" Colen demanded.

"I've answered enough questions," Sheena said flatly. "You've no right to be prying into my life."

"Enough bickering!" Jamie intervened sharply. "Colen, the lass isna destitute. So for me to insist she stay here for her own good is no longer reasonable. You'll take her back to Aberdeen."

Colen turned on his heel and stalked from the room. Sheena was so happy that it was several moments before she realized she was alone in the bedchamber with James MacKinnion.

Fearfully, she looked at him. His eyes were on the open door through which Colen had departed. It struck Sheena suddenly that if she hadn't known *who* he was, she wouldn't have feared him at all. She recalled the night before, when she had first seen him, when she had felt anything but fear. She had actually been quite attracted to him. He was still the most handsome man she had ever seen. And seeing him now, without being unnerved by his steady gaze, she was once again fascinated by him.

"He's a stubborn lad, and no mistake," Jamie said with a long, drawn-out sigh. "It seems I must be taking you to Aberdeen, lass. I'm sure he willna do it."

"*You* take me?" She felt her stomach turn queasy. How to get out of this new fix? "You've been kind indeed, but I . . . canna accept. I'll find my way back alone, thank you."

"Nonsense," he replied sternly. "I dinna take responsibility lightly. I've told you that. I'll see you safely to your aunt. 'Tis well I speak with her too. She needs to understand the folly of leaving you unescorted."

Sheena froze. Speak with Aunt Erminia? He'd learn who they were and kill them both!

"You command many men," she said quickly, fearfully. "Any one of them could take me back. 'Tis no' necessary that you go."

Seeing the fear in her again, he snapped, "You'll go with me or you'll stay! Now which will it be?"

Sheena didn't answer. She couldn't. She would sooner have stayed there, seeing him every day with others nearby, than spend one moment alone with him on some lonely moor. She would have to find some other way to leave.

"Well, lass?"

"I . . . I willna go with you."

"You'll be telling me why, Sheena," he said very quietly.

She found the courage to answer truthfully. "I dinna trust you no' to hurt me."

Anger drained away, replaced by utter confusion. "Why would I hurt you? You're a bonny lass, Sheena. I would never hurt you."

When she remained silent, he said, "You dinna believe me?"

"I only wish I could," she replied truthfully. "But I canna."

Jamie was silent, staring at her thoughtfully. Her

fear of him was infuriating, for he had done nothing to cause it. But she would not be leaving, not without him. She had made the decision herself.

"'Tis glad I am you'll be staying, lass," Jamie said with a half-grin.

Sheena was taken aback. "Why?" she asked warily. "I'll still no' marry your brother."

"And glad I am to hear that, too." Jamie chuckled, so contrary to his previous mood.

Sheena was thoroughly confused. "Glad? But you gave Colen your blessing."

"With reluctance, I assure you."

"I dinna ken. If you dislike me so—"

Jamie's laughter cut her off. "How wrong you are, lass. But no wonder, since I've done naught but shout and lose my temper with you."

He paused, then said, "But 'tis wanting you for myself I am. And there you have it, why I'm glad you're staying. I'll be proving to you you've no reason to fear me."

He turned and left the room then, leaving Sheena alone with her amazement and chagrin. No reason to fear him? He had given her the greatest reason of all!

Chapter 15

C OLEN rode furiously from the castle. In a fine temper, he galloped to Mackintosh land and released himself by harassing crofters, scattering herds, and causing mischief wherever he could. For that reason, it was night when he finally returned and learned that his precious Sheena would be staying after all. Jamie added crossly, after telling him the news, "She might be staying, lad, but I dinna think we'll be seeing much of her."

"Why not?"

"I believe she plans to tuck herself away in that tower and keep hidden from us. It's what she did today."

"Did she no' come down to supper?"

"Nay."

"She went hungry?" Colen exploded.

"Dinna fash yourself, brother." Jamie's tone was calm. "Our aunt appears quite taken with the lass. She went to see the girl—taking a tray of food for her." Jamie grunted. "'Twas no' easy explaining to Jessie what all the fuss is about."

Colen grinned. "I can imagine. Did you tell Jessie she has a rival?"

Jamie scowled darkly. "Now why would I be telling her that? I've enough on my mind without adding more trouble."

"'Tis just as well." Colen baited his elder brother. "No need to have an empty bed waiting to be filled, eh? Who would fault you for keeping a bird in hand?"

Jamie didn't answer. Maybe it was true. He had told Jessie as little as possible about Sheena. He had not known precisely why, but he began to see a grain of truth in what Colen implied, and he didn't like it. Such selfishness was unworthy of him, never mind that he had been unaware of it until that point.

"Well said, Colen. I'll be rectifying the situation tomorrow."

Colen was surprised, and he quickly realized that in baiting his brother he had only spited himself. With Jamie unencumbered by his present mistress, he would be free to devote himself fully to pursuing Sheena.

"Now wait, Jamie," Colen said hastily. "I was only jesting. Dinna deny yourself, or Jessie, because of my foolish talk."

"But you were right, lad. 'Tis no' fair to Jessie to pretend my interest is the same. No, better to end it now, after only one encounter."

"One?"

"Dinna look so shocked." Jamie chuckled. "I'm

no' the ruttish stag folks take me for."

"Humph!"

Jamie shrugged. "In truth, I've no' had much desire for Jessie since I met the lovely Sheena."

"'Tis no' like you to be so . . . particular," Colen grumbled, not at all pleased.

Jamie ignored the gibe and said, "The dark-red-haired lass in the tower is a jewel to outshine any other. I'll have her or have no one."

Recognizing Jamie's iron determination, Colen knew then and there that his brother was as obsessed with Sheena as he was, perhaps even more so. It was an upsetting realization.

"You'll no' be having her unless she wants it!" he warned sharply. "I mean it, Jamie."

"Have you ever known me to take a lass who wasna willing?" Jamie countered.

"I've never known one to refuse you, so how can I know what you'll be doing when this one does?"

"I'll no' force her, lad," Jamie said calmly.

"Sheena is hard to resist," Colen said relentlessly.

"But you've no' touched her," Jamie reminded him.

"True, but it has no' been easy. 'Tis a battle I fight with myself, keeping her at arm's length. So I'm asking you, Jamie, can you consider her feelings above your own. Can you leave her be, as I have, if she doesna want you?"

Jamie's brow wrinkled in a frown. "I've told you I'll no' force the lass."

"So you have, but you're a man accustomed to

133

getting whatever you want *and* no' having to wait for it. I'm wondering if you can wait, Jamie, or even go without something you want badly."

"You're asking too many questions, lad," Jamie replied irritably.

"You dinna like the idea of defeat?"

"I dinna like all this prying. If you find me conducting myself badly in this matter, then I give you permission to point it out—when and if that happens. Till then, lad, leave it be. I canna say now what I will or willna do, any more than you can."

Colen didn't push, but he couldn't shake off his uneasiness. He knew his brother's temper and impatience. How would Sheena fare?

"So she would rather stay here, where she doesna want to be, than ride alone with you to where she does want to be?" Colen asked.

"She's naught to fear from me, but I must prove it to her," Jamie sighed.

"If you can keep your temper," Colen replied, "she may stop being afraid of you. To be truthful . . . I hope she doesn't," he finished fervently.

Chapter 16

S HEENA fell back on her pillow, grateful for the downy softness cushioning her aching head. Lydia had just left. Sheena was grateful for her thoughtfulness and for the food. It was comforting to know there was a kind soul there, someone who cared. But Sheena wished Lydia hadn't come, for unwittingly, the older woman had added to Sheena's fears.

She was much too perceptive. The whole time she chatted about mundane things, putting Sheena at ease, she had been studying her intently. Then, all at once, she had said bluntly, "You've the hair and eyes of a Fergusson! I knew there was something familiar about you, but it only just came to me. That hair, so darkly red, 'tis the same color as Niall Fergusson's hair was." Sheena had been too stunned to speak, and the woman had rambled on. "I've never seen another family with such hair. Are you a Fergusson?"

"I . . . I've said who I am."

135

"Och, so you have." Lydia had sighed. "Dinna mind me, hinny. 'Tis only I've seen the way our Jamie looks at you. He has a feeling for you, and no mistake. Only . . . it has long been a wish of mine that he marry a Fergusson lass to put an end once and for all to our horrible feud. So here I am, trying to make a Fergusson out of *you*. But I know in my heart he would never marry just to please me. 'Tis just as well you're no' a Fergusson. Then again, if you were, you wouldna admit it, would you?"

Lydia had left then, quietly closing the door without waiting for an answer. She had apparently guessed the truth. What if she told Jamie? Lydia had not seen a Fergusson for forty-seven years, yet she had seen the resemblance Sheena bore to her grandfather. Jamie had seen her father recently, and her brother, as well. He had not noticed the resemblance, but would he if Lydia pointed it out to him? Of course he would.

Sheena thrashed around on the bed, her headache getting steadily worse. What was she going to do? If James MacKinnion found out who she was, he would kill her. His desiring her would make no difference then. She should have let him take her to Aberdeen. But her fears there were doubled— being ravished by him on the way, and then being killed when she met her aunt and learned who she was.

The fears invaded her sleep when sleep finally came. Her dream was the nightmare she lived while awake. She was riding through the streets of Ab-

136

erdeen, sitting atop a powerful horse. James
MacKinnion was behind her, his arms locked
around her so she would not fall, and binding her
so she could not escape, either. Then there was the
nunnery, and Aunt Erminia standing in front of it,
waving excitedly, happy to see Sheena safe. Aunt
Erminia was unaware of the danger, and there was
no way Sheena could warn her. Then the horse
stopped, but Sheena was not allowed to dismount.
Those strong arms still held her, getting tighter,
cutting off her breathing so she couldn't speak. He
asked the question she knew would come, whether
her aunt was Erminia MacEwen. Sheena screamed
to prevent him hearing the answer, but he heard it
anyway and she was thrown to the ground. She
looked up and saw her enemy, sword in hand, a
look of terrible rage on his face. She screamed
again as the sword was raised, screaming again and
again, waiting for it to descend and cut her to
pieces. But instead a hand covered her mouth to
silence her, and then the sword and enemy were
gone. Someone had saved her and was comforting
her, whispering soothing words, letting go of her
mouth as she began to cry with relief, holding her
close to dispel her fear.

She realized she was no longer dreaming. She
was in the tower room, dark because the candle
had burned out. The comforting arms were real. A
man was sitting on her bed, holding her close
against his bare chest, a wide muscular chest. The
arms were terribly strong.

"Colen?"

"What frightened you so, lass?"

His voice was muffled in her hair, but she sensed real caring and said, tears in her voice, "I dreamed your brother was going to kill me."

Did she imagine the tensing of his muscles? She shouldn't have spoken. The poor lad, how was he to deal with her revulsion for his brother? He was loyal to the older man. And she couldn't explain.

"I'm sorry, Colen," she offered. "I know you dinna ken why I fear him so."

"Explain it then." The voice was low and still muffled.

"I canna make it plain," she said.

"But he's never hurt you," said the voice.

"No, not so far."

He took her head between his hands, his face so close she could feel his breath. "He would never harm *you,* Sheena," he said huskily. "How can I make you see that?"

Before she could answer, Colen was kissing her. She was more than surprised, not only by the first touch of a man's lips, but by the tenderness of it. Colen was usually so rough. This was a gentle brush of lips, soft, warm. The tingling of his fingers on the back of her neck spread down her back. She had to forcefully remind herself that this was Colen, a mere lad.

She tried halfheartedly to move away, struggling when she couldn't put any real distance between herself and him. He laughed deeply, and somehow she knew it wasn't Colen. There was too much strength, too much authority in the man.

"G . . . go away," she stammered, horrified to find herself in Jamie's arms.

Jamie kept his face close to hers. "Have I hurt you?" he demanded, though not roughly. "Have I?"

"Nay."

"Was the kiss so terrible?

He didn't let her answer. His mouth closed over hers again, but this kiss was different—gentle, yet so overpowering she thought she might faint.

When the kiss ended, Sheena was filled with an awed feeling, a feeling of wonder. She was so relaxed, so at ease. It was several moments before clear thought returned. She tensed, then, and fear ruled again.

Jamie was joyful. Sheena had responded. She had been soft and pliant in his arms, letting him hope she was not as repulsed by him as she had been.

"You yielded to me, Sheena," Jamie said gruffly. "You liked my kissing. So dinna push me away and deny it."

"Let me go."

Jamie sighed, released her, and stood up. "There. You see how agreeable I am?"

Sheena sensed the anger underlying his words and knew the cause. If she showed her fear, she would increase his anger.

"Will you leave now?" she asked meekly.

"You dinna like my company?

Sheena sighed. How like a man to turn stubborn when angry!

"I'm sorry I've upset you, Sir Jamie, but I didna ask you to kiss me."

"But you didna mind it, either. You may wish otherwise, but you liked it, and for a moment you were mine. If 'twas only your passion I wanted, I could have taken it. I think you know that."

Sheena trembled. Was it true?

"What prevented you?" she dared to ask him.

"I'm wanting more from you than just a quick tumble."

Sheena gasped at the crude remark. "You'll no' be getting even that!"

Jamie laughed, delighted. She had set aside fear long enough to let her temper loose.

"I'll no' be your mistress!" she snapped, furious at his laughter.

"Nor will I ask you to be."

Sheena frowned. "I dinna ken. You say you want me, then you deny it. Are you amusing yourself at my expense, James MacKinnion?"

"Never, lass," he breathed softly. "I'm wanting you badly and willing for you to know it. I've never given a lass such an advantage 'afore."

"If you think I'm grateful, you're mistaken."

"It doesna please you that I am taken with you?"

Sheena was becoming most exasperated. "You've a high opinion of yourself, Sir Jamie! 'Tis understandable enough, you being laird of such a fine castle and no doubt sought after by many. You're a fine looking man, too, I'll say that plainly. But I'm no' flattered to receive your attentions."

"You'll tell me why you dislike me so."

His tone was harsh. How, then, could she tell him she knew him to be cruel, vengeful, and murderous? She had to keep in mind that Lydia knew too much.

"I just want to be left alone," Sheena said softly, skirting the issue altogether. "Have I no' the right to refuse you? I did your brother."

"Aye, you have the right. But you've yet to hear what it is you're refusing."

"I dinna care."

"'Tis cruel you are, lass, no' to even give me a chance. I wouldna have thought that of you."

Sheena flinched. It was true. Being hard was wrong, and it was not the way to handle James MacKinnion, especially when he couldn't know her real motive.

"I'm sorry, Sir Jamie. You're right. The least I can do is listen to you."

"By the saints, but you try a man sorely!" Jamie exploded.

"What did I say—?"

"Never patronize me, Sheena MacEwen. I'll bear your fear, your anger, and your loathing, but I'll no' be played for a fool!"

Sheena's eyes gleamed. "There's just no pleasing you, is there?"

"A little honesty would be appreciated."

She gasped. "I *was* honest, and for that you called me cruel!"

"So I did—and so you were." And then, to Sheena's amazement, he chuckled. "I like your spunk, lass. Never be afraid to show it with me."

141

"Och, you're impossible!"

"No more than you are, m'dear," he replied lightly, and Sheena grinned. How easy it would be to like him if he were not a MacKinnion—*The* MacKinnion.

"I do believe I've weathered the storm," she remarked impulsively.

"Do you now?" Jamie said, delighted by her change of mood. "And was it such a bad storm?"

"Nay. I suppose not."

"I hope you'll be remembering that in future."

"Maybe I will."

Jamie laughed heartily. "You're a rare one, lass. 'Tis no wonder I'm thinking of handfasting myself to you."

Sheena was not prepared. "Handfasting? You jest!"

"Nay, I'm willing to commit myself, and I want the same of you."

This was much too serious. "You honor me, Sir Jamie, but I must refuse," she replied uneasily, her voice as soft as she could make it.

"I'll no' accept that."

"You must," she said firmly. 'I'll no handfast with you or any other man. I dinna hold with that loose commitment."

"And I'll no' marry a woman I've no' tried!" he retorted just as firmly.

"'Tis glad I am to hear it, for I'm no' wanting to marry you anyway," she said hotly. Didn't he think highly of himself!

Jamie was silent, fighting to overcome rage. He

swallowed hard and managed a level tone.

"You'll give me the courtesy of thinking on my offer?"

"Very well."

Expecting another harsh dismissal, Jamie was overjoyed. It was a little thing he'd won, but it was enough for the time being.

"I misjudged you, lass. You can be reasonable after all." Sheena said nothing to that, and Jamie grinned. "I'll be leaving you now, but I'm thinking I'll have one more kiss 'afore I go."

His mouth silenced whatever protest she might have made. The first tender kisses hadn't prepared her for this. Jamie released his passion for a brief moment, and Sheena was incredulous at her unresisting compliance. She should have been pushing at him, anything but what she was doing. She was captive of a will stronger than her own.

He left the bed and went to the door. "You'll be thinking over what has been said and done, lass. And there'll be no more hiding in this tower. I want to see you in the hall tomorrow. And, henceforth, have pleasant dreams."

Then he was gone, and the door closed. Silence prevailed. Pleasant dreams henceforth? She was living the nightmare she had had—and had told him about! Or perhaps she was still dreaming. There was something not quite real about what had transpired in the dark. Better to believe she had never awakened, that James MacKinnion had not come into her room and said and done so much. Much better to have only dreamed it all. Much better.

Chapter 17

THE pounding on the door woke Sheena abruptly, getting louder and louder before she could reach it and throw it open. She was furious to be awakened in such a rude manner. Seeing Colen standing there grinning as if he hadn't made enough noise to wake the dead only made her angrier.

"Must you make such a racket?" she snapped.

"Must you take so long to answer?"

"I was sleeping!"

"Och, 'tis late for that," he replied.

"I dinna care what time it is," Sheena retorted. "I'll be going back to bed now."

"Nay, lass." Colen shook his head, still wearing that infuriating grin. "You've been ordered to appear below, and so you shall."

Sheena had been in the process of yawning, but that stopped her. "Ordered? Who dares order me? *Him?*"

Colen chuckled. Her indignant expression was

just what he'd expected.

"He says he warned you last night no' to be hiding up here any longer."

"But I . . . I had hoped . . ." She swung around. What a fool she was to think wishing something away would make it go. "What else did he tell you about last night?" She turned back, facing him squarely.

"More than he cared to admit."

"Then you know he asked me to handfast?"

"Aye."

Sheena frowned at his expression. "And what do you find so amusing about it, I'd like to be knowing?"

"You'll tell him nay. He's expecting an answer today and is waiting for it now. An impatient man, my brother. He canna stand waiting for anything, especially something he is no' certain of getting."

"But today?" she gasped. "He said I could think on it." She began to pace the room. "And what will he do when I refuse him, Colen? What do you think?"

"He'll no' give up any more than I did. You're the first he's asked to handfast, so you see he's quite serious about you, Sheena."

"But I would never handfast. 'Tis a man's convenience, and one I dinna believe in."

"Yet, 'tis considered honorable, especially in the Highlands," Colen pointed out.

"Maybe, but how often does it really lead to marriage? You have a man and woman handfasting for an agreed-upon time, and in all respects they are wed. Yet when that time is over, the man can reject the woman publicly, and they go their separate ways."

"The woman has that privilege, too."

"True, but the man is no' changed by it, or thought the worst of for having failed. But the woman is no longer a maiden and is known to have failed, no matter the reason. You think another man considering her will no' think long and hard about that?"

Colen shrugged. "I've never thought of it that way. But handfasting is a tradition older than both of us, and I'll no be arguing over it now. I'm no' the one asking you to handfast. I dinna need time to see if we can be happy together—I know we can. 'Tis Jamie you'll have to be telling all this to, for after the tragedy of his first marriage, he's sworn never to marry again unless he's tried his bride-to-be."

"This is all beside the point, Colen. I'll no' be handfasting *or* wedding your brother. Now I've asked you what he'll do when I tell him so, and you say he'll no' give up. What does that mean, Colen?"

"I dinna know what he'll do, Sheena, truly," Colen replied gently. "I suppose he'll ask you again and again until you say yes. But Jamie's never met with anything like this 'afore and how he'll handle it is uncertain." He brightened. "Then again, you can solve everything by telling him you'll wed me. He'll leave you alone then."

Sheena plopped down on the bed, angered by his

suggestion, however lightly given. "You do think all this is amusing, this fix *you've* put me in! Aye, 'tis your fault I'm here. 'Twould serve you right if I did marry your brother!"

"If that is what you want—"

"What I want! Sweet Mary!" She shot off the bed, raging. "You know what I want! Take me away from here. You can—he'll let you. Take me away 'afore he kills me!"

"Dinna talk like that!" Colen shouted back. How could she say anything so shocking about his brother?

Sheena glared at him, her blue eyes sparkling with jewel-like radiance. "Do this, dinna do that— 'tis all I've heard since I've been here! No' even my father ordered me about like this. If you were not so much like my brother, I'd be hating you like I do Sir Jamie!"

"You've a brother?"

She clamped her mouth shut and walked past him through the door. Colen caught up with her on the stairs, but she wouldn't stop.

"Sheena!"

The stairs leading to the second floor were circular and narrow. Sheena wouldn't look at him, but concentrated on her footing instead.

"Leave me be, Colen. The great laird is waiting."

"*Have* you a brother?"

"Aye, a brother, a father, sisters, cousins! I told you I've family, but would you believe me?"

She stalked down the second floor passage to the

stairs that led to the hall. Colen was right beside her, growing just as angry as she was.

"We've been over this 'afore, Sheena!"

"Aye, but we never reached truth," she stormed. "You are selfish, Colen, selfish and stubborn. If you had any feeling for me at all, you'd see I hate it here and take me back to where you found me!"

"To what good?"

Sheena was so enraged that she shrieked, "For my good!"

She had just about reached the open archway into the hall. A man stood there, a handsome man of lean build. Whether he had been about to leave the hall or enter it, Sheena couldn't tell. He was looking up, drawn by her voice. What had been an expression of open curiosity turned to awe when Sheena took the last few steps and stood before him. She was a vision of dark-red-haired fury.

Sheena was struck with acute embarrassment, knowing this man had heard her tirade. Oh, the arrogance of the laird who had given the order to drag her down there! What sport for these Highlanders to see their laird abuse a Lowlander! She must never give him an excuse to berate her in public.

Colen was right behind Sheena, but the man didn't see him. He was blocking their way into the hall, and although Sheena was too flustered to point that out, Colen was not.

"Your pardon, Black Gawain." He spoke curtly.

Black Gawain's surprise gave way to a winsome smile. "Och, Colen, where are your manners? I've no' met this lovely lass—"

"Nor need you!" Colen snapped.

"Have a heart, lad."

"Nay, you have a care," Colen returned, unrelenting. "She's spoken for."

"Is she now? By you then?"

"The lad is mistaken." Sheena took matters into her own hands. "And I am Sheena, late of Aberdeen, sir."

"And desirous to return there?"

She blushed. "You heard that?"

"I assure you 'twas no' intentional."

Colen was bristling over Sheena's behavior and Black Gawain's obvious interest in her. What chance did he have when older, more experienced men offered suit? He did not consider Jamie a threat, not really, not the way Sheena felt about him. But Black Gawain was an unexpected challenge.

"You've detained us long enough, Black Gawain," Colen said coldly. "My brother awaits us."

"Och, well, I've business with Sir Jamie myself," Gawain said agreeably.

"Naught that canna wait, I trust?"

"'Tis sorry I am to be disappointing you, lad, seeing as you're eager to be rid of me. No' that I blame you, mind you." Gawain grinned, his eyes caressing Sheena admiringly. "But the girnal's in need of repair because of the heavy rains we've been having. I'll be talking to Sir Jamie now, and so you'll allow me, lass. . . ."

He offered his arm, and Sheena took it, remarkably at ease with this man and surprised by the fact. Darkly handsome he was, and gallant—for a Highlander. Is that what makes him likable? she asked herself. She had been too much in the company of the rough, overbearing MacKinnion brothers, that was it. Black Gawain had manners, courtly behaviour she would take for granted at home but had been missing at Castle Kinnion.

Sheena managed to appear calm as they approached the laird's table. She was even able to meet those hazel eyes, cloudy green just then, and inscrutable. James MacKinnion was keeping his feelings tightly hidden, as was she.

Jamie arose, marveling anew at her beauty, her flawless skin, those bright, clear blue eyes, the masses of hair floating down the gentle curve of her back.

Quite formally, Jamie took Sheena's hand. He had given this much thought. "I had begun to think our guest wouldna join us. You're no' ill, I trust?"

Sheena's gaze fell from his. "Just weary. I didna sleep very well."

"We have that in common, then," Jamie murmured softly with unmistakable meaning. He pulled her closer, offering her the chair next to his, forcing her to sit.

Sheena was flustered by the blatant reminder of Jamie's desire. Black Gawain was standing back a little way, also confused by the remark. Sheena wished she could explain to Black Gawain, or protest. He could make an ally. But was he not Jamie's man? Would he even speak to her again, now that Jamie had made his interest in her clear?

Just as Colen stepped forward to take the chair to Sheena's left, Black Gawain moved smoothly in front of him and took that position. Colen was angry enough to challenge his cousin, and would have if Jamie had not given him a sharp look of disapproval. With heightened color, Colen turned away and left the hall. Jamie turned that dark look on Black Gawain.

"What brings you here, cousin?"

"Do I need a reason to come to this hall?" Gawain grinned.

"You provoked my brother."

"Did I? Well, young Colen has a thing or two to be learning about the ways of fighting for a fair lass."

"And you'll be teaching him?"

Sheena squirmed, her nerves jumping. The underlying anger was growing. They were talking over her, as though she weren't there, yet the fight was because of her. Her hand was still being held by the man she feared. His fingers were surprisingly warm, strong.

"What is this about, Jamie?" Gawain sighed. "The lad says she's spoken for, but she says nay."

"So she does." Jamie's tone softened. "But I'll thank you to withhold your interest until she says nay to me, as she has to my brother."

"I'll say—"

Sheena was cut short by a warning pressure from Jamie's fingers. She wasn't fool enough to test the man just then. If he wanted to hear her answer when they were alone, so be it.

"You'll say what, lass?" Black Gawain prompted. But when she shook her head, he didn't press it. "No' made up your mind, eh?" He leaned back reflectively. "Well, well, so that's the way of it. I must say, I never thought to see you and Colen fancying the same woman, Jamie."

"It has been known to happen in many families," Jamie replied, his casual tone a little forced.

"So it has," Gawain agreed. "And what of Jessie Martin? I thought—"

"'Tis over," Jamie said curtly.

"Is it now? But does she know that?"

"You ask too many questions, Gawain. This is none of your concern."

Gawain smiled. At that moment Jessie came hurrying over, looking provocative in a blue silk gown. She gave Jamie a bright smile. He swore silently. He hadn't had time to speak to her, and now Sheena was there. Sweet Mary!

"Dinna leave, Sheena." Jamie squeezed her hand before letting it go. "I want to talk to you when I'm through."

She looked at him beseechingly. She understood who this woman was, and what she was to Jamie.

"I know what you're about to do, Sir Jamie, and I'm asking you no' to do it on my account. You'll regret it."

He smiled at her gently before he left the table to intercept Jessie, steering her to the hearth. Sheena sighed. This mistress of Jamie's was a strikingly beautiful woman. She did not deserve to be treated so callously. Sheena's guilt grew when voices were raised.

"You canna mean it, Jamie. 'Tis too soon!"

"Lower your voice, Jessie."

"Nay! I'll no' go!"

"You will!"

"Och, God," Sheena gasped, covering her face with her hands. "How can he be so cruel?"

"Dinna waste your sympathy on a slut, lass," Black Gawain said.

"I would have expected more charity from you, sir," she said stiffly.

"Och, now, dinna look at me that way. Jessie Martin is a calculating, deceiving woman. She's only getting what she deserves."

"What do you mean?"

"Our Jamie wanted naught to do with her," Gawain explained. "He knew her game and what she was after. Anyone who knows Jessie does. But she was out to have him, and there's only so much enticing a man can withstand."

"I'd prefer no' to be hearing of this."

"I only thought you'd be wanting to know, since you'll be taking Jessie's place."

Sheena's eyes flared. "He's no' asked me to be his mistress," she said indignantly.

Gawain looked suitably shocked. "Forgive me, lass. I was only assuming . . . I mean, Jamie's sworn never to marry without trying his bride first."

"So I've heard," Sheena retorted.

"He's asked you to handfast then?" At her reluctant nod, Gawain chuckled. "Well, well, I never thought to see it. He's no' handfasted 'afore, you see. He's never found a lass he'd be willing to commit himself to."

"I dinna see handfasting as a commitment," she said sharply. "'Tis only free license for an immoral love. I dinna believe in—"

She was cut short as a hand dug into her hair, yanking so viciously that her chair toppled over and she found herself on the floor.

She couldn't move. The wind had been knocked out of her. She could see the face of her attacker above her, a face contorted wildly by rage, an ugly visage replacing the beauty she had seen earlier in Jessie Martin. A hand with its bent fingers and long nails was coming at Sheena's face, yet she couldn't seem to move, to cry out. She could only stare at those clawlike fingers, mesmerized as they got closer and closer. . . .

The hand was gone. Jessie stumbled backward, yanked away by Jamie.

"Enough!" Jamie roared. "Or I'll lay you out as I'm tempted to do!"

"I dinna care!" Jessie cried. "You turn me out for this *tart* your brother brought home. Why?"

"I'm no' obliged to explain to you, Jessie. 'Tis over and that is all you need know."

"I'll no' stand for it!" the woman screeched. "You used me, Jamie!"

"No more than you did me," he replied, his voice controlled and cold. "You'll be paid for your trouble, if that is what worries you."

"Curse you, Jamie MacKinnion!" Jessie hissed,

her green eyes gleaming fire. "You'll be regretting this, I swear you will. And she will, too!" Jessie turned her murderous eyes on Sheena. "You're welcome to him, for he'll be treating you this way as soon as a new lass catches his eye. The man is a faithless bastard!"

Jamie gripped her arms and shoved her away from him. "Gawain, if you please, take her out of here. And find someone deaf to escort her home. I wouldna wish this hagborn tongue on anyone who can hear."

Gawain was thoroughly amused. He chuckled as he moved to take Jessie's arm. "She just needs a little reassurance. I'm just the one to give it to her, if you can do without me for a day or two."

"Suit yourself," Jamie said. "As long as you know what you're doing."

Black Gawain laughed as he took Jessie out of the hall. She went willingly enough, her confidence restored by a new admirer. Gawain listened to her indignation with only half an ear. Cruel, selfish, fickle, were just a few of the words Sheena overheard before the hall quieted. What had happened was unbelievable. The humiliation. The scorn. All so unnecessary.

"Sheena."

All that she was fighting to control was revealed in the look she turned on Jamie. "How dare you subject her to that? How dare you subject *me* to that?" Her voice was but a whisper, but filled with such outrage that Jamie was taken aback.

"I didna know she would make such a fuss. Are

155

you hurt, lass?"

"'Tis a fine time to be asking!" Sheena's voice rose. "You had no right to insist I stay here and be put through that."

"That isna why I asked you to stay." His temper was wearing thin, and, quickly, she lowered her gaze. She was provoking him to the very thing she feared the most—his anger.

"I think enough has been said and done this day." She spoke very softly.

"Now what is this?" he demanded. "So much anger canna disappear that easily. If you wish to shout at me, do so. Dinna hide your spirit behind a meek surface. I'll no' stand for that, Sheena. Dinna pretend wi' me."

"Very well, Sir Jamie," she said stiffly. "I hate what you just did, and agree with everything that woman said of you. I asked you no' to do it, but you wouldna listen to me. Now you've no one, for you certainly don't have me."

Jamie grinned, surprising her. "We'll see about that, lass."

"There'll be no handfasting!" she snapped, infuriated by his easy humor.

"We'll see about that, too," he assured her. "Now come, you've no' eaten."

Sheena ignored his outstretched hand, exasperated by this new mood of his. "I've no appetite now. If you'll excuse me. . . ."

Jamie sighed. "Very well. But you'll be riding with me today. Be ready in an hour."

"Nay!" she gasped.

"Be ready, Sheena."

She walked away. Another order, and one she would have to obey. She could challenge him only so often, she knew. The man misused his power cruelly. Yet how much could she do about it?

Chapter 18

T IGHT-lipped, temper simmering, Sheena glared furiously at the wide back riding before her. She had not said one word to him when he came for her at noon, or as he escorted her to the stable and helped her mount a mare. She had not acknowledged his compliments or his attempts at conversation. His high-handedness was more than she could bear.

She was, at that point, forced even to abide his charity. The gown he had given her fit her well. She and Lydia were the same small size, and only the tightness in the bosom made it apparent that the gown was not Sheena's. It was lovely, powder blue, with full sleeves that turned back to reveal white fur cuffs. There was a matching fur-lined cloak with a pearl clasp. Under other circumstances, the gown would have been appreciated.

She hadn't been paying attention to where he was leading her, but suddenly she realized that they were not riding down to the valley, where flat land would allow an agreeable ride. As they rounded a steep crag, Sheena looked back. She could no longer see the castle. They were riding neither up nor down the mountainside, but following a worn pathway. There were no crofts there, no sign of life except a few trees and berry bushes.

A shiver of fright ran down her back. Out there, no one would be able to hear her cry. There were only the two of them. She was utterly at his mercy. Why, he was even holding her horse's reins, leading her.

"Where are you taking me?" Sheena shouted, but Jamie didn't answer. Nor did he turn around to look at her. She tried to force down her rising panic. "Sir Jamie, please! I wish to go back!"

"Dinna sound so frightened, lass. You've no reason to be," he replied calmly, still without looking around.

If Jamie had seen Sheena's expression, he might have relented. Then again, he might not have. His very purpose in taking her away from the castle to where they could be alone was to prove to her that she could trust him. Also, he wanted to give her a way of enjoying herself. He knew she liked to swim. Of course, he was not going to tell her he had seen her swimming in a glen!

Jamie grinned. He couldn't deny his motives were selfish. He hoped for gratitude, at the very least, a smile from her or a lighter mood. And he could try his damnedest to see again the girl who had laughed and giggled only the night before.

Sheena devoted herself to silent prayer. Her only

hope was for a miracle, something extraordinary to save her from—

Jamie stopped his horse suddenly, and Sheena's mare stopped, too. Sheena held her breath until Jamie turned at last and looked at her. Her breath escaped in a long sigh then, for the look he gave her lacked evil intent. She had never seen a more winsome smile. Remarkably, even her anger disappered, along with her fears. A shyness came over her then, so unlike her. She became flustered when Jamie dismounted and lifted her to the ground. "I came here often when I was a wee lad," he said simply.

"Did you?" she responded, as though they were accustomed to normal conversations.

She saw sparkling water, a lovely little pool on the other side of a burn, next to what appeared to be a man-made dam. A high pile of boulders below the pool hid the water from the valley side.

"Did you make the dam?" Sheena asked.

"Nay. It has been here longer than I can remember. 'Tis a peaceful place. Many's the time I've sat on the rocks there and watched the day pass on the surface of the water. But the rocks form a good base for jumping, too, if you've a mind to dive."

"'Tis deep?"

"Aye, the deep slope is what caused the pool to form easily. To be sure, it makes a fine swimming place."

Sheena was looking at the water wistfully. It did indeed seem a fine swimming hole. Not as secluded as her glen at home, yet private enough, and lovely.

She tried to picture Jamie swimming there but couldn't. Imagining him as a youth was impossible. This man surely had never been a boy!

"Do you still come here sometimes?" Sheena ventured softly.

"No' for many a year. I canna seem to find the time anymore. Then again, I only swim in the warm months, and 'tis too cold for it already this year."

Sheena could have laughed. She was used to swimming in the early spring and late autumn, and in weather colder than this. Oh, how she would like to swim now! If only she were alone. She sighed. To feel the cold water surrounding her, caressing her. She hadn't had a decent bath since being brought to Castle Kinnion, only sponge baths. If only she were alone, she thought again.

"Why did you bring me here?" Sheena asked bitterly.

Jamie turned away. "I thought you would appreciate the tranquillity. Apparently, I was mistaken."

"But I *do*," she assured him, sorry she had sounded so ungrateful.

He turned back, the corners of his mouth lifting slightly. "Then I'm glad I took the time to bring you here. But alas, we canna stay."

"Why?"

"There are others who require my time, lass. But mayhap I will bring you back here, if that is your wish."

"Today."

He laughed. "Mayhap."

161

"Then could you leave me here?" she asked hopefully. "I've a great need to be alone . . . for a while."

He gazed searchingly into her eyes. "If I thought I could be trusting you no' to set out for Aberdeen, I just might grant your wish, lass."

"Take the mare then. I canna get far without her."

"Aye, I could do that, but you could still wander off and lead me the devil's time finding you."

"And if I swore to stay here, to be here when you returned?" she ventured.

"Would you?"

"Aye," she answered quickly, and waited, breathless.

He made her wait several long moments, his expression betraying nothing. Finally he sighed.

"I suppose 'tis a matter of trust—my trusting your word. And as I'm wanting you to trust me, too, the trusting between us must start somewhere."

Sheena's eyes gleamed. "I can stay then?"

"Aye."

"For how long? I mean, how long before you return?"

He grinned. "I'll give you at least an hour, whether I finish 'afore then or no'."

Sheena turned away so he couldn't see how much this small gesture meant to her. "I thank you," she said softly.

"It pleases me if I have made you happy, Sheena."

He sounded so serious that she turned around to look at him again, worried over what he might be making of this. But she found him grinning.

He mounted his horse and grabbed the mare's reins. "I'll be taking your mare, as you suggested," he explained. "Just so you're no' tempted."

As he rode away, back toward the castle, she smiled. Was that charming, agreeable man really her enemy? she asked, then chided herself. He *was*. She would have to guard against that charm. It mattered not at all that he was devilishly handsome, or that he could dispel her fears with a smile. He was still James MacKinnion, sworn enemy of her clan. He might trust her all he wanted—but she would never trust him.

Chapter 19

S HEENA lay stretched out on a smooth rock, basking in the sun slanting through low-lying clouds. The water had indeed been cold, but that had not diminished her delight in the least. She had enjoyed herself thoroughly. Now she was warming her chilled body. It had been much too long since she had enjoyed herself so.

Sheena's hour of privacy was drawing to an end, and she could no longer lie there letting the sun caress her bare skin. She had to dress and dress quickly. She hurried into her clothes, grinning as she thought, How surprised he would have been to find me like that! I'll wager he would have been too shocked to take advantage.

She saw him the moment he rounded the steep crag that hid the castle from view. He galloped over, pulling her mare along. Sheena frowned. Why was he in such a hurry?

"Is something wrong?" Sheena called out to him.

Jamie chuckled and slid off his horse, leaving both animals to graze on the heath. A few long strides brought him around the pool, and he climbed up the rocks to Sheena.

"Can a man no' be eager to join a bonny lass?" He grinned. He reached her side and shoved a sack into her hands.

"What is this?" she asked.

"I recalled that you've no' eaten yet today, so I brought along a wee bit of food for you."

Sheena opened the sack and then looked up at him. "A wee bit? This sack is full."

"Well, 'tis not *all* for you," he replied lightly. "Come, sit with me."

Sheena hesitated. He was in such high spirits, and he seemed so utterly pleased with himself for some reason. Why?

She turned a little, so she could sit facing him.

As soon as they were settled, Jamie grabbed the sack from her and began tossing things to her, a skin of wine, bannocks, half a roasted hen, ginger cakes. She started laughing as the food began to spill out of her lap. "Enough, Jamie!" she cried.

Jamie settled back against a rock, stretching out his long legs. Sheena relaxed, a grin on her lips as she watched him rummage through whatever else there was in the bag. He finally settled on the other half of the hen. They ate, and she watched the play of clouds across the blue sky. She watched Jamie, too, unable to stop from looking his way every so often. Every time she did, her eyes met his and she looked away, flustered. It was ridiculous, the way her eyes were continually drawn to him, almost of their own accord. There was a sort of unreality to what was happening, enforced by the silence. Her pulse picked up its beat each time their eyes met, and she felt a warm, giddy rush. The wine, no doubt. She shouldn't have drunk so much. It made her cheeks hot. No. She was blushing under the constant regard of those hazel eyes.

At last Sheena reluctantly broke the silence. "Should we no' go back?"

"There's no hurry."

Jamie had no intention of leaving yet. He had long ago decided to devote this day to her. It had taken much willpower to leave her alone here. And as he had had no pressing business, it had meant even more willpower to stay away a full hour. But he had wanted her to have her swim.

She was certainly changed! Not a bitter word had crossed her lips since he returned, and there was no fear in her eyes when she looked at him. Instead she blushed, and most becomingly. It was all Jamie could do to still keep his distance.

Sheena got up to wash her hands, kneeling by the water's edge. The rock was too high, and she had to lie down on it to reach the water. As soon as she ran her hands through the pool, Jamie lay down close to her, the whole length of his side pressing against her, his hands cupping the water. She knew she should have jumped right up then, but she didn't. For some reason she couldn't move at all.

His hand caught hers as it trailed in the water,

and he slowly raised it, holding it to his lips, his eyes on hers. Keeping his gaze on her, he began to suck the drops from her fingers. Tingling spread up Sheena's arm and rushed down her back. All the while, he was moving closer and closer. Swiftly he closed the distance. He leaned over her, kissing her ever so softly. His tongue running along her lower lip and then slipping inside her sweet mouth.

If Sheena had thought about what was happening, she might have stopped it. But she had abandoned thought. There was no fear, either, only a strange, warm rush flowing through her. She reveled in it. Nothing that felt so good could be bad.

Jamie pulled them away from the water and gently pushed her down onto his plaid, which he had spread out on the smooth rock before joining her at the water's edge. She had a glimpse of thick, curly hair at the opening of his tunic. Then his mouth covered hers completely, his tongue exploring, and the warmth rushed through her again. Those large, strong hands moved across her cheeks, along her neck, down her arms, while his lips clung to hers.

Vaguely she realized the clasp of her cloak had come undone but dismissed the thought. The lacing on her bodice was unraveling, and Jamie's fingers were tickling just above her breasts. Thought pushed past the warm, rushing feeling: did he mean to undress her?

Sheena brought her hand up to push him away, but Jamie caught the hand and moved it to his cheek.

"You . . . must stop . . . Sir Jamie."

Her voice was no more than a breathless whisper, and, looking at her, he smiled a knowing smile. His eyes moved over her face, admiring every facet of it. Then his lips followed the path of his eyes, his breath warm and caressing, mingling with hers as he licked her lips ever so gently.

"You taste of ginger, and I've no' had dessert yet," he murmured.

Dessert? Did he mean to devour her? She started to protest, but he cut her off.

"Hush now, Sheena. Let me taste of your sweetness." His voice was beguiling. "Let me."

His mouth closed over hers again, and again she felt herself losing control. He plundered her, sucking away her breath, her will.

He let go of her hand then, and the hand instinctively moved to his neck. This time, when she again felt his fingers working on her lacings, she didn't move to stop the magic.

Jamie peeled back the edges of her gown, and she shivered as his hand closed over her warm breast. The large hand moving across her breasts, exploring, gently squeezing, touching where no man had ever touched before, took her beyond the point of protesting.

Jamie felt it. She was his now. He knew it, gloried in it. He was near exploding with need, hard and throbbing, and she moved against him, making it worse. With any other woman it would have been unthinkable to restrain himself. But this was Sheena. He desired her above all others. He had aroused her, and he wanted her to know the full force of that arousal. He wanted her need to be as great as his.

His lips moved to the side of her neck, and as he kissed the sensitive area below her ear, she moaned, trembling. His hands slipped under her back, lifting her, and she gasped as his hot mouth closed over her breast. She grasped his head with both hands, gripping his hair. She was on fire, and the heat moved lower, bring an ache to her whole being.

"Jamie! Ho, Jamie!"

They both heard it. Jamie looked up, his eyes flashing dangerously when he saw his brother coming around the steep crag.

"I'll throttle that lad, so help me I will!" Jamie swore between gritted teeth. He looked down at Sheena. She was frowning, and in an instant she released him, the color draining from her face. Her eyes widened accusingly as she gazed up at Jamie.

"Dinna look at me like that, Sheena," he said levelly. "You've done nothing wrong, and I've done nothing I'll apologize for. What happened was meant to happen, and we'll be finishing it some other time. Now lace yourself quickly. I dinna want my brother seeing you."

The color returned to her face, hot color now, her cheeks crimson. She turned away from him, mortified. Oh, God! What had she done?

She fumbled until she had her bodice tightly closed, then turned to pick up her cloak but found Jamie holding it out to her. She grabbed it, unable to meet his eyes. She never wanted to meet those eyes again.

"Are you all right, Sheena?"

Colen had reached them, stopping his horse just across the burn.

"Nothing is amiss, Colen," she answered, her voice shaking. "We've been for a ride."

Colen raised a brow. "And a swim? Do you no' think the weather's too cold for swimming?"

"How did—?" She caught herself. Of course, her heavy braid was still wet. Slowly, she inhaled deeply. She was suddenly fed up with both men. She started around the pool to her mare, walking quickly.

"Where do you think you're off to, lass?" Jamie called.

"To the castle. I can find my own way, thank you," she retorted angrily.

"Sheena!"

She didn't look back. She swung up onto her horse, positioning herself astride, her skirt hiked to her knees. Digging her heels into the mare, she jumped the burn, surprising both men, and galloped off.

"She rides with unusual skill, and no mistake," Colen remarked as he gazed after her. "You wouldna think MacEwen would possess enough horseflesh to let his women learn to ride."

He looked back at Jamie, flinching under the murderous regard he hadn't expected. "If you were no' my brother," Jamie said icily, "I would take pleasure in killing you right now. What the devil brings you here?" he finished with a shout.

"We've guests at the castle," Colen explained quickly. "Will Jameson has come to look over your horses and he carries a fat purse. I thought you'd want to know."

"He could have waited until I returned, Colen. He'll no doubt be staying the night as it is."

"True. But I had no way of knowing I'd be disturbing you, Jamie. I'm no' sorry I did," he added, then chuckled at his brother's black scowl. "You'd best cool off with a swim now. Don't worry. I'll see that Sheena returns to the castle safely."

He rode away before his brother could get his hands on him, and he didn't try to hide his grin.

Chapter 20

SHEENA entered the living quarters through the servants' entrance, so she would not have to pass through the hall. She ran up the stairs leading to the second floor, along the corridor to the tower, and up more stairs to her room. When she opened the door, she saw two gowns folded on the window seat, and bolts of cloth to make more. The sight brought tears to her eyes, for a new wardrobe seemed to imply that she would never leave there.

She threw herself on the bed, sobbing, then quickly sat up. Her breasts were sensitive, her nerves raw.

"God, what has he done to me? I canna even touch myself and no' be reminded . . ."

How had it happened? She couldn't begin to answer. She knew only that she had been drugged with a heady magic, and she recalled everything, every moment. She blushed.

"He's a devil with a devil's magic, and he works a potent spell. I need to get far, far away from

James MacKinnion."

The one who had made Sheena cry came to her door much later that day. She had slept a little, worn out by confusion and tears. Since waking, she had been combing out her lustrous hair while sitting on the window seat, trying to calm her jangled nerves. But when she saw Jamie, her pulse picked up its beat again, and when he spoke, she jumped.

"You must like this room. You spend so much time in it," he commented with a lazy smile.

"At least I am alone here. Or I *was*," she said pointedly, backing away from him. "Why have you come?"

"To escort you to the hall. We've guests, and it grows late."

"I suggest you attend your guests alone," Sheena replied stiffly.

"I wish to have you at my side," he said.

"But I wish to stay here."

"Now who do you think will be getting their wish?" he said with a grin.

"Is that an order?" she asked sharply.

"Aye."

Sheena cried furiously, "Just who do you think you are?"

"Laird of the MacKinnions," he answered smoothly.

"But I'm *no'* a MacKinnion, and I dinna take kindly to your ordering me about. You've no rights over me!"

"Enough, Sheena." He cut her off. "I'll no'

debate with you. Now I dinna give orders often—"

"You most certainly do," she said.

He frowned. "But when I do, my orders will be obeyed."

"'Tis no' fair!" she cried. "You take advantage of your position."

"Nay, lass, I dinna do that, or I would've had you where I want you 'afore now." She blushed and looked away. His tone softened. "'Tis minor things I insist on, and I wouldna have to insist at all if you didna hide yourself up here."

"'Tis a matter of freedom, Sir Jamie, and you're denying me mine."

Jamie chuckled. "You would be a hermit if I let you. Have you no' learned yet that woman's will is less than man's?"

"Only if woman lets it be so," Sheena said quickly.

Jamie sighed. "I dinna know why I put up with this. Dinna make me force you, Sheena. Come along."

Sheena barely managed to keep herself from shouting. What would defiance accomplish? She was helpless. They both knew it.

But she still had her pride. "Move away from the door, then."

"Why?"

"So I can pass."

Jamie grinned and stepped back, bowing. "Your wish is my command."

"Would that it were, I would no' be here now,"

she said sharply, as she passed him smoothly. She kept up her pace, staying always a little ahead of him, until she reached the arched entrance to the hall. The large room was full of people, and noisy. There was a festive air.

"A feast in honor of our guests," Jamie whispered behind her. "'Tis no' often we have guests and an excuse for festivity."

"Your guests are important?"

"Nay, 'tis only Will Jameson and some of his retainers. Will lives east, across the river."

"Friend or foe?"

Jamie chuckled. "Well now, I can never be sure with old Will. He professes friendship, yet he does try to rile me. I think he just likes to live dangerously."

Sheena stiffened. "Do I detect a subtle warning, Sir Jamie?"

"Come now, Sheena," he admonished lightly. "Must I guard every word I speak? Dinna hunt for hidden meanings."

"Your meaning was clear enough and not hidden," she returned resentfully. "A person must live in fear of your anger."

"Not you, Sheena."

His warm breath near her ear sent shivers over her.

"Your . . . your guests await, Sir Jamie," she said weakly.

"They can wait a moment more." He turned her around to face him, but she wouldn't meet his eyes. "Look at me, Sheena. Give me the answer I've been waiting to hear all day."

She kept her gaze lowered. "I dinna know what you mean."

"You do," he replied softly. "And I've been patient."

"Patient?" Her eyes widened incredulously, and she looked directly at him. "You call only one day's waiting being patient?"

"For me it is." He grinned. "I thought to have the matter settled 'afore we returned from our ride, but I hadn't anticipated the interruption of our . . . dalliance."

Sheena blushed. Oh, how she wanted to forget that afternoon! Now there he was, sure of victory, just because she had been snared by his spell for a short time. Didn't he realize his magic worked only when he touched her? He needed a setdown, and she ached to give it to him.

A smile curled her lips, and Jamie took heart. "You'll be telling me what I want to hear, lass?"

"This is no' the time, Sir Jamie."

He frowned. "Why not?"

"I dinna think my answer is . . . what you're wanting to hear."

He stared at her hard, and she watched a muscle tighten along his jaw. Then his chest expanded as he took one deep breath. In the awful silence, she heard her heart drumming. Her own chest tightened, for she was holding her breath.

He's going to kill me, she thought wildly. For refusing him!

"You were right, Sheena," he said at last. "This

is no' the time."

"What?"

Her surprise made him feel a little better. "We spoke of trust today, but you're no' ready yet to trust me, so I'll be giving you more time. I'll wait."

"But—"

"I'll wait, Sheena."

The subject was closed. He took her arm and led her into the hall. The arrogance of him! So he would wait, would he? Let him wait until the stars fell from the sky!

"Sir William, may I present Sheena MacEwen, late of Aberdeen."

"I am—" William Jameson turned his gaze on Sheena and caught his breath. "Delighted."

Sheena managed a nod before Jamie sat her down in the chair next to his and took his own, placing himself between her and the agreeable-looking stranger. She leaned forward to see the man who dared rile the laird of the MacKinnions, but Jamie leaned forward, as well, blocking her view. She surveyed the hall, meeting eyes wherever hers wandered, finally looking back at their table, uncomfortable under so many questioning gazes.

Food was served immediately. It was grouse stuffed with buttered wild cranberries, roasted venison, boiled carrots, and sugar rolls and scones to dip in sweet heather honey. But Sheena could not do justice to the food, not with so many eyes turned her way. What must these people think of her, sitting in the place where Jessie Martin had been only the day before? Had it really been only two days since she'd met Jamie MacKinnion?

"It seems like a lifetime."

"Did you say something, hinny?"

Lydia MacKinnion was sitting beside her, on her left. "I didna see you," Sheena said apologetically.

"I only just came in. I understand you had a pleasant ride today."

Sheena's cheeks stained. "And who was it told you that?"

"Why, Jamie. He said you enjoyed yourself immensely, and 'tis glad I am. Sheena, the lad's taken with you. It does my heart good to see he's finally ready to stop philandering and settle on one lass."

Sheena nearly choked. "But *I'm* no' ready—I assure you."

Lydia patted her hand. "I understand your reluctance, hinny. Jamie is a formidable man, like his father. Robbie could be a terror—but never with those he loved. He, too, found a woman who was right for him, and he loved her till the day she died—longer, perhaps."

"Loved her? But Colen says his mother and father fought all the time. Why, the tower where I sleep was where she went to escape him."

"Aye, they did fight." Lydia smiled with fond remembrance. "But how they loved. It seems to be the way with true love."

Sheena was aghast. "I must disagree, m'lady. There is peace in true love, and sharing, and—"

"You know a great deal about it, do you?" the older woman said with a smile.

"Well, 'tis how it should be, surely."

Lydia chuckled. "And I'm sure it is with lovers of mellow temperaments. But when two strong-willed people love each other, they canna help but clash wills sometimes."

"I suppose."

"Now Jamie, he has the devil's own temper and can be a wee bit intolerable at times. If the lass he weds has little spunk, he will dominate her completely. But if she has a will to match his . . . I'll wager she'll win more battles than she'll lose."

Sheena's curiosity was piqued, despite herself. "And why is that?"

"Because of love, m'dear. Why else would Jamie take a wife? He's no one to tell him to, now his father's gone. He's in no need of an alliance through marriage, for he has many strong alliances as it is. Riches couldna tempt him, for he has enough wealth. So why would he commit himself to one woman, when he has any woman he wants just for the asking? Love, m'dear, is the only reason Jamie would marry."

Lydia began filling her plate then, and Sheena turned away, grateful to have the disturbing conversation ended. Love? There was no love in hand-fasting, and no honor, either. And handfasting was all Sir Jamie offered her. How easy for him, when he could back down before the final commitment. How convenient. But he would not use her that way; she would leave first. It was time she devoted herself to doing just that.

Her only hope was Colen. She looked up and

saw him at the opposite end of the table, looking downright sullen. She was undoubtedly the reason. If only she could make use of his resentment to help her get away. But his resentment might just work against her, as well. Who did that leave? Black Gawain was gone. Lydia seemed entirely on Jamie's side. That left only William Jameson. He was not answerable to Jamie, and he seemed taken with Sheena.

She leaned forward to look at him carefully and was surprised to find him almost unrecognizable. Anger made his face paler, his red hair seem brighter, his soft brown eyes hard, damning. Worse was his tone of voice. An argument was in progress, and getting out of hand.

"You were to marry my sister, Jamie," William was saying bitterly. "When you took her in, when you flaunted her as your mistress, I didn't interfere, for she swore to me you promised to wed her!"

Incensed though William was, Jamie was calm. "Libby lied. It was understood from the start that there would be no marriage. She knew it well, and still she decided to stay here."

"You used her, Jamie, like all the other women you've used and cast aside!"

"My women are never unwilling." Jamie's voice was rising now. "Your sister came to me of her own choice and left the same way—only richer, with a fat purse of gold to take her where she wanted to go."

"And where is that?" William demanded.

Jamie laughed. "So you canna find her? Is that what this is all about?"

"She could be dead for all I know."

"Nay, Will, you'll find she's living royally somewhere where she wants to be. You see, she knew I would provide generously for her. 'Twas all she wanted from me, a way to escape you."

"That is a lie!"

"Is it?" Jamie countered. "I wonder what riles you most, Will, that she came to me, or that she didna return to you?"

"Bastard!"

Jamie rose abruptly, and William Jameson paled, realizing he had gone too far. There was an awful silence as Jamie looked down at him. Sheena couldn't see his furious expression, but she saw the hardness of his back, the clenched fists.

His voice held an icy edge. "I'll be excusing myself 'afore I take your insults to heart and forget you're a guest in my home. But you'll be gone from here by morning, Jameson, and you won't find a welcome here again."

Jamie walked away stiffly, and Sheena sighed with relief. She turned to Lydia.

"And what was that all about?" She whispered because William Jameson was still sitting only a chair away from her.

"He's a bitter man, hinny, Will is. His parents died long ago, and he raised his sister himself from a wee bairn. But he devoted himself too much to her, and his love smothered her. 'Tis no wonder he doesna ken her desire to be away from him, but the

181

truth of it is, she is a spoiled and fickle lass and never returned his affection. I came to know her while she was here, and I didna like her one bit. She thought nothing of ridiculing her brother to us, painting a picture of a man pathetically worshiping his own sister. The man is lucky to be rid of her, but I'm afraid he'll never see it that way."

"Will Sir William leave then?"

Lydia laughed softly and leaned closer to whisper. "He's a bit of a coward, hinny. He'll be leaving any moment now."

Sheena wondered if that was so, but as she turned, she saw him standing up, calling his men together. A minute later, they all stalked furiously from the hall.

Sheena panicked. There, walking angrily away, was her last chance. She quickly made her excuses to Lydia and crossed the hall, apparently on her way to the south tower. But as soon as she passed under the arched entrance at the end of the hall, she dashed to the left instead of up the stairs. Then she was out in the courtyard and running toward William Jameson.

He was by the stable with four retainers, waiting impatiently for their horses. Sheena failed to consider the foolhardiness in approaching a stranger. She saw Jameson only as a means of her freedom.

"A word, Sir William, if you will," she called out.

"What is it?" he snapped. Then he turned and saw her. He was quite startled. "Well, well, Sir Jamie's new whore, is it?"

Sheena flinched. "Nay, but 'tis what he would make me. I beg your help, Sir William. I must leave here."

"And what stops you?"

"He does. He'll no' let me leave here alone."

William's eyes widened. "You are a prisoner, then?"

Sheena wrung her hands, wondering how to explain. "'Tis . . . most complicated, Sir William. The MacKinnion would take me to Aberdeen himself. But he'll no' let anyone else take me. So if I want to go I must go with him, and I fear being alone with him. Do you ken? I fear him, and I loathe being here."

"And you want to get away?"

"I want to return to Aberdeen, where I've kin. He's asked me to handfast, and I've refused, but still he keeps me here. Will you help me, Sir William?"

"Handfasting, eh?" William said thoughtfully, and then he laughed mirthlessly. "Aye, I'll help you, lass. 'Twill be a pleasure."

She didn't like the sound of his laughter, but she pushed the feeling aside. She had to go with Jameson . . . or else stay where she was.

Chapter 21

COLEN pounded on the door to Jamie's bed-chamber, then burst inside. He was livid with the rage that had been building all day. Finding the south tower empty just now had sent him running to his brother. There was just so much he would stand for.

"I warned you, Jamie . . ."

Colen stopped, seeing Jamie stretched out on top his bed alone, fully clothed. A quick glance around the room told him it was otherwise empty.

"You had best be explaining yourself, brother." Jamie sat up.

"I . . . I thought to find Sheena here," Colen said meekly.

"Much as I'd like to be finding her here myself, lad, you can see she's not here. What made you think she would be?" Jamie demanded.

"Today . . . at the pool, when I saw you."

"Ah, so you saw more than you let on," Jamie said thoughtfully. "Well, had you no' come along

184

when you did, she'd be mine now."

"You swore you'd deal with her honorably!"

"And so I have every intention of doing. Have I no' asked her to handfast? And as soon as I've tried her and know for certain she's no' like my first wife, then I'll wed her."

"If she'll have you."

"Well, she wasna fighting me off today, lad."

Colen felt his chest constrict. No, she hadn't fought his brother off, and that was why he had been so furious all day. Jealousy was new to him. Jamie was winning, despite Sheena's fear of him. Colen had been so certain Jamie wouldn't have a chance.

"Where is she then, Jamie?" Colen asked with all the dejection he was feeling.

"What do you mean?" Jamie demanded. "'Tis late. She's in the south tower."

"Nay, I went there, but she wasna there."

"Still in the hall?"

Colen shook his head. "I looked everywhere else 'afore coming here. She's no' in the castle, Jamie. That can only mean . . . ."

"Jameson," Jamie finished, his intuition honing in on the culprit.

But he continued to sit, staring at the floor, a blank look coming over him. Colen didn't know what to make of him.

"Well?" Colen asked sharply. "Are you just going to let him take her?"

"We've no claim on her, lad. I've no right to bring her back," Jamie said very quietly.

"You held yourself responsible for her. Are you forgetting that?"

"Only while she was here, lad."

"But what if she comes to harm with Jameson?" Colen cried.

"Enough! You think I dinna *want* to bring her back? I would like nothing more—but my hands are tied. If she were friend or foe of the Mac-Kinnions I could do something, but the MacEwens are neither. Jameson knows that. He could raise a complaint with the king if I took the lass from him without a reason. That's what's needed, lad, a valid reason. You find me one, and I'll bring her back, no matter who Jameson turns her over to."

Crossing the river at that late night hour was a cold, dangerous business. But the horses had crossed in the same area many times before, and only one balked at the frigid water, dousing its rider. Luckily that horse was not Sir William's, on which Sheena rode, trying in vain to relax against the strange body.

They had not turned east to Aberdeen, but were riding west, to Sir William's home. Sheena accepted this. After all, it was late. She couldn't very well expect to be taken the long way to Aberdeen just then. And the important thing was getting away from Castle Kinnion. She was safe now, her fears farther and farther behind her with every mile.

Where, then, was the peace of mind she had expected?

Chapter 22

"**S**IR Jamie!"

Jamie turned from his contemplation of the fire. One of his retainers was hurrying across the hall, leaving a trail of dripping water behind him. Poor Alwyn had been soaked through by the storm raging outside. His bonnet was askew, beads of water clung to his red beard and bushy brows, and his knobby knees were bone white and shaking.

"A bit chilly outside, is it?" Jamie said, grinning and shaking his head at Alwyn's condition.

"That it is," Alwyn agreed.

Jamie ordered blankets, and Alwyn stepped closer to the fire. The weather had taken a turn for the worse the day after Sheena's disappearance, five days before. Jamie had spent two days in Aberdeen, a waste of time as it turned out. He had searched everywhere for Erminia MacEwen, even spent half a day at the poorhouse, set upon by beggars. But no one had heard of a MacEwen nun.

Lies. He should have known.

His thoughts were as dark as the sky. He had been willing to humble himself. If he had found her, he would have pleaded with her rather than lose her. But what if he couldn't find her?

He gave Alwyn his full attention. "How far down was the party sighted?" It was Jamie's sister's party, traveling in the storm.

"Yer canna see sae very far wi' rain as thick as this, but they're just outside."

"And which sister is it who's ventured out in this wretched weather?"

"Mistress Daphne."

Jamie scowled. "I should've guessed. No doubt Jessie Martin's spun some wild tale about her treatment here, and now Dobbins' come to learn the truth of it."

"I didna see Dobbin Martin."

"Who did you see out there?"

"Well, I do believe 'tis The MacDonough escorting yer sister."

"The hell!" Jamie growled. "How dare he come here after wedding a Fergusson?"

"Did he? Yer've had news?"

"No' recently, but what was to stop him? If he's here to petition peace for his bride's kin, he's in for a sore disappointment." Jamie clenched his fists, anger mounting. "Curse the man! Has he brought his bride with him?"

"I canna say, Sir Jamie," Alwyn replied, growing exceedingly uncomfortable so near Jamie's anger.

"If he has, she's no' to be let through the gate.

Go, give the order now!"

Alwyn was aghast. "Yer'd turn a poor lassie away in this weather?"

Jamie stared hard at the man. After a few moments, he sighed. "I suppose that woudna be very hospitable of me, would it now? You're right. And now I think of it, I've a mind to look over this particular Fergusson. She's old Dugald's favorite, you know."

"Is she now?"

Jamie chuckled, a chilling sound. "That she is. And if she dares to enter the lion's den, then let her. Whether she leaves it or no' is another matter. Aye, bring them all to me here in the hall."

"But the Fergusson lass may no' be here at all, Sir Jamie," Alwyn pointed out.

But Jamie had turned back to the fire. He was remembering his time in the Fergusson dungeon and the vengeful thoughts he had directed at Dugald's family. He had almost been forced to marry one of Dugald's daughters. Almost. And then he remembered the lad who had saved him from marriage, and he grew uncomfortable with his spiteful thoughts. It would hardly be fair for him to harm the sister whom young Niall had risked so much to protect, not after the lad had freed him.

Curse MacDonough for bringing her here and putting him in such an absurd position. To accept a Fergusson into his castle, and as a guest! He couldn't toy with her, strike fear into her, couldn't even ransom her—all because of a debt owed one small lad.

Jamie's curiosity was keen. At last he would finally see what he had so very narrowly escaped being tied to. Well, not exactly the lass herself, but one of her sisters. How much difference could there be? The encounter should at least distract him from thoughts of the one who had implanted herself in his heart, the one whose image would torture him for eternity.

A voice called out, and Jamie turned to look at the bedraggled group of people making their way toward the fire. Besides MacDonough and four of his men, Daphne had with her three servants, two men and one woman. A party of nine. Jamie recognized the girl as a servant who had accompanied Daphne before. No Fergusson there.

"Is this all of you, then?" he demanded, kissing his sister in greeting.

"If 'tis Dobbin you're looking for, he didna come." Daphne spoke softly as she returned his kiss, then stretched her hands out to the fire. "He's preparing to attend court at the week's end, and as I wasna going to attend myself, he agreed I could come here instead—for an extended visit."

"So soon after your last visit?"

"We stayed no time at all then, Jamie, as you know," Daphne said stiffly. "Am I no' welcome?"

"I've no' made up my mind about that yet," Jamie returned disagreeably. "If you've come on Jessie's behalf—"

"Now why ever would I be doing that?" Daphne asked in surprise. "You know I've little liking for my husband's cousin. If you're worried I've come to take her home, you've no need. I like it better that she's here. I only hope to see very little of her during my stay."

"But I sent her home, Daphne. She should have arrived 'afore you left."

"Och, well, she's no doubt found another man 'atween here and there. She'll make her way home in her own good time," Daphne speculated. "But 'tis glad I am you didna fall for her and her scheming ways."

Jamie flinched. Then his eyes narrowed as he looked more closely at his sister. Her blond hair was wet and matted, her face tinged with blue, her body shivering convulsively. He gave no further thought to Jessie. She must have convinced Black Gawain to let her stay with him. That bothered Jamie not at all.

"Get you to your old chamber, Daphne, and warm yourself 'afore you're taken ill."

"I'm welcome then?"

"Aye," Jamie said, although his voice lacked warmth. "But we'll discuss the matter later, for I'm thinking 'twas no your idea alone to come visiting."

Daphne said nothing to that. He's no' angry at me, though, she thought as she hurried away with her servants in tow. She knew he was displeased by her foolishness in venturing out in such deplorable weather, but it was nothing compared to the anger she felt Jamie direct at Alasdair. No wonder the poor man had not wanted to come here alone.

She had done Alasdair a favor by letting him escort her here. But she had warned him that her presence would make no real difference to Jamie. He would be finding that out very soon.

Jamie made Alasdair wait while he summoned food and dry clothing for his guests. That much he would do in light of the clan friendship that had existed in their fathers' day.

"Taken to hiding behind women's skirts, have you?" Jamie said at last.

Alasdair MacDonough flushed crimson. They were still standing by the fire, Alasdair's men partaking of food at the tables, away from them. He was thankful for that, for an insult could be ignored when not overheard by anyone. And he was here to renew his alliance with the MacKinnions, not tear it apart completely.

Alasdair decided to try for a little levity. "'Tis a pleasant enough place to hide, if one must hide."

Jamie was not in the least amused. "I dinna like your dragging my sister up here, Alasdair, any more than I like anything else you've been doing recently. And I have to tell you, you've picked the worst time to be here, for I'm in no agreeable mood. At least you had the grace no' to bring your wife."

"But I didna marry."

Jamie's only indication of surprise was a slight raising of his brow. "The wedding was postponed?"

"Nay. I broke the betrothal."

Jamie burst out laughing. "Did you now? Well, well," he chuckled, his spirits greatly improved. "So if you've no' come to plead a wife's cause, why are you here?"

"To renew our alliance. I hadna seen or heard from you since well 'afore the betrothal. I wasna sure how you felt about it."

"I didna like it, and no mistake, but since you came to your senses, there's no hard feelings."

"And if I had wed the lass?"

"We would no doubt be enemies one day."

"But, Jamie—"

"Dinna take me wrong, Alasdair." Jamie cut him off. "I wouldna have ended the alliance *because* of your choice of bride. But your alliance with the Fergussons wouldna have been mine. You ken? The feud would have gone on as usual, but with you in the middle. Eventually you would have had to choose sides."

"No' if your feud ended."

"There's no chance of that, now they've begun it again," Jamie said tersely. "Did you no' learn of my sojourn in the Fergusson dungeon?"

"Learn of it?" Alasdair replied bitterly. "'Twas what led to the breaking of my betrothal."

"Well then, I fear I've greatly misjudged you. I didna think you would choose sides 'afore the wedding."

"Dinna mistake me, Jamie. 'Twas no' a matter of choosing sides then, though I might have been forced to it if I'd know you were there. You see, I was unaware of your capture until after you were gone."

They blamed you for my escape then?"

"The lass was quick to accuse me, to be sure,"

Alasdair said coldly.

"'Tis no wonder you withdrew your suit."

"I was furious, and no mistake. But you know for yourself who the guilty one was, Jamie. Now, dinna take offense, but the fact is, she betrayed her family in aiding you, and any lass who would betray her own family might betray a husband some day. I couldna very well marry her after that. Don't you agree?"

"You mean to say your betrothed was blamed?"

"Who else? Her own cousin saw her near the dungeon and was quick to say so."

Jamie laughed, unable to help himself. This was wonderful. So the lad had not suffered for his help, and the favorite daughter no doubt got off lightly. He would have liked at least one Fergusson to suffer for his humiliation, just so long as it was not the boy.

"I dinna see any humor in it, Jamie," Alasdair said testily. "I've regretted breaking the betrothal a hundred times since, for I did want that girl more than I've ever wanted any other."

"Och, well, there are indeed lasses who can get into a man's blood, and no mistake," Jamie concurred, sobering.

"But none so beautiful as she," Alasdair said wistfully.

"Beautiful, is she?" Jamie smiled. Alasdair had assumed he knew what the lass looked like. "You think so?"

"You jest, Jamie." The older man gasped. "Why, there's none with red hair so dark, blue eyes so crystal clear, or skin so white and flawless. They dinna call her the jewel of Tower Esk without good reason."

Jamie sat up, his stomach wound into a knot. The description mirrored the image that was so constantly in his mind. There could not be two girls so alike, could there? It was just too unlikely, too . . .

"Her name is just as lovely, I suppose?" Jamie prompted.

Alasdair's eyes snapped. "Why do you toy with me, Jamie? Can you no' see I'm suffering over the loss of her?"

"Of course. Forgive me, Alasdair. But I did warn you I was no' in the best of moods. I havena been since first seeing Sheena. Mayhap I was taken with her, too."

Jamie waited breathlessly. Would Alasdair say, "Sheena's not the name of the lass I'm talking about"? Or was he right?

Alasdair grinned, confirming everything. "Och, well, your dilemma is worse than mine. To have tender feelings for your enemy's daughter! Even if the old man would be giving her to you to end the feud, she'd no' like that one bit. Willful she is, and wants to choose her own mate. I would go to Aberdeen and try to win her for myself again if I thought she'd have me. But the truth is, she was never keen on our match. 'Twas her father's wish, and of course you know why he chose me."

Jamie sat back and closed his eyes. He was no longer listening. A flood of memories rushed through his mind one after the other. The coincidences. The similarities. Sheena being at the glen on Fergusson land the first time he saw her. Niall's hair like hers, the father's eyes like hers. The boy's curiosity over what Jamie would have done with the girl at the glen, his anger over the answer. Sheena's accusations against the MacKinnions, her fear and distrust of him, her desperation to get away. And, finally, there being no "Erminia MacEwen" in Aberdeen. He'd stake his life there was an Erminia *Fergusson*.

Jamie shook his head. He might have put it together at any time, but he hadn't. Maybe he hadn't wanted to, had avoided making connections, not wanting Sheena to be a Fergusson. Now he realized it didn't matter at all. His feelings about her, his wanting her, were not going to change.

"Did you hear me, Jamie?"

"What?" Jamie focused on Alasdair.

"I said old Dugald would probably be agreeable to your suit, if you were so inclined."

"He's already refused to give her to me," Jamie said absently.

"You asked for her then?"

"'Twas the condition for my release from his prison that I marry one of his daughters," Jamie explained. "But Sheena wasna offered."

Alasdair laughed wryly. "The others dinna compare to her."

"So I suspected at the time."

"Och, well, you were saved from that—and by Sheena herself. I always wondered why she helped you."

Jamie thought quickly. He wasn't going to betray Niall now.

"She helped me because she feared me. She thought her father meant to give her to me."

"Yet you knew otherwise."

"Aye. I used any means to get out of there, and I'm no' sorry. Better to cultivate a small lie than to have a poor lass forced on me as a bride. You know my temper, Alasdair."

"That may be, Jamie, but 'twas Sheena who ended the loser, banished for helping the enemy."

Jamie sat up. "Banished?"

"I was surprised myself, but the old man was hurt by her betrayal, her being his favorite and all."

"So that is why she was in Aberdeen," Jamie mused to himself.

"She still is in Aberdeen, as far as I know."

Jamie relaxed. It was only a harsh-sounding word, "banished." And if Sheena had not been sent to Aberdeen, Jamie would never have seen her again after that time in the glen.

He thought for a while. Sheena must have willingly accepted the guilt in order to protect Niall, while Niall had let Jamie go so as to protect her. The lad wouldn't have let her take the blame unless she'd insisted. How ironic! In trying to keep her from Jamie's clutches, the brother and sister had in fact led her straight to him.

"I wouldna worry over it, Alasdair," Jamie said lightly. "The fact is, Sheena is old Dugald's favorite, and he'll forgive her in time."

"I suppose. But I wonder if I'll ever forgive myself for the burst of temper that made me lose her."

"Look at it this way, Alasdair. You're probably no' alone in wanting her. Many men have and many more will, but only one can win her."

"The one who does will be a lucky man, and no mistake." Alasdair sighed.

"That he will." Jamie grinned, feeling quite lucky himself at the moment. "And now I must be leaving you, though I do indeed thank you for coming. You're welcome to stay, of course. I should be returning in a few days."

"And where are you off to in this weather?" Alasdair asked, surprised.

Jamie laughed, unable to contain his bubbling mood any longer. "To Aberdeen, to win a bonny lass."

"Sheena?" Alasdair was growing bewildered.

"Aye."

"But she's your enemy, Jamie. At least she sees it that way."

"Exactly. My enemy—and an easy prey to capture."

Jamie was smiling as he left the hall, but he didn't fool himself, not really. It would not be easy to break through a lifetime of animosity. But he would win her heart. He knew he would. And where Sheena had had the advantage of knowing just who he was, now he had that same advantage. How to *use* his knowledge was another matter.

Chapter 23

WILLIAM Jameson lived not in a castle or a tower house, but in a simple fortified tower near the river Dee. Atop a small knoll, it was a dismal place indeed, bleak, cold, without the least comfort or cheer.

Upon arriving, Sheena was shown to a small room and locked inside. She made excuses for that—the late hour, a simple precaution to protect her. She would be gone in the morning, so what did it matter?

How naive. How utterly foolish. But it was her own fault, putting her trust in a stranger, and a Highlander at that.

All was made clear the following morning when Jameson paid her a short visit. Without mincing words he told her he would not be taking her to Aberdeen any time soon, that she would be his guest for however long he chose to have her, that she would have no say in the matter.

Sheena nearly cried. She had escaped a

luxurious prison, where she'd had good food, warmth, comfort, and a little freedom, for a dirty, cold, isolated room, very little food, and no freedom at all.

Some of the fear was lessened that night when Jameson came to see her again. By then he was pathetically drunk, for drink had been meant to bolster his courage. Through slurs and leers, he told her he would have her as Jamie had taken his sister. But his attempt at rape was laughable because he was so besotted. Fortunately for her, fear and liquor unmanned him, and he left her, red-faced with shame.

She supposed Jameson was too embarrassed to face her again, and indeed many days passed. She was alone, a prisoner, growing more and more dejected.

"Och, anything is better than this, even Jamie's amorous pursuit!" she told herself.

When had she started thinking of him as "Jamie"? She wasn't sure, but she had. And she started remembering. It seemed she could recall every word they had ever said to each other, every moment spent in his presence, his touch—the magic.

This was crazy! She'd thought she'd escape him! Had he moved permanently into her mind?

"I canna stand it! The four walls are doing this to me, blank walls, no one to talk to! No fire, foul food, and a silent servant to bring it! Another day and I'll go mad!"

William Jameson paced nervously before his hearth, the only area in the narrow hall that was lighted. It was quite late. He had been sleeping but was awakened with the disturbing news. A rider had been sent ahead to warn of The MacKinnion's imminent arrival. He would be there any moment.

What had kept him? Jameson had expected James MacKinnion long before. More than a week had passed since he'd taken the girl. He had begun to think Sheena had lied, that MacKinnion was not interested in her after all. But no matter what had kept him, he was coming now. The moment Jameson had craved was at hand. He had to keep control, stop himself from showing what pleasure he got out of twisting the screws on that blond bastard.

Boots sounded on the stairs, many boots, and then Jamie appeared in the doorway across the short hall, six retainers behind him. He waved them back and crossed the hall alone. He was wrapped in his plaid, which added considerable bulk and made him appear twice his size. Coming out of the shadows, he was a formidable sight. A bit of green doublet showed beneath the plaid, but there were no stockings to protect him against the cold. His knees were bare above high boots. A sword swung at his side. Jameson took in every detail, as though memorizing.

But it was Jamie's approaching face that made William catch his breath. The haggard look, lips drawn in a tight line, cheeks red from the wind. The eyes, reflecting the fire, glowed with a green light.

Jameson trembled.

Jamie spoke. "I've no' slept for two days, Jameson. I'm tired, and I've wasted two trips to Aberdeen. You tell me what you think you're doing, keeping the lass here."

William smiled tightly and gave a little shrug. "She wanted to stay with me."

"I don't think so," Jamie said.

"You're welcome to have her back, of course," William quickly assured him in a congenial tone. "In fact, I'd be glad if you'd take her off my hands. I confess I'm bored with her already."

"Bored?" Jamie ran a hand through his hair. Lord, he was tired. "You'll be explaining that."

"What is to explain, my friend? Usually one whore is as good as another, but this one has only bonny looks and nothing else. I was surprised. I thought a man of your temperament would like a more . . . lively lass. *I* certainly do."

Jamie's hand shot out and gripped Jameson's plaid, pulling him so close their faces nearly touched. "Are you saying you bedded Sheena?"

"Now I'd be a fool to admit it, with you ready to thrash me for it."

"You'll tell me or I'll kill you!" Jamie growled.

William tried to move, but he couldn't break Jamie's grip. His confidence was evaporating quickly, yet he had to bluff his way through this or be lost.

"You're no' being reasonable, MacKinnion. If you had a claim on the lass, you should've made it known. I only took what was offered. 'Twas she

202

who begged me to take her with me. 'Twas she who begged me to let her stay here."

"And I suppose she begged you to bed her?"

There was no answer, which was answer enough. A low growl, very much like pain, came from the depths of Jamie. He shoved the older man away. He wanted more than anything to tear him apart, to beat him until there was nothing left to beat. But damn the man to hell, he was right. Jamie had no claim on Sheena. And, banished from her home, without family, she could do as she chose with her life. But not any longer, by God!

"Get her down here, Jameson, quickly, 'afore I forget what's reasonable and what isna reasonable."

Jamie was left alone in the hall then, staring at the fire, its heat no match for the jealousy burning him. He tried to remind himself he had no real right to Sheena, but that didn't stop the hurt. He would rather have the pain of a hundred wounds than a tortured spirit.

"Sir Jamie?"

He swung around sharply. There was a timid smile on her face, but it vanished when his eyes met hers. Cursing himself, he knew he would not blame her for what had happened. He was not her keeper. She had every right to make her own choices. But Will Jameson? That puny, sorry excuse for a man? He shut his eyes against the pain. Sweet Mary, he would never understand it! But he would not blame her. Well, he would *try* not to, anyway.

When he opened his eyes again, some of the fury was gone from his gaze. But Sheena kept her distance. She had been about to thank him for rescuing her, but she wasn't so sure she wanted to be rescued by him. How angry he looked!

Jamie watched her watching him, saw the wary look in her eyes. He should have been used to her fear of him, but he wasn't. And she did not look well. She was wearing the same blue gown she had left in, and it was in terrible condition. Dark crescents had formed under her eyes. She was so pale. Maybe she was unhappy with Jameson. Or maybe . . .

"You will be coming with me, and I'll hear no nonsense about it," he ordered tersely. "Where's Jameson?"

Sheena looked behind her, then shrugged. "I dinna know. He brought me down here, but I guess he was too afeared to face you after—"

"'Tis just as well." Jamie cut her off gruffly. "I'm sore tempted to kill the man." He shouted at the rafters then. "You hear that, Jameson? Dinna let me *ever* catch sight of you again!"

Sheena's eyes widened in amazement. And when he grabbed her arm and escorted her roughly from the hall, she went right along. Did he know she had been kept prisoner there? Maybe he was not angry with her after all, but with Jameson. To be so furious over her, this was certainly not what she had expected.

Jamie's retainers gathered the horses, and Sheena saw quickly that there was no extra horse for her. She let Jamie help her up onto his big gray stallion, tensing when he joined her. The others rode off, leaving them to follow at a slower pace.

With Jamie's arms wrapped around her, Sheena felt herself growing hot despite the biting wind. She half turned so he could hear her. "Sir Jamie, is it to Aberdeen you're taking me?"

"Nay."

She ignored the curtness of his reply. "But I want you to. I would rather go to Aberdeen."

"Would you?" he asked darkly.

Sheena frowned. "You said you would take me there. Well, I'm asking you to."

"If you longed so for Aberdeen, then you should have had Jameson take you there while you had the chance," Jamie snapped. "My offer is withdrawn, Sheena. Permanently. Dinna be asking me again."

"But . . . why?" she cried.

"It has been pointed out to me that I have been negligent in no' putting my claim on you. I will remedy that as soon as we return by announcing our handfasting."

"I refuse!" she gasped.

Jamie said coldly, "It can be done without your approval. 'Tis only a matter of a formal announcement to my kin, for them to know I commit myself to you. I should have done it sooner."

"That is barbaric, and no' fair! You canna force me, Jamie. Only my father could force me into a commitment I oppose."

"And if he did?"

"He wouldna give me to an oaf like you!" She

was growing angry, and quite forgot herself. "I willna agree, and I'll be telling your kin I willna agree. So if you try to take me, 'twill be rape and you know it!"

"Curse you woman! Rape for me, but willingness for Jameson, eh? How could you, Sheena?"

"How could I what?" She gasped, quite confused by then. "What are you accusing me of?"

He drew the horse up abruptly and gripped Sheena's shoulders painfully, making her face him. His eyes were smoldering. Even in the dark, she could see it. She held her breath, terrified.

"He offered you naught, yet you gave yourself to him willingly. I offer you a binding commitment, and you refuse me. All right. I know why you refuse me. I know the reason, and I'll overcome it. But by the saints, Sheena, I'll never understand what you saw in Jameson!"

Her eyes had grown wider and wider, and when he was finished she struck out at him in a blind rage. He caught her hand and shoved it behind her back, bringing her even closer to him.

"How dare you accuse me?" she hissed furiously. "I'm a maiden still, though I'll no' be proving it to *you!* And even if I werena pure, 'tis none of your concern. Aye, think whatever you like. I hope you think the worst! Then you'll no' be wanting me!"

He kissed her, because he wanted to shut her up and because he just couldn't help himself. Lord, what she did to him! No one had ever caused him so much yearning as this small wisp of a girl. Or so much pain, either.

He let her go. His voice was now a gentle caress. "I still want you, Sheena, you can be sure of that. And I'll have you, too, soon, and when that happens, you'll wonder what all the fighting was about, m'dear."

He rode faster to catch up with the others, and Sheena was left wondering. He had given her no chance to reply.

Chapter 24

"**S**TILL up, lad?"

Colen jerked awake to find his brother standing over him. He saw that Jamie was exhausted but unharmed. Then he slumped back down in his chair by the fireside.

"I wasna tired," Colen answered sulkily. "With you gone, I've been sleeping late mornings, and I stay up later."

"Do you?" Jamie grinned.

"And where were you off to without telling anyone?" Colen demanded angrily. "That's twice now in two months you've taken off without explanation. Sweet Mary, do you think no one here worries when you go off like that?"

"Were you worried?" Colen remained silent, and Jamie sighed. "Och, well, I see you're upset, and I'll be saying I'm sorry. I *am* sorry, Colen. It shouldna happen again."

"Will you tell me about it? At least you took some men with you this time. Was there trouble?"

208

"Nay, lad, I just went to Aberdeen."

"Again?" Colen was surprised. "What made you think you would have better luck this time?"

"Did you no' speak to MacDonough while he was here?" Jamie asked.

"Nay, he left soon after you did," Colen replied. "And I was at Black Gawain's during his visit. Did you know he has Jessie Martin with him?"

"He's welcome to her," Jamie said without surprise.

"Well, that's a fine attitude," Colen grumbled.

"And why are you forever expecting me to be overcome by jealousy, lad? When an affair is finished, 'tis finished. I didna exactly pursue Jessie in the first place."

"It just doesna seem right, her going to Black Gawain after being with you. She isna just a . . . a serving lass. She's Daphne's cousin by marriage."

"I dinna see what difference her status makes. If I'm no' bothered about it, lad, then neither should you be—unless you had a liking for her yourself."

Colen reddened. "Nonsense. She's too . . . full around the curves for my taste."

"You like them slimmer?" Jamie chuckled, enjoying his brother's discomfort.

But Colen refused to be sidetracked. "Did you find Sheena this time?"

"She wasna in Aberdeen." And before Colen could ask another question, Jamie went on, "She was still with Jameson." His voice took on a cold edge.

"But why?"

209

"The why of it you'd no' be caring to hear."

"I dinna ken."

"Nor do I," Jamie said sharply. "But she was there."

"You had no luck in getting her to return with you?" Colen asked, afraid of the answer, whatever it might be.

"She's here, Colen, and she'll no' be leaving again."

Colen sat up. "She agreed?" he asked, incredulous.

"I didna ask. She had no chance to agree."

"But you said you wouldna force her. And you said you needed a reason 'afore you'd bring her back."

"MacDonough gave me a reason."

Colen rose from his chair. "Will you be telling me, or must I ask her?"

"She doesna know."

"By the saints, Jamie, must everything you say be so cryptic?"

Jamie grinned. "I'm sorry, lad. I suppose you may as well know, but no one else is to know—especially Sheena. Do I have your word?"

"Aye! Tell me 'afore I perish. What reason could The MacDonough have given you?"

"He didna marry his Fergusson bride, lad. She was banished to Aberdeen—where you found her."

"Fergusson bride? *Sheena?* I dinna believe it!"

"'Tis true, Colen. I never told you 'afore, or said anything to her, either, but I knew her when you brought her here. I had seen her 'afore—in the spring—on Fergusson land. When you said she was a beggar, I thought it must be so, for I had seen her bathing in a glen in the early morning, which was not something a Fergusson would do, not just after a raid."

"Exactly. So she canna be a Fergusson."

"But Sheena is headstrong. Did she no' leave here the first chance she got? Did she no' swim in the burn that day even though I warned her the water would be too cold? She does as she pleases. No doubt she behaved the same way at home, as well."

"But a *Fergusson?*"

"Aye, and old Dugald's favorite daughter, too. MacDonough described her, which is what convinced me. Think on it, lad. Does it no' explain her fear, the fear neither of us could find a reason for? When I first came upon her in your chamber, she was most agreeable with me. She even teased me. She wasna afraid of me. 'Twas no' until she heard my name that she was frightened."

"Now that you mention it, she went sort of crazy when she learned who I was, shouting that she had to leave, she couldna stay here. I had to slap her to calm her down."

"You did what?" Jamie exploded.

Colen squirmed. "Och, Jamie, she slapped me back."

Jamie started a slow smile, and then he laughed heartily. "Did she?"

"It may be amusing now, but it wasna at the time, I assure you," Colen grumbled. "Lord,

211

everything is changed if Sheena's a Fergusson. What are you going to do?"

"I've brought her here, and nothing has changed. I'll still be handfasting with her, whether she agrees or no'."

"'Twould be a mockery if you forced her to it. She doesna believe in handfasting. Marriage would be another matter, though I dinna see how you can force her to that, either."

Jamie scowled. It was the truth, and it was not to his liking. Before, he had been willing to wait for her agreement. Her willingness mattered. True, all brides became compliant, whether the marriage was to their liking or not. But he didn't want to begin on a sour note. Yet he refused to marry her without trying her first. He would not make that mistake again. And others had tried her. Jameson had insinuated he found her lacking. Curse it! And curse Jameson!

"I'm too tired to be discussing this now," Jamie said abruptly.

"At least tell me why you're no' explaining that you know she's a Fergusson."

"To make her aware that her deception is over would be placing a sword in her hand. She would attack me at every turn for past actions that have nothing to do with her and me, things between our families. Think you I could stand that and no' retaliate?"

"But what of her fear of you, Jamie? That centers on your finding out who she is, what you will do to her when you do find out. Yet you know, and you mean her no harm. She should know her identity doesna matter. Then she would see her fears are groundless."

"I'll be proving that to her at any rate," Jamie replied confidently. "But I'll no' have her using clan hatred as another excuse to refuse me."

"I'll wager that *is* her reason."

"Aye, but she canna tell me so. Can she?" Jamie grinned, but it wasn't a convincing grin.

Chapter 25

S HEENA left the security of her tower room that next morning, meaning to test the extent of her freedom. She wore her green gown, clean now. It was still shoddy, but it was her own. She left her hair loose and flowing, without even a ribbon or cap to bind it.

She did not go directly to the hall, assuming Jamie was still there. She walked along the gallery, where she could look down into the courtyard at the activities there, or out over the mountainside, where the river Dee could just be glimpsed through the trees. A bit of sun broke through the dark clouds to kiss her face, probably the last warmth she would feel till spring.

Though she was seen by many, no one stopped her. Satisfied that no order had been given to deny her freedom of the inner castle, she decided to try her luck at the gate, and descended through the east tower. The winding stairs were narrow. She passed only two rooms on the way down, guard rooms she supposed, this tower being at the front of the castle. She wondered how the large, burly retainers with all of their battle regalia managed those narrow stairs. She learned the answer before she reached the bottom, where she found her way blocked by a man.

He wasn't a castle retainer, though. In the dim light from the open doorway at the bottom of the stairs, she recognized Jamie's cousin. Black Gawain was surprised to see her. He didn't step aside. "Well, well, so you're back."

"So I am," Sheena replied curtly, despising that smug tone.

"Alone, I see. Has your young watchdog given up?"

"If you mean Colen, he's no' my watchdog, as you put it."

"Yet you do need one, you'll agree."

"What for?"

"Well, if you dinna feel you need protection from rogues like me . . . who am I to differ?" He grinned at her.

Sheena was not amused. "Let me pass, Black Gawain."

"But we've no' had a chance to get acquainted. And 'tis no' likely I'll find you so conveniently alone again."

He took a step closer to her, and Sheena retreated. Then he took another step, slowly, as if stalking her. She didn't quite know whether to take him seriously, but she wasn't pleased with his game.

She put out a hand as he backed her into the shadows. "Just what do you think you're doing, sir?"

His hand moved over hers, imprisoning it, then his other hand circled her waist. He was pinning her against him. "Risking all, m'dear. But 'tis worth it."

His lips came down to cover hers. He was very gentle until Sheena began to struggle, and then he held her so tightly she couldn't move. Her chest hurt from the tension of it. His kiss became savagely passionate, bruising her lips against her teeth. She thought her neck would snap. If only she had a dirk! Just as she thought her chest would explode, he moved away.

"Och, Sheena, you drive a man to do what he knows he shouldna," Gawain breathed huskily. "But there's no harm in a kiss, after all."

No harm! She wanted to scream at him, but she sensed the danger was over, so she said only, "Release me, sir. I'm no' without the courage to kill you for what you've done!"

He chuckled, but he released her and stepped away nonetheless. "'Tis no' you I fear, lass, but your laird."

"Jamie? He's no' my laird."

"Nay?" He grinned wickedly. "Then I've risked nothing. Mayhap I'll be stealing more than just a kiss."

The scream died in her throat. Once again she was crushed against him. He groped at her breasts. She was sickened. This was real danger.

Then she heard steps, voices coming down the stairs, and Gawain let her go, cursing. She squeezed past him, racing out of the tower into the open courtyard. She slowed, then stopped altogether to take a deep breath and thank the fates for sending whomever had been approaching.

That had been too close, too damned close. Did she have to worry about being attacked in every dark corner? There was one hope, however, and she went on to the gatehouse. But she had only to look at the gatekeeper before he shook his head at her.

Where did that leave her? Without any protection at all? She wasn't about to give herself over to one man in order to protect herself from other men. There had to be a better way than that.

Colen was the only one at the laird's table when Sheena entered the hall. She strode over to him angrily.

"I demand your protection, Colen," she stated boldly. "You owe it to me."

"Do I?" he asked. "And do you expect me to fight my brother for you?"

"Nay, I dinna expect that. But 'tis no' Jamie I'm worried about, not just now."

He looked at her lips, and she touched them, then grimaced. They were swollen. Curse Black Gawain!

"I'm asking you for help," she said flatly.

"Why do you no' go to my brother? I'm sure he will be happy to offer you protection."

"But at what price?" Sheena snapped. "I'm no'

ready to sacrifice myself!"

"Sacrifice?" he chuckled. "Aye, I suppose you would look at it that way."

She frowned. This was getting her nowhere. And he was acting so strangely.

"You dinna care then?" she asked.

"I dinna think you will consider my brother's attentions so terrible." His tone was bitter.

"What do you mean by that?" she demanded.

"I saw you lying with Jamie by the burn," Colen replied. "You werena exactly fighting against him, Sheena."

Her cheeks flushed bright rose, but she wouldn't admit anything. "He took advantage of me, Colen. He's stronger than I. But I'm no' wanting him, if that is what you think."

"Marry me then, if you're so set against him. 'Tis the only way, for otherwise he'll have you."

"There must be another way."

Colen shook his head. "I give up on you, Sheena. I dinna know how my brother stands your constant rejection of him, but I've had enough of it. He's welcome to you."

She had not expected that. Somehow, she had felt she could always count on Colen. And he was telling her not to.

"So you'll no' help me?"

Colen sighed. "You've no' let either of us put a claim on you. And as for protecting you, well . . . you'll have to deal with my brother. I brought you here, and I'm sorry for it now, but you managed to escape, and 'tis Jamie who brought you back.

218

You're his now."

"Why did he drag me back, Colen? And what right has he to keep me here?"

Sheena just barely heard his answer as Colen walked away. "You'll have to ask him why."

Chapter 26

SHEENA did the only thing she could do, and locked herself in the south tower. She was determined to stay there until Jamie agreed to let her leave Castle Kinnion. It did seem the only solution. She would not be accosted there, not with the door locked. She had gathered enough food from the table to last her several days. Jamie wouldn't know that, of course. He would think to starve her out.

When he returned to the castle that evening and found her door locked, found she wouldn't answer his demands to open it, he broke it down. Sheena stood in her room, facing his anger, no locked door to shield her.

"You'll be telling me what that was all about!" Jamie commanded. "I know you heard me call. Why the devil did you no' answer?"

Sheena gathered her courage about her.

"You had no right to break the lock, Sir Jamie. If I had wanted you in here, I would've let you in."

"Your silence wasna telling me that."

"And if I had said go away, would you have heard me through all the shouting and pounding you were doing?" she retorted.

Jamie's frown darkened, but she went on, "I've a right to privacy. Your father never broke down your mother's door. He respected—"

"I'm no' my father!" Jamie cut her short. "There'll be no locked doors 'atween me and what *I* want. And once we're well mated, you'll no' be wanting them either."

Sheena gasped. "Your confidence is extraordinary. And misplaced. I will always want a barrier between you and me!"

She stood, hands on hips, breathing heavily, chin jutting out, and Jamie's anger fled. He chuckled.

"Och, but you're lovely with that fire in your eyes." He grinned. "'Tis easy to see I'll never be able to stay angry with you for long."

That statement from James MacKinnion, a man who carried anger to its worst conclusions? She didn't believe what she'd heard.

"I dinna like being toyed with."

"You dinna like, you dinna like," he mimicked. "Is there anything you *do* like, lass?"

"Freedom."

"Where have you ever known freedom?" he asked pointedly. "You were under your father's rule 'afore you fell under mine."

"He allowed me freedom."

"Did he? Allowed it? Or did you just take it?"

Sheena couldn't meet his steady gaze any longer. The man had too much insight.

221

"That doesna signify," she replied uneasily. "But the fact is, I'm still under his rule, no' yours. I'll be doing what *he* says, no' what you wish."

"Will you?" Jamie chuckled. "Well then, perhaps I should find him and put the question to him. A MacEwen would relish an alliance with a MacKinnion."

"Nay!" she gasped.

"'Twould certainly be putting an end to all this pointless arguing."

"Nay!" Sheena repeated forcefully.

"Well now." Jamie pressed his point home. "If I want to find him, I'll find him."

Sheena suddenly realized what he'd said. "You'll never find him. Go ahead, waste your time trying," she said confidently.

But Jamie knew exactly where her confidence came from. "'Twill no' be difficult. A talk with your aunt in Aberdeen should enlighten me."

She was cornered. "I hate you, James Mac-Kinnion!"

"Do you?" he said sharply, growing tired. "Well, I've no doubt of that, lass, no doubt at all. But 'tis the name you're hating, no' the man, and I'm sick and tired of it." Her eyes widened, and he added quickly, "You didna object to me when we first met. 'Twas only after you learned my name that fear took you. Explain that. Can you?"

"I dinna have to explain anything to you," she said weakly.

"Ah, of course not," he said mockingly. "Your way of dealing with an issue is to ignore it. So let *me* explain, if you will: you've heard tales, terrible tales that made you fear me 'afore we even met. Speak up if I'm wrong, Sheena." She stayed silent, and he continued. "I'll no' ask you what you've heard. I'll no' even deny there's truth to some of those stories. But given the travelings of tales, you have to allow for some exaggeration."

"Less of one than the other, I would imagine," Sheena replied tartly. "More truth than exaggeration."

"*Some* truth, Sheena. No' enough to condemn me," he said earnestly.

"But enough to know you're no' to be trusted."

Jamie's brows drew together, and his lips formed into a hard line. "Look at me, Sheena," he commanded brusquely. "You take away my name and look at me as I am. Have I ever given *you* reason to fear me? Have I ever threatened your life or caused you any harm?"

"You have!" she answered readily. "You order me around. You talk of handfasting when you know how I feel. You bully me at every turn."

"Cursed stubborn female!" Jamie shouted. "My only crime is in wanting you. And if you would be honest, you'd be admitting that is no crime at all. You're no' as opposed to my desire as you say you are."

"I am!" she cried. "I swear—"

"Sheena, 'tis time to have done with all this foolish fighting."

He moved, and suddenly there was almost no distance between them anymore. "Come to me,

223

Sheena." His voice was soft. "Follow your heart for once."

She didn't. But she didn't move away, either. She knew she needed only to stand there, and he would come to her and put his arms around her. She remembered the feel of those arms. She closed her eyes, recalling exactly how she'd felt when he kissed her. Her eyes flew open at the touch of his fingers on her back, pulling her gently to him. He made no further move. He just stared at her intensely, his eyes probing hers. Was he trying to see the truth?

"Sheena," he breathed softly. "I know what happens when I kiss you, but mayhap you've forgotten and need reminding."

"Nay, I've no' forgotten. 'Tis your devil's magic that makes me like your kissing, and only that."

She said it with such conviction! "Magic, eh? How you delude yourself! The only magic is the pleasure that comes when two people want each other with equal intensity. The devil has nothing to do with this."

"Why do you do this to me?" she cried in frustration.

"I have a need to be near you, Sheena, to hold you, to touch you. Now tell me," he asked, "am I hurting you? Nay, 'tis only holding you I'm doing. And a kiss or two I might steal."

His mouth lowered to hers, but Sheena cried out in pain.

"What is this?" he demanded, seeing the slight swelling. "What caused this?"

"I . . . fell," she said ineffectually.

He stared hard at her and then suddenly exploded. "By God, woman, you're lying!" He shoved himself away, afraid he would strike her. "Only back one day, and you've already given yourself to another man!" he thundered. "Anyone but me, eh? Jameson was bad enough, but now one of my kins has been with you!"

"How dare you accuse me?" she shouted in outraged fury, reaching out to slap him as hard as she could. "First Jameson, now this! Mayhap you like thinking I'm a whore, to ease your own guilt, but I must disappoint you. 'Tis only a husband I'll be giving myself to willingly. One of your kin indeed! I hate you all, for you're all the same to me! Savage brutes!"

"Then how—?"

"I was attacked! But what difference does it make who attacks me, you or someone in your family? I'm no' safe under your care, 'tis why I locked myself in here. And still I'm no' safe—from you!"

Jamie fingered his face, his eyes glowering. Sheena backed away, appalled to realize what she had done. But the cause of his furious look wasn't her slap.

"You were raped?" he asked in a deadly tone.

"Nay, it didna come to that—this time. But the fact is, you brought me back here and said I canna leave, yet you have done naught to protect me. Am I to live each day in fear of every man here, including you?"

225

Her accusation cut to the quick, because she was right. It was his fault. He and Colen both had brought her here without explaining her presence to the others.

"You'll be telling me who it was attacked you, Sheena," he said in a deceptively calm voice.

"Why?"

"An example will be made, to ensure your future safety."

"Of course. A fine solution," she said sarcastically. "Punish the man for having the same brutish nature you have. Punish him because you are laird and he isna. Are you any less guilty than he is?"

"My intentions were made clear from the start."

"And that excuses you?" she snapped. "Well, his intentions were made clear, as well, so you must excuse him, as well."

"Sheena—"

"Nay, you'll hear me out! I'll no' tell you who the man was, for he knew I was without laird here. I told him so."

"Then you could have avoided the attack?"

The reprobation was clear, and Sheena's chin jutted out indignantly. "I'll no' claim an intimacy with you that isna true, even to protect myself. There is only one solution here, Sir Jamie."

"To let you return to Aberdeen? Nay, there is another solution."

He seemed more furious than ever, and began pacing the floor, Sheena watching him nervously. After an eternity, he spoke very quietly.

"We will be wed."

He turned to look at her, seeing confusion cross her face, then anger. She couldn't know that the words were just as hard for him to say as for her to hear.

"Will we?" she demanded, incredulous. Did his arrogance have no end? "How will you manage that? I have no intention of agreeing."

"We will be wed!" he repeated coldly.

Anger fled, replaced by uncertainty. Was there some way he could force her? Something she hadn't thought of?

"Just last evening you spoke again of handfasting. What has changed your mind?"

"Handfasting willna make you willing, or have *you* changed your mind?" he countered.

"But you said you wouldna marry an untried lass."

The reminder only fueled his anger, and he answered cruelly. "That applied to a maiden. We both know you've been tried. And since you havena taken your life over it, you must have found it to your liking. 'Twas a frigid wife I wasna wanting, you see. You'll no' be that, will you?"

Sheena caught her breath, her cheeks flaming, and retaliated just as sharply. "You mean to rape me then? You think that will make me agree to marry you?"

"Nay, lass." He smiled coldly. "We will be wed soon, so I can wait to have an obedient wife, willing to please in every way."

"Never!" she screamed, but he turned his back on her and walked out. Her screams became louder. "You canna force me! Do you hear?"

She sat down on the bed, her head in her hands. She was right back where she'd started, terrified of marrying a Highland chief, recalling all the stories about him, about his wife, his raids. She heard Niall saying that he'd beat her and rape her and make her suffer all her life. And she knew that was just what he meant to do, make her suffer. His cold fury proved that. There had been no heartfelt declaration, no talk of love. Lust was ruling him, and, in the end, lust would make them both suffer.

Chapter 27

SOON after Jamie left her, two men escorted Sheena to a chamber near Jamie's. She didn't object, for she wouldn't have slept at all with the door to the tower room broken. Her new room didn't have an inside lock, but it wasn't locked from the outside, either. The two men didn't go away. They were there all night, and the next morning, they followed her to the hall. They were there to guard her. They stuck to her for two days. On the third day, as she sat at the table with Jamie and Colen, eating porridge and cream, she began worrying about Jamie's attitude. He was too calm. Indifferent. Aye, indifferent described him perfectly. Where before he hadn't been able to keep his eyes off her, now he never looked her way. Could she hope it was over, that he had given up? Or was he keeping her in suspense? If he had some plan, what was he waiting for?

The man who ran into the hall before the meal was finished received everyone's attention. Visibly upset, he stopped at the laird's table, a look of utter disbelief on his face.

"A word, Sir Jamie. Quickly!"

"You may speak freely, Alwyn," Jamie sighed. "You are always making too much of minor incidents."

"You're no' going to believe it, Sir Jamie," Alwyn gasped. "But I swear every male Fergusson alive is outside our gate."

Sheena blanched, swallowing quickly before she choked. Her eyes riveted on Alwyn. Her kin, here? All of them outside the castle? But she was inside! They would attack, not knowing she was there!

"So this is how you settle it, Jamie. 'Tis a bit underhanded, if you ask me." Colen's disapproving voice broke through Sheena's panic. His meaning was not quite clear until she looked at Jamie. He was smiling at her, such a self-satisfied smile.

Sheena gasped. There being no point in pretending any longer, she said simply, "How long have you known?"

"No' long, m'dear," Jamie said. "I had a visitor while you were sojourning with Jameson. Alasdair MacDonough—I believe you know him? He had much to say about the betrayal of his bride-to-be."

"But you had never seen . . . how could you know?" Sheena demanded.

"We can discuss that later." Jamie's smile deepened as he got up from the table. "Right now, I dinna want to keep your father waiting." He signaled to her guards and ordered sharply, "Take the lady to her chamber and see she stays there. She's no' to leave it for any reason, you ken?"

Her arms were gripped, gently but firmly, yet she couldn't just let them lead her away. All manner of horrible visions flashed through her mind . . . her kin slain, her father, her brother. . . .

"Jamie!" she cried, stopping him as he turned to leave. "You must tell me what you plan. Please!"

His expression softened, and his fingers brushed her cheek. "Do you know that's the first time you have used my name without formality."

"Jamie! Please!"

"Dinna fash yourself, lass," he said gently. "I didna send for your father to kill him."

"You sent for him?"

"Did I no' say we would be wed soon?" he grinned.

He left her then. Suddenly it was all clear. He had not changed his mind, he had only been waiting, waiting for the one person who could force her to marry him—her father.

Jamie leaned over the parapet, getting the best view of all the horses at his gate, some burdened with two, even three men. It did indeed look as if every male Fergusson alive was at Castle Kinnion. Jamie was amused. His message to Dugald had been clear enough, stating that he was in possession of the jewel of Tower Esk. If the old man could afford to ransom her, he was to come alone to Castle Kinnion.

He certainly was not alone! But then, the only plaids Jamie could see were Fergusson plaids. No

231

other clan was involved—yet. Of course, that was not to say the MacAfee, MacGuire, and Sibbald clans weren't on their way. But Jamie doubted it. If he had thought it would come to bloodshed, he would never have sent the message.

Jamie saw Dugald moving to the fore, his son beside him. He was glad the boy was there. If Sheena wanted to disobey her father, the lad could help persuade her not to.

"James MacKinnion!"

"I'm here, old man," Jamie called down, leaning over the battlements so Dugald could see him. "So we meet again. I must say I like this meeting better than our last encounter."

Dugald glared up at him, and Jamie chuckled. Then Colen spoke from behind him. "So you've met him 'afore. How?"

"Dinna ask me questions now, lad. I've my life to settle here."

"And I hope she makes it a miserable life indeed!" Colen rasped bitterly.

"Och, now, I didna expect you to be a poor loser, Colen," Jamie replied, still talking over his shoulder. "You knew I meant to have her. You gave no objections then."

"I thought you would be leaving it up to her. I didna think you would be bringing outside influences into it. You're forcing her, and that's the truth."

"To marry me, lad. That's what this is about," Jamie explained. "Marriage, no' handfasting."

A flicker of surprise crossed Colen's face, then

he turned and walked away. Jamie sighed. Colen had managed to prick his conscience, and he was very near to having second thoughts. But, well, Sheena felt something for him, he was sure of it. That wasn't something a man could be mistaken about. If he weren't sure, he would never have done this. Nor would he have pursued her against such terrible odds. He regretted his brother's disappointment, but he was not going to let that deter him from having what he wanted.

"So, Sir Dugald," he called down, "will you come inside, so we dinna have to be shouting at each other all day?"

"And have you take me prisoner, as well?"

"I have the only prisoner I want," Jamie replied. "She's worth more to me than you are, I vow it."

"And who's to say this is no' a trap, Mac-Kinnion?" Dugald called up.

"I am. Come now, man. I could kill you now if that was my intention."

More than a dozen weapons poked over the wall at Jamie's signal, demonstrating the truth of his words. He gave another signal, and the gate opened. He was no longer asking Dugald to come inside. He was leaving the older man no choice.

"I'm coming with you," Niall said to his father.

"And let him have at his mercy all that is dear to me? Nay. You will stay outside his walls."

"'Tis my sister he has in there!" Niall said angrily.

"And I'll be getting her back!" Dugald growled. "Dinna argue. Och, but you're getting as bad as

Sheena. Disrespect, 'tis what's wrong with both of you."

Dugald rode through the gate, anger giving him courage to enter the enemy camp. Jamie had already left the wall and was waiting in the courtyard. Dugald rode to him and dismounted. There were no retainers nearby. If he had wanted to, Dugald might have drawn his sword. But that wouldn't have been honorable.

"Come into the hall," Jamie offered. "A tankard of ale will make bargaining easier."

Dugald followed Jamie, and still no retainers came near them. The two lairds sat at the laird's table, Dugald beginning to think he might not have walked into a trap after all.

"I must welcome you, your first time here," Jamie said congenially after the ale was served and they were alone again.

"I never thought to set foot in this castle," Dugald replied gruffly.

"You wasted no time getting here, however."

"Did you think I would?" Dugald's eyes narrowed. "How much, MacKinnion?"

Jamie sat back and looked thoughtful. "I can safely say you canna meet the price I would set for her."

"So this was a trap!" The old man rose, furious. "No less than I could expect from a MacKinnion!"

"Sit down, Sir Dugald, and hear me out. 'Tis your daughter's honor you are bargaining for."

Red-faced, Dugald took his seat. "I want to see Sheena."

"You will, after we have settled her future."

"*We?* How dare—?"

"Come now, Fergusson. Were you no' determined to settle *my* future when you had me as your prisoner? The situation is only reversed. *You* didna ask for ransom. The condition for my freedom was to marry one of your daughters."

"So what is it you want now, MacKinnion?"

"I want Sheena," Jamie said simply.

Dugald's face turned redder, and his eyes blazed. "You canna have her!"

"Ah, well, but you see I *do* have her," Jamie said calmly.

Dugald seemed to crumble. It was true. He looked away. "Did you . . . have you . . . harmed her?"

"She's not been harmed or dishonored here, Sir Dugald. If she's no' a maiden, it wasna my doing."

"My Sheena isna like that!"

"*That* is in need of debating," Jamie replied coldly. "She has been away from you for some time. You canna know how she has conducted herself during that time."

"You say so, yet you still want her?"

"I do."

"Why have you brought me here?" Dugald demanded abruptly. "You already have Sheena at your mercy. Was this to torment me? Will you be telling me now all the things you'll do to make her suffer?"

Jamie chuckled. "You'll have to forgive me, Sir Dugald. I suppose I have been a bit vindictive in

235

no' telling you 'afore now that I want Sheena for my wife."

It took a moment to sink in. "Your wife?" Dugald sat back, stunned. "But you said you'd no' marry one of my daughters."

"I know what I said." Jamie cut him off. "But you didna offer me this daughter."

"Because I wanted a special man for her, someone I could be sure wouldn't mistreat her."

"And you thought I would? You surprise me, Fergusson. I may have been your enemy from the day I was born, but I am still a man who can appreciate a beautiful woman. Your daughter is more than beautiful. Mistreat her? I want only to make her happy."

Dugald stared hard at Jamie, trying desperately to see the truth.

"Does she want to marry you?"

"She doesna."

"Then how can you make her happy?"

"Her objection is that we are enemies. Of course, if we are wed, that will no longer be the case. Will it?"

"Of course not," Dugald agreed.

"Too, she does fear me a bit. But that is only natural after all the exaggerated tales she has heard of me. She will get over her fears quickly enough. I'll give her no cause to fear me."

"So I'm here to *order* her to marry you?"

"Ask, order, plead, whatever it takes to obtain her compliance. Remember, 'twas you who wanted the alliance between us, an end to our feud. You'll have it through Sheena."

"And if she doesna agree?"

"I know you've raised a stubborn daughter, Sir Dugald. But I mean to have her, *and I will,* one way or another. I am a determined man. The lass will never leave this castle except as my wife. That is a promise I make you. You can relay it to her if she balks."

Chapter 28

NIALL sat by the fire, across from Jamie. After Dugald and Jamie had talked, the whole clan had been offered the warmth of the hall, and food. Niall knew what the agreement between his father and Sir Jamie was, for his father had come downstairs blustering over Sheena's stubbornness awhile before. But one look at Jamie and he had gone back upstairs to try again.

Niall was not surprised that The MacKinnion wanted to marry Sheena. He wondered if Sheena knew that James MacKinnion had seen her in the glen, or that trying to find her again had got Jamie captured.

Watching the Highlander, Niall almost laughed. He was as nervous as any bridegroom, worrying over what was happening in the part of the castle where Sheena was staying, and throwing tantrums. He hadn't spoken one word to Niall, didn't seem even to know he was there, but instead kept his eyes turned to the end of the hall where Dugald had disappeared. It was just as well. Niall wasn't eager to speak to Jamie. He was still in awe of the large man.

"'Tis well our father never lived to see our hall overflowing with Fergussons."

Jamie turned and looked at Colen coolly. "If you've come to argue more with me, I'd rather no' be hearing it."

"No' to argue, Jamie. But I canna contain my curiosity. Has it been settled?"

"Her father is still with her."

"And who is this?" Colen asked.

Jamie noticed Niall then, and smiled at him. "Sheena's brother, Niall," he said to Colen. To Niall he said, "And this is my brother, Colen."

Niall's light blue eyes were huge. "Och, you're as big as he is!"

Colen laughed. "So I am—almost. And did he tell you we were both wanting your sister?" He kept his voice light.

Niall looked from one brother to the other. "But you're younger than she is," he blurted innocently, not realizing what a sore subject it was.

"So I've been told—one too many times," Colen replied curtly.

"You mean you'd no' mind dancing to her tune? My sister has a knack for getting her way, you know. Even our father canna contend with her when her temper's up." Jamie chuckled, and Niall said firmly, "I wouldna laugh, MacKinnion. You'll no' have an easy time of it."

Jamie grunted, making Colen laugh. "I suppose

I should be grateful I've lost her to you, brother. I think I'd prefer a wife I can handle."

Jamie fingered his cheek, remembering the slap. Sheena was indeed a lass to contend with. But she could be tamed. He had no doubt about that.

They went on, the three of them, swapping stories about the girl, until Colen left to visit Daphne. His sister had been in bed, ill, since her arrival.

"I'll be telling Daphne the news, if Aunt Lydia hasna already done so. 'Tis all she can talk about, how happy she is Sheena's a Fergusson," Colen said in parting. Then he suddenly added solemnly, "Just never hurt her, Jamie. 'Tis all I ask." He turned away abruptly.

Jamie stared after his brother, a frown creasing his brow. "Sweet Mary, my own brother thinks me a brute," he muttered.

Niall heard him. "Then you really havena touched her? I mean . . .?"

"I hate to disappoint you, lad, but I'm no' the ravisher of women you assume I am."

"The impression you gave when last we met was no' encouraging. You did say—"

"You've no' need to remind me," Jamie interrupted. "But I was angry then, Niall, with you and with your father. The truth is, your father never offered me Sheena. But if you hadna thought so, then you would never have let me go. So I let you think he had."

"Sheena wouldna be here now if she hadn't been banished," Niall continued thoughtfully. "She had a great fear of you, James MacKinnion. Does she still? Is that why my father is taking so long?"

"She did fear me, I'll no' deny it. But what she feared was my learning who she was. Even knowing how much I wanted her, she thought I'd do her harm if I discovered she was a Fergusson. Today she learned it made no difference to me. I'd never harm her. She knows that, deep in her heart, but she's too stubborn to admit it."

"What are you saying, MacKinnion?"

"That I believe she feels the same about me as I do about her."

Sheena burst into tears the moment her father left her room. Not five minutes later, Niall was knocking on her door, ready to continue where her father had left off. What was she to do, when the two people she cared the most for were insisting she marry The MacKinnion?

Her father hadn't been kind about it. "The feud will be over," he had said. "Our kin will be safe."

As if the fate of them all were in her hands. He had made it sound as terrible as he could.

"You want us all to die?" he had stormed. "He says you'll no' leave this place unless you're his wife. Can I go home, knowing that? Nay, 'twill mean war now, the bloodiest war yet. Is that what you're wanting? Are you that selfish, Sheena, lass?"

How he had heaped on the recriminations! He had thundered, and he had threatened. His last words had been, "You'll do it!"

And then Niall. She was so happy to see him,

but he ruined their reunion. "You'll have to be marrying him, you know. And 'tis lucky you are, I'm thinking."

Lucky! Could no one see her point of view? "What of the raids, the killings?" she finally demanded, furious with her brother, her father, all of them. "What of his first wife, who died rather than be married to him? And what of love? He's no' spoken of love."

"And if he did speak of it?" her brother asked quietly.

Sheena never answered. She didn't know why she had mentioned it at all. Grasping at straws was what she was doing, reaching out desperately. But whenever she reached out, she found herself clutching at nothing. Was there no help for her? Had they taken everything away?

Chapter 29

THEY were married in the late afternoon on that very day, bound by a kirkman whom Jamie had summoned the day before. In the presence of her clan and his, before God, Sheena became wife to The MacKinnion.

The clans, also, were bound by the marriage. The Fergussons were delighted. It was a day for great celebration—a marriage and the end of a bitter feud. For most, it was a day to be happy.

There were, however, some who were not pleased. Those who had recently lost loved ones to the feud, for example, of whom Black Gawain was one. He refused to attend the wedding or the festivities that followed. His current mistress was also quite bitter. Harboring a hope that she might get Jamie back after he had finished with the red-haired Lowlander, she had stayed where she was. That was the only reason for the relationship with Black Gawain, staying at Castle Kinnion. The marriage dashed hope for Jessie.

But Sheena was by far the most miserable. Her wedding day felt like a day of execution. Now that she had been given to the savage MacKinnion, her life became his to do with as he chose. And once his lust for her cooled? Then he would remember that she was a Fergusson, always his enemy. He would remember, and he would never let her forget. She ought to have worn black, instead of the lovely gown Lydia had worked on so hard and so swiftly. It was made of lime green silk, and the bodice had been cut with a V of white lace, the wide sleeves trimmed with white fur. She knew very well that such a special gown was meant for a special occasion. So Lydia had known all along!

Watching her father, so pleased with himself, and her brother enjoying himself, only added to her misery. Couldn't they understand what they had done to her? Why did nobody care about *her?*

And her husband? The last time she had dared glance his way, he had not looked like a newly wedded man. Was he already regretting what he had done and the finality of it?

He got up, startling her, and walked away from the tables where the splendid feast was laid out. She was happy to see him go and considered sampling a bit of food. There was roasted venison, Highland grouse stuffed with wild cranberries in butter, smoked fish, mutton pie, stewed beef, kid, pigeons, and capons. And the sweets! Cream crowdies, ginger cakes, sugary nutmeg cakes. She would get fat, that's what she would do. He wouldn't want her if she was grotesquely fat.

But Jamie didn't go far enough away, and Sheena never filled her plate. He went to her father and had a few words with him, laughing. It stung, how glad her father was to have her wedded to The Mac-Kinnion.

Jamie returned. He took her hand and forced her to rise. She looked at him questioningly, but his expression revealed nothing and he said nothing. He tugged at her, expecting her to follow. She held back.

"You'll be telling me where we're going, Sir Jamie." Her tone was obstinate.

Jamie turned around to face her, giving her hand a sharp tug, making his point. "So you'll be giving me trouble already?"

"If you'll just give me a reason why you're taking me away . . . ?"

"I dinna need a reason, wife. You *are* my wife?" He put the question coldly. "You do agree you are my wife, Sheena? Say it."

She looked away from the hard hazel eyes. "I agree," she murmured.

"I didna hear you."

"I agree!"

"Then you'll also agree I need no reason to have you follow me?" he pressed his point.

Her head snapped up, and her eyes, deeply blue, sparked with anger. "So it's to be that way, is it? Now you've got what you want, you've no thought for my feelings? But then, you never did."

Before her eyes, Jamie changed. The stiffness left him, and his expression softened. He even grinned, shamefaced.

"I'm sorry, Sheena. There's no excuse for my acting this way. 'Tis just . . . och, never mind. 'Tis for your sake we're leaving. You're no' enjoying yourself."

"Was I supposed to?"

"Now, lass," he said reprovingly. "Let us have a wee bit of peace, eh? For your father's sake at least? Would you have him regretting he gave you to me?"

"As if he would," she said bitterly. "And what did you tell him just now?"

"Only no' to get himself alarmed if we dinna return for a while."

"A while?" The words rang ominously.

They stared at each other. The look in Jamie's eyes was quite clear. Sheena shook her head slowly, feeling so peculiar. Somehow she found the words to speak and even managed a calm voice.

"We have guests. And I've no' eaten yet, nor have you."

Jamie held up a hand to silence her. "You've naught to fear, and I'll show you that. Then you can return and be at ease, and you can smile for a change. Sweet Mary, Sheena! 'Tis your wedding day, a day to remember."

"I'm no' likely to forget!" she snapped. "And as to why I canna smile, 'tis simply that I've naught to smile about, being married to you."

Jamie was cut deeply, but he hid it well.

"We'll leave now, Sheena," he said in a level tone.

"But . . . but I've no' even met your sister yet," Sheena protested. "What will she think of me, leaving without saying hello?"

"You have met her, Sheena. You met her and spoke no' two words to her, though she left a sickbed to be here. What she thinks is that I've made the same mistake twice, for you've been sitting there at the table acting exactly as my first wife did on her wedding day. I'll have no more of it."

Sheena was surprised. Could memories of his first wife pain him still? She had never considered that. She thought about it as they walked from the hall, up the stairs, to the door, where Jamie stopped.

"Our chamber," Jamie said softly as he held the door open, letting go of her at last.

Sheena walked inside slowly. It was a large room, with a large French bed, linen sheets pulled down, large pillows fluffed. She quicky tore her eyes away from the bed. There was a standing chest for clothes, a table with stacked papers all weighted down. Across from the table was a tier of lit candles. A comfortable chair was positioned before the fire. Most intriguing was a cabinet containing exquisite glass ornaments, large and small: birds, animals, a glass boat, a bell, and many other things. Sheena had never seen the like.

"They were my mother's," Jamie said. "Handed down to her by her Norman ancestors."

Embarrassed by her own staring, she turned away from the beautiful collection and moved to the fire. Keeping her back to Jamie, she held out her trembling hands to the flames.

"Will you have some wine, Sheena?"

She jumped, then glanced at him sideways. He was waiting for her answer. She nodded hesitantly and watched him pour a rich red wine into a large goblet. He brought it to her, and she took the heavy container in both hands and drank it down without once pausing to breathe.

Jamie's eyes were on her, slightly amused. Amusement at her expense? The wine was warming her, spreading a delicious languor. Weakness, when she had to face her enemy? She gripped the goblet, debating whether to ask for more. Would more fortify her or make her succumb? She had to get a grip on herself.

Behind her, Jamie was in agony. Never in his whole life had he been more unsure of himself. Staring at Sheena's stiff, unyielding back, he waited. It had to be right. It had to be perfect. From the time he'd first seen her, shrouded in mist, he had wanted her. And now she was his.

The most beautiful, most desirable of women, and he was loathe to touch her, loathe to frighten her.

"I'll have more wine, Sir Jamie, if you please."

As she handed him the empty goblet, their eyes met. What he saw in those deep blue eyes twisted his heart.

"Why is it you still fear me, lass? Have I no' proved you've no need? I swear I'll be more gentle than any lover you've had 'afore me."

"I've had no others."

She didn't say it indignantly, as she had before, just simply and quietly. Jamie caught his breath. His heart filled with sudden joy.

"If you can say that now, when you know I'll be finding out 'afore we leave this room, then it must be so. Och, Sheena, you canna imagine how happy I am to be knowing it. You canna imagine what hell I suffered when I thought Jameson—"

"And why should it make a difference to you, James MacKinnion?" Sheena snapped.

"Why?" He was shocked.

"Aye, why? You believe in handfasting and the taking of innocent lasses. How many maidens have you had and set aside without a thought to what their eventual husbands would be thinking?"

"Enough, Sheena. I wed you thinking you had been with another, so you see it made no real difference to me, but I canna deny I'm glad there's been no other. If that makes me selfish, so I am. Here, if it will help," he said gently, and filled her goblet.

She looked at it and shook her head despondently. "Nay. Nothing will help except if you take pity on me and let me go."

"And have you live with fear even longer? I wouldna be so cruel."

She gasped and looked up, ready to face him, but he had set the wine aside, and his hands touched her shoulders, resting there with a gentle weight. She could feel his chest against her back. Her hair, the sides swept up to fall backward with the rest, was out of his way, and his thumbs rubbed against the curves of her neck.

"Let me put your fears to rest, Sheena, for all time," he breathed.

His lips brushed the skin just below her ear, and a tingling spread down her neck and over her shoulders. Sheena succumbed. She tilted her neck to the side to give him more access, and his lips took complete advantage.

If he hurt her, then he hurt her. But if he didn't? How wonderful to think she might be wrong about him! How extraordinary to think she could feel something other than hate and fear.

She was unable to dwell on the discovery, however, for he caught her tightly in his arms. His lips touched hers with such incredible tenderness. It was the same as the day at the burn. Thought deserted her, and sensation took over. She had the feeling of floating, feather-light, supported only by his arms. Her body was soaring through the sky, soaring. . . .

How long they stood there by the fire, Sheena didn't know. She was dimly aware of a change in Jamie's kissing, an increase in urgency. But it was only when the warm breath of the fire touched her bare skin that she became completely aware. Her gown and petticoats lay in a pile at her feet.

She was bared to the eyes of a man—and not just any man. Bright color flooded her face and neck. She tried to cover herself, but Jamie pushed her hands away while his own circled her waist to pull her close. And then he was kissing her again, and she didn't know whether to give in to the warmth that was rushing through her or fight to escape.

She was still undecided when he picked her up and carried her to his bed, laying her down gently. He began to remove his own clothing. She was free for the moment and had a chance to run, but Jamie sensed her thoughts, and while he caressed her with his eyes, he soothed her with words.

"You dinna have anything to fear, Sheena. I'll never hurt you. 'Tis cherishing you I am. You're more precious to me than anything I ever dreamed of. Can you no' sense that, sweetheart? Can you no' see I want only to make you happy? And I swear you will be happy. I swear you'll no' regret being my wife."

He knelt on the bed and bent over her, cupping her face in his large hands. "'Tis too long I've waited for you, too long I've been wanting you. Just trust me a little, Sheena, 'tis all I ask."

Why shouldn't she? He was going to have her. Why not make the best of it?

But the decision was not really Sheena's. Her body was in control, more than willing. His lips had been warm, and soon they became hot. Her fingers tangled in his thick hair, pulling his head back a little, for she was afraid of the intense heat. But Jamie's tongue was dancing circles around one taut nipple and then the other, and Sheena pressed him closer, the feeling exquisite.

When his mouth returned to hers, Sheena returned his kiss so wholeheartedly that Jamie leaned back to look at her. His eyes were bright, and he smiled at her with such warmth. She smiled back, fully and freely. It was the first time she had smiled at him since learning that he was The MacKinnion. Was all forgiven? It was more than Jamie had hoped for.

Her blood was fired. There was a need she didn't understand, a desire to have his body closer, closer. Sheena jerked and cried out as his fingers suddenly slid between her legs. But he didn't stop, and once the shock had passed, she didn't want him to. His fingers explored, causing delightful spasms. She could have suffered that blissful torture forever. Jamie prolonged it just long enough.

She would never be more ready for him than she was then, and he knew it. His change in position was swift and, before she knew what he was doing, he plunged into her. Sheena caught her breath. Then she sighed. She had expected pain, much worse pain, not that tiny tearing that was soon forgotten. How kind of him to have done it quickly, making it much easier. She felt only a fullness now, deep inside her. He didn't move, and she couldn't guess why he was so still.

Jamie was silently waiting for her accusations to start. How he had hated hurting her! If only she would say something, curse him.

She did speak, with her body. Sheena instinctively understood how she needed Jamie. She moved under him, forcing him out of her, then moved her hips upward to take him back, taking him whole.

Jamie shuddered in relief and delight. His hands gripped the sides of her head, holding her still for a kiss. While his lips plundered the sweetness of her mouth, his hard member explored the warmth enveloping him. He had never felt so strong, so masterful, so enthralled. He drifted into the mist where he had first seen her, floating ever closer to her, intoxicated by her feel, her scent, her warmth.

If Jamie was in awe, Sheena was in shock. Each thrust of Jamie's powerful body brought her to a higher plane. She had felt a rush of blood through her body before, but now there was a flood, all directed to the small area that was on fire. But the flood didn't put out the flame. It nourished the fire instead, gathering there, every part of her swirling round and round that fire.

She knew she couldn't contain it. Too great an intensity was building. It was going to kill her, explode and shatter her to pieces. She couldn't possibly survive this.

The moment was at hand, and Sheena knew it. But instead of her life flashing before her eyes, she saw only Jamie's face in her mind's eye, that handsome face grinning with a secret knowledge that she understood at last. The floodgates burst, and Sheena screamed, but the scream was smothered by Jamie's ravenous lips. There was no end to the waves washing over her, pulsing against every nerve. She heard him moan, knew he was dying the same sweet death. They plunged downward together.

He was so still, so heavy. She floated high above him, gliding ever so slowly, dreamlike, delighting in her new world, the peace of it, the warmth, the delicious—movement of his lips?

Her eyes opened a little. He was looking at her, too, his hazel eyes a warm gray-green. He was still holding her head, his thumbs moving softly on her cheeks. His lips touched her with a feather-light movement she wasn't sure she felt. He kissed her chin, her cheeks, her eyes. He leaned back to look at every bit of her face, and a smile curled his lips, a smile of utter contentment. If he were a cat, she thought, he'd be purring.

Sheena's eyes were round with wonder. "I'm seeing you, James MacKinnion! You're real, then?" she gasped. "I'm no' dead?"

His smile widened. "I dinna think so, sweet-heart."

"But I thought . . ." Bright color washed her cheeks. "How foolish of me!" She thought a moment, then rushed on, not quite meeting his gaze.

"'Tis just . . . I never knew what it would be like, Jamie. I knew there would be pain at first, I did know that. But the rest . . ." She lowered her eyes, willing to admit everything, yet still just a little embarrassed with this new intimacy. "No one could have prepared me for it," she continued, awed. "I was frightened by the intense feelings, since I didna know to what end they would bring me. And when they increased, I knew there would be an explosion. I feared the worst. I thought I would surely die, yet I wouldna have stopped you for the world."

Hesitantly, she looked up, meeting his eyes again. He was not looking at her with triumph.

Pride, aye, but not a conquering pride. The look in his eyes spread a warmth through Sheena that surprised her. Tenderness? Maybe even . . . love?

"You're no' alone in what you felt, Sheena," he murmured softly. "I canna say I've no' been pleasured 'afore, but never like this. In all the years since I've called myself a man, I never felt anything to compare. I knew, somehow, it would be this way with you. I always knew."

"You could've told me," she chided.

"Would you have believed me?"

"Nay," she answered simply. "Will it always be so, Jamie?"

"For us it will, I do believe so."

She giggled, squeezing him. She was happy, surprisingly, amazingly, happy. Who would have thought it possible?

"Nay, Jamie," she teased with a sigh. "I dinna think it can ever again be like this first time. But we can try to make it so. Often, eh?"

He laughed deeply, kissed her soundly, and laughed again. "By the saints, you're a jewel, Sheena. And to think I feared you might be like my first wife. What a fool I was! I ought to've known better."

Sheena confessed, "I had crazy thoughts when the fire was in me, and no' just of myself dying. I thought you were the devil, and no mistake. I also thought . . ." She stopped.

"What?"

She shook her head. "Nay, I'll no' repeat those thoughts."

"Och, but you will. You've got my curiosity riled," he said lightly.

"You'll be angry, Jamie, and I dinna want to spoil—"

"As if you could," he interrupted with a grin. "There's nothing you could say to make me angry at this moment. But never fear making me angry, sweetheart. I do have a temper, as you can attest. You'll see it no doubt, time and again, but I'll never harm you, I swear." She still hesitated, and he added, "Come now, lass. You must learn to trust me."

She sighed. "'Tis only when I thought I would die, I thought of . . . of your first wife . . . that she had died that way, too. In your arms. Happy." As he tensed, she added quickly, "I know how ridiculous it was to even think it. I canna believe you even touched her, for if you had, she would never have killed herself."

Jamie's eyes were inscrutable, but his body was tense, as if he was fighting for control.

"Och, Jamie, I'm sorry. But you see, I thought the worst of you 'afore today. I believed the stories. I may as well say it."

"Say it all, m'dear, by all means." His voice was hard as an iron blade.

Sheena did. "The story was your first wife killed herself because of your brutal raping of her on your wedding day. I believed the story because I never heard any tale to the contrary. I heard only of rape, murder, and mayhem. Is it any wonder I couldna tell you who I was, any wonder I believed you

256

would kill me if you knew? I was wrong," she said. "Wrong about you and about your wife. Wasn't I?"

He was enraged that she felt she had to ask him that. Could she not see clearly enough who he was?

"Maybe wrong, and maybe right," he said sarcastically.

Her eyes filled with tears, and Jamie was instantly remorseful. He shouldn't have been so hurt by her mentioning Ailis Mackintosh. She had been trusting enough to confide in him, and he had done just what he had sworn he wouldn't do.

"Och, Sheena, 'tis a brute I am, and no mistake. Of *course* the stories were wrong. I've never taken a woman who didna want it so. As for mayhem, well mayhem can at times be unavoidable. And murder? I'll no' deny I've killed men in battle. I've even sentenced one of my own kin to death, one who was deserving of that justice. But I've never murdered for the sake of killing, Sheena. No killing is to my liking, but what Scot hasna killed or wounded another in his lifetime? Is your father innocent of fighting and killing? Will your brother still be innocent of it 'afore long? Will you blame me for a life I canna change? For doing what I must do?"

He waited. He waited a long time. Finally she whispered, "I won't."

Jamie smiled, relieved greatly. "Then let me put your mind at rest about one thing more, sweetheart. You were right in thinking I never even touched my first wife. The wedding was arranged by our fathers. I had never seen Ailis Mackintosh

257

'afore we were joined in marriage. Nor did anyone warn me that she was a weak, fanciful lass, and utterly terrified of men—no' just me, Sheena, but all men, including her own father. She was dead 'afore I came to her that awful night. Her serving lass later confessed the poor thing's fear of men and that she was forced into our marriage and had sworn she would kill herself 'afore she'd let a man touch her. Her father apparently didna believe she would, and hadn't told me of the threat. He still didna accept it and blamed me and my family for her death. We've been enemies with the Mackintosh clan ever since."

"So that is why you swore you'd never marry a lass unless you'd tried her first?"

"Do you blame me? 'Twas horrible what Ailis did, a bitter shock. Any lass who looked at me in fear after that I stayed well away from. Is it any wonder your fear upset me so? You I couldna stay away from, as much as I sometimes wanted to. It didna help to know it was only me you feared, and not men in general."

"Och, well, you know why now."

"Aye. A foolish reason," he said.

"I didna think so."

He grinned down at her, his eyes reflecting amusement. "Even when I kissed you and you enjoyed it?"

"I didna enjoy it!" she protested.

Jamie chuckled. "A liar to the end, eh? Well, let us see if you'll admit now to enjoying my kissing."

And he kissed her. And she did enjoy it. And what followed was as lovely as could be imagined. Their guests were forgotten for a good while longer.

Chapter 30

JAMIE closed the door to his chamber, then pulled Sheena to his side, his hand resting possessively on her waist. Their eyes met, and Jamie smiled warmly. Sheena smiled back, and the smile stayed on her lips as they walked down the corridor.

Sheena was happy, truly happy for the first time in a very long time. And Jamie? He had laughed in delight when she put her lovely gown back on and blushed to find it so full of wrinkles from lying where they had left it. Everyone would know what they had been about. How could she dare return to the hall?

But she had seen the humor, too. What did it matter? They had been gone so long, everyone would know anyway. Either right then or in the morning, she would have to face their knowing. And Jamie was strutting so proudly, like a cock just come in from the henshed.

They passed the room where Sheena had stayed

those last few days under guard. But even that couldn't put a damper on her mood. How frightened she had been, and all for nothing. Jamie would never hurt her. And now she could be herself again, without performing, without always being on her guard. She wondered how Jamie would like the real Sheena Fergusson.

They approached the hall, but Jamie slowed suddenly, and Sheena looked up to find him frowning. Then she realized why. The hall was quiet, eerily so. Had everyone gone? Why?

"Jamie—" she started to ask, but he shushed her, and they continued down the stairs.

Confusion doubled when they entered the hall and found it not deserted at all. It was just as crowded as it had been. Yet the silence was oppressive. Most of the people were standing, and there was such a solemn look on every face that she felt prickles of unexplainable fear up her spine.

She didn't want to go into that large room at all, but Jamie forced her with him to the middle of the two trestle tables, where everyone's attention was centered. Her father was there, as were dozens of Fergussons, all standing beside and behind him. Black Gawain was there, and Colen, and many more MacKinnions than Fergussons.

Sweet Mary, they're going to fight, she realized. But Jamie would stop it. Thank God they'd come in when they had! Why? What could possibly have happened to set the clans against each other again?

The reason lay at Black Gawain's feet, and Sheena paled on seeing that it was Iain Fergusson, her cousin. Blood spread across his chest, making it impossible to tell exactly where he had been wounded. But wounded he was, and unconscious—or dead. Dear God, not Iain. Such a kind man, so sensitive. He cared nothing for fighting or raiding—only for his animals. How many times had she and Niall spent whole days with Iain, learning habits of wild creatures, laughing over the antics of a beaver, awed by his great shaggy aurochs?

The noise started all at once, the accusations, denials, anger. No one was making any sense, and it only got louder and louder, not clearer. Everyone shouting at the same time made Sheena ready to scream. But the figure of Jamie leaning down to examine Iain was more effective than any call for order could have been. He was probably the first to see if Iain was still alive.

Jamie stood up at last, utter disgust on his face. "What madness is this?" he demanded. "You stand here glaring and shouting at each other while a man bleeds to death!"

"Is he dead, then?" Colen was the one to ask.

"Without tending, he will be 'afore long."

Colen nodded and gestured to men to carry Iain to the hearth. Water would be heated there to clean his wound. But Dugald delayed that, obstinately instructing his own men to care for Iain.

Once Iain was carried away, Jamie stepped forward, growing angrier by the second. Such childish theatrics these were, intended as insult and taken as insult.

"I'll no' take issue with you, Sir Dugald, until I

hear what has happened," Jamie said with deliberate evenness of tone.

"Take issue all you want, MacKinnion. But if you're wanting to know what happened, ask your man there. See if he dares tell the truth."

Dugald's finger was pointed at Black Gawain, and Jamie eyed his cousin with considerable surprise. "You? What have you to do with this? You werena even here for the wedding."

"I came after you took your leave—and your pleasure—with your new bride."

The rudeness of it was bad enough, but the unmistakable bitterness in Gawain's voice disturbed Jamie. He was reminded of the spring raid, and how Gawain had behaved when he found his sister dead. Hell-bent on blood and revenge. Did he still hold that grudge? Had Iain been his revenge?

"You stabbed the man?" Jamie asked without preamble.

"I did."

"An accident?"

"Nay."

Jamie took a deep breath, holding himself in check. There was not an ounce of remorse in Gawain. If anything, he was belligerent on purpose.

"You'll be telling me why."

Jamie's tone was sharp, leaving no mistake about his rising temper. Black Gawain wisely took note of it and was less bellicose as he said, "You've no need to worry I was without cause, Jamie. The man rose to attack me. If he was slow and cloddish and my dirk found him first, whose fault was that?

The first attack was his."

"But he wouldna have attacked you!" Sheena gasped. "I know Iain. He wasna a fighter."

Jamie gave Sheena a sharp look. She was not to interfere.

"Who else can tell me what happened here?" he demanded, looking around.

"You doubt me, Jamie?" Black Gawain asked.

Jamie eyed him steadily. "Since when is only one side a fair accounting?"

"I can be telling you what happened here." A Fergusson spoke up. "'Twas no' the way he says."

"You saw it all?" Jamie was being very careful.

"I was next to Iain at the table," the man explained. "I couldna help but see it all."

"And what part wasna as my cousin claims?"

"Nae part," the man said without hesitating, his accent thickening with his emotion. "The MacKinnion came, and nae sooner did he sit down, he started in on poor Iain. Boasting he was, of raiding us. Laughing, too, he was, over how many Fergussons he'd killed. He was baiting Iain, and nae mistake. He should've come to my side, and he'd hae found what he was after. But Iain was only disgusted wi' his blathering. He rose to leave, *no' to attack*. He would've walked away if this one hadna gone for his dirk and stuck it in him."

Silence reigned once again. Sheena was appalled, believing her kinsman completely. Didn't she know all too well what kind of man Black Gawain was? Hadn't he attacked her, as well, without provocation? A different kind of attack, but still an attack.

Jamie was in a quandary, unable to believe it of his cousin. The same age, the boys had grown up together. Would Gawain deliberately provoke a fight? He couldn't have changed so drastically in the months since his sister's death, could he? There had to be more to it.

What was Jamie to do, take the word of a man he didn't know over his cousin's version? Yet he had to make a decision. The tension in the room was getting very bad. It was obvious that all his clan believed Black Gawain and the Fergussons believed their man. Even young Niall stood on his seat, viewing the scene below with his hand on the hilt of his sword. Could Jamie stop the men from fighting?

"Were you looking for a fight, Black Gawain?" Jamie had to ask the question.

"No' looking, but no' backing down, either. If I had wanted to fight the Lowlander, I would've challenged him outright, no' goaded him to it."

Jamie sighed. His decision would not be greeted well by Sheena's clan. "What we have then is an error in judgment, a misconstruing of simple actions. I'm thinking it can only be called an accident, however unfortunate it was."

"Are you now?" Dugald spoke up, his face mottled with anger. "And I'm thinking we'll be getting no justice here!"

"Concede. It was an accident, Sir Dugald," Jamie offered in warning. "There are no' enough witnesses to prove otherwise."

"I need only one witness!" Dugald roared.

"I need more! This is not a clear case!" Jamie roared back.

"Then wait till Iain recovers!" Sheena shouted before her father could say anything else. She was torn apart, knowing where this was leading. She couldn't stand it. And all over Iain, peace-loving Iain.

"To what end, daughter?" Dugald rasped. "The MacKinnion would only find other excuses no' to mete out justice, even if the truth were clear."

"I beseech you—"

"Nay!" Dugald cut her off sharply. "But dinna fear I'll soil this day with vengeance. We'll be leaving here, and you with us, 'afore there are more *accidents.*"

"She doesna go, Dugald." Jamie's voice was deceptively soft.

"She's wed to you, MacKinnion." Dugald glowered at him. "But by your own words, you did say she wouldna be forced to stay here."

"She can leave—when I say. For now she stays."

Sheena held her breath. Her father and her husband stared at each other for so long, not one more word passing between them, that she thought a battle was inevitable. She knew her father was placed in an intolerable position. It was either fight or back down. A Fergusson back down? When his whole clan stood behind him? Yet, as always when against the MacKinnions, the Fergussons were outnumbered.

His face dark with rage, Dugald Fergusson turned on his heel and left the hall without another word. Sheena was forced to watch the rest of her clan storm out of the hall. Then Iain was carried out, still unconscious. He was in no condition to be riding, yet ride he would, and probably die on the long trek home.

Even Niall did not look at her once as he left. Sheena moved toward her brother. They had to have at least a few words before he left. But Jamie's restraining hand on her shoulder kept her beside him, and she could only stand there, unable to prevent it, while her family left. Deep down she wondered if she would ever see them again.

Her chest ached, and she would have cried if not for the heavy hand on her shoulder. It reminded her that she was in the midst of the hated Mac-Kinnions. She wouldn't let the enemy see what this was doing to her.

"Sheena?"

Jamie's voice was soft, and she was reminded of his earlier tenderness. Did he think nothing had changed? Didn't he know everything was shattered?

She lifted his hand and shoved it away from her before she turned and looked squarely at him, her eyes filled with pain and condemnation. "Dinna touch me again, Jamie—ever," she whispered brokenly, all her pain in her voice.

"Sheena—"

"Nay!" she sobbed. Nothing he could say would change any of it.

She ran from the hall before they were shamed in front of his kin. Jamie stared after her, wanting desperately to follow, to make her see his side of it, but he feared his own temper, so he didn't move. He watched until she was out of sight.

Chapter 31

WHEN Jamie entered the chamber, Sheena was asleep in the chair by the fire, still dressed, her hair flowing over the side of the chair to form a shimmering red pool on the floor. Her arms were crossed over her breasts, her feet tucked under her skirt. Had she just fallen asleep there, or was she making a deliberate point by not sleeping in the bed?

Jamie added wood to the dying fire before he sat down at Sheena's feet to stare up at her. She looked so peaceful without the glimmer of tears in her eyes. Aye, he had seen the unshed tears, and the pain. But how to make it right with her?

He picked up the dark tresses lying on the floor and fanned them through his fingers. Their wedding day! What an utter fiasco, except for that little time together. How could she forget that time? Didn't it matter at all?

He wasn't going to wake her and hear more accusations. Enough angry words had been thrown at him that night. Colen had accused him of being ten kinds of a fool, and Aunt Lydia had had her say, as well, upbraiding him severely for letting the feud start again. But neither of them had made him admit he might have made a mistake.

It was actually Black Gawain who had made him consider the possibility. His cousin showed not a whit of remorse for what had transpired, enjoying himself on Jamie's wedding day though Jamie no longer could. Jamie's temper finally got the best of him, and he ordered Gawain from the hall, sick of the sight of him, sick over the fates that had turned Sheena against him again.

Sheena woke to see Jamie sitting on the floor near her, her hair entwined in his fingers. She stiffened and yanked the hair away from him.

Jamie turned to her, his eyes gleaming brightly in the firelight. He stood up and held out his hand, but she made no move to take it. He sighed. "Come to bed, lass. It has been a tiring day, and we can both use the rest." She still didn't move, so he added, "I'll no' be bothering you, if that has you worried."

Her eyes rose slowly to meet his, and when he saw how much anger was there, he wondered again if he could ever make it right with her.

"I only waited here to tell you I'll no' be staying in this room with you," she said.

"You will indeed stay here," Jamie replied adamantly.

She glared at him. "I want the tower room repaired, Jamie!"

"Nay! Dinna force it, Sheena," he warned her. "I'll no' be gossiped about as my father was whenever my mother got the sulks. I warned you 'afore there'd be no doors 'atween us."

"You'll sleep on the floor then!"

"I'll sleep on the bed!"

"Then I'll—"

"You'll cease this blathering now!" he stormed. "I've said I'll no' bother you. Leave it be." She seemed ready to continue shouting, and he said tiredly, "Go to sleep, lass." He began to remove his clothes.

Sheena turned away from him and stared at the fire, still standing in the center of the room. They had both carefully refrained from mentioning the real issue. She knew that if Jamie dared to try to justify his doing nothing to Black Gawain, she would say things she might regret.

Jamie wasn't going to discuss it, he had decided. He didn't have to explain himself to anyone. Sheena had no right to question him. If he let her sway him now on any issue, it would always be so. He couldn't allow that. She was only a wife—albeit a beautiful, tempting curse. Be damned to her!

He lay down on the bed but couldn't rest.

"I'll no' stand for this, Sheena."

"What?" She turned to face him, and he sat up. "This anger 'atween us. This room is no place for it."

Her eyes narrowed. "This room is the *only* place for it!" she hissed. "Or would you rather I be telling you what I think of you in front of your kin?"

271

"Tell me now and get it over with," he said, bracing himself.

"You're a coward!" she cried. "You didna dare pass fair judgment for fear your kin would cry favoritism on my behalf. You couldna bear that, to be accused of being partial to your wife. So you did what was wrong in order to save yourself that!"

"I didna do wrong, and partiality had naught to do with it, Sheena."

"For me, nay, but for Black Gawain it did. You canna tell me otherwise."

"Would you rather have seen your kind forced to arms?" he asked. "The atmosphere was too heated, Sheena. My kin would never have stood for a judgment against Black Gawain. Why should they? They believed him. They would never have considered the word of a Fergusson, two Fergussons, a dozen, no' over a MacKinnion. Too many years of hatred have made it so. They believed Gawain."

"Nay!" she cried. "If you had waited till Iain recovered, you'd have seen his story would be the same as my kinsman's—without Iain's having heard it. That would have been proof. You could have waited, Jamie."

"It is done. I canna bemoan it now."

"You could," she said bitterly. "But you willna because you dinna care."

"Och, Sheena, it wouldna make any difference to change my mind. Can you no' see that? All that matters is *further* bloodshed."

"I see only that my father will never forgive you

for the injustice you dealt my clan."

"I saved them any more fighting!" he returned sharply. "Is that injustice?"

"So a Fergusson is never to be dealt with fairly? Is that what you're telling me, Jamie?"

"Sheena, 'twill all take time. The feud is over, it ended when I made you my wife. I'll no' be starting it again, no matter what. In time, old grudges will be forgotten. We'll even visit your father and make it right with him. It will just take time."

"And what of Black Gawain?" she demanded. "Is he to get away with what he did?"

His face was set in a hard line. "I've no' said I agree with you that he's guilty."

"But he is!"

"Then if he is, I'll deal with him in my own way!" Jamie replied in exasperation.

"Will you? Or will you just forget about it once you think I have?"

Jamie sighed. "You have to understand about Gawain, Sheena. His sister was killed in the spring, when your father saw fit to resume the feud. Gawain was—"

"What?" She cut him short. "*We* didna begin the raiding again. *You* did!"

"Och, Sheena, no more lies."

Jamie watched the play of emotions cross her face, from hurt, gone quickly, to anger, there to stay. He became incensed. Why was she holding on to that ridiculous claim? Was she really so ignorant of her father's treachery?

Her blue eyes flashed dangerously, and she

began to speak, but he stopped her.

"Enough is enough, Sheena," Jamie warned darkly.

"Enough? Aye, and 'tis I who've had enough of you!" she cried.

Swinging his legs off the bed, he reached for her, but anger gave her the strength to jerk away. He reached for her again, and her temper exploded, knowing how futile would be her efforts to fight him off. While she had the chance, she slapped him with all the strength she had. Even when Jamie raised his hand to hit her back she regretted nothing.

But he didn't strike her. Her eyes were shooting great sapphire-blue sparks at him, daring him, yet he couldn't.

"Why do you hesitate?" she demanded, her voice a whip. "I dinna fear you anymore, Jamie. You couldna hurt me more than you already have."

"I canna hit you."

"Why not?"

His chest ached as if pressed by a great weight. "Because I think it would hurt me more than you," he said, furious with himself for feeling that way. "Now why is that?"

She didn't know. Her throat constricted tightly, and she didn't understand that either. And then he was kissing her, crushing her in a powerful embrace, and she understood at last.

No sooner had the kiss begun than there was hammering at the door. Jamie broke away and wrapped himself in his plaid before bellowing, "Enter!" After the irascible welcome, the entering was most hesitant.

Sheena sank down on the bed, dazed. She was amazed to feel her anger vanquished by the simple touch of Jamie's lips. How was that possible?

"I didna want to be disturbing you, but 'twas necessary," Colen was saying to Jamie.

The portentous tone drew Sheena's full attention.

"Be done with it, lad," Jamie prompted when he saw Colen's hesitation.

"There's been a raid, Jamie. Hamish and Jock were wounded, and it doesna look as if Hamish will recover."

Jamie's face turned to stone. "How many livestock lifted?"

"None. All were killed, and the croft fired."

Sheena drew her breath in sharply as Jamie's eyes pierced her. She knew what conclusion he had drawn.

"Nay!" she cried, coming off the bed to stand before him. "Nay, he wouldna have done that."

"But he did," Jamie said. "'Tis the same as in the spring—no' a common raid, but slaughter and perverse destruction. And I let it happen. I didna think he would have the effrontery to exact revenge for what happened today, so I put no extra guards around."

"But you're wrong, Jamie!"

He turned to Colen again. "How many in the attack?"

"Jock swears to at least half a dozen."

"Did he see them well?"

There was a lengthy silence before Colen mumbled, "Well enough."

"Then tell my wife, if you will, the colors they wore," Jamie commanded.

Her eyes pleaded with Colen, but he could not lie. "I'm sorry, lass, but the colors were indeed your father's. I wish I could tell you different."

She looked at the two of them, Colen doleful, Jamie holding on to his emotions tightly.

"Your kinsman was mistaken!" she raged at them. "And you're detestable, both of you, to think otherwise!"

"Leave us and ready my horse!" Jamie ordered Colen.

"You canna do this, Jamie. You canna ride against my clan!" she shouted at him.

"You are presuming to know my intention," he replied harshly, turning to dress.

"I suppose you feel your father was justified?" he asked her after a silence.

"I didna say that. But put yourself in his place. If my father hadna given you justice where it was deserving, would you have sought justice on your own?" He glared at her, and she added bitterly, "You would have, and you know it. But my father canna afford to, and you know that, too. He wanted no more of this feud. He did everything he could to protect himself against it."

"You forget the alliances he's made through your sisters. They were all wed soon after you were banished, I was told. Your father may feel he now has the strength to continue the feud against me."

"Then why did he give me to you as wife?"

"I forced him to it!"

"Did you?" she shouted. "Then what of the strength you say he has now? If he is so powerful that he can fight you now, Jamie, then he would have fought you then. Instead, he agreed. And he argued till he was blue in the face to get me to agree. I wish to God I had defied him!"

"I'm beginning to wish you had, too!" Jamie retorted furiously. before storming out of the room.

Chapter 32

SHEENA woke the next morning to find herself alone. She pulled herself up to a sitting position, but she didn't have the will to do any more than that. She just sat there. Her eyes hurt, for she had cried herself to sleep. Her whole body seemed to hurt from the terrible sobs that had racked her.

A pointless thing, crying. It didn't change anything. And it certainly didn't make her feel better.

She stared out the window at the dismal sky, dark with clouds. Morning, and Jamie had not returned. So he had gone to Angusshire. It was daylight now. The MacKinnion always struck in daylight. Was he attacking Tower Esk at that very moment?

A horrible image of a bloody battle came to mind, and she shook her head against it. But the image would not go away, and she began to hear screams and cries as well. Her father's. Niall's.

Her hands covered her ears, and she leaped off the bed and paced furiously to drive the image away. She couldn't stand not knowing what was happening at home. And if the agony of wondering was not terrible enough, she would have to be waiting when Jamie returned, his hands bloody. She would have to face him, knowing what he'd done to her family.

She wouldn't! She would leave while he was gone. No one would would dare stop her this time. She was The MacKinnion's wife. She would take a horse and be well away before he returned.

But where would she go? She couldn't ride straight for home and risk coming upon Jamie. She would go to Aberdeen and her Aunt Erminia. That was better. Together they would find out if she still had a home to return to, and a family.

She opened the door but stopped short, finding the servant Gertie there, about to knock.

"I've brought yer things, lass," Gertie explained as she entered. "I thought yer might like to be changing 'afore yer come down to greet the guests."

"Guests?"

"Aye, they've been arriving all morning," Gertie said as she laid the gowns on the still-rumpled bed, tsk, tsking as she did so. "Did yer only just awake, lass? 'Tis late, you know."

Sheena frowned. "How late?"

"Och, nearly noon it is. We were beginning to wonder if yer'd be coming down or no'. Doris was saying as how yer might be 'afeared to, after what happened. But I told her yer've more spunk than that. It wasna yer doing, what happened."

279

Wasn't it? Sheena thought ruefully. If Jamie hadn't wanted her so badly, would he have kept her at Castle Kinnion? Would he have wed her? There would have been no wedding, and no "accident," as Jamie called it. Her father would be safe at Tower Esk, and she would have been returned to Aberdeen. Perhaps she might not have been whisked away by Colen in the first place. It was all her fault, the fault of her looks. Her beauty had always been a curse—would it always be so?

But here was a kindly soul who didn't blame her, even though she blamed herself.

"Will yer be wearing this lovely blue gown, lass? It do bring out the color of yer hair, making it glow as if 'twere on fire."

Sheena looked at the gowns, Lydia's lovely ones and her own threadbare one. "I'll wear the green." It was her own.

Gertie's look registered her disapproval. "As yer wish," she said tightly. "But if yer dinna mind my saying so, yer should be telling the laird 'tis high time he was seeing to yer needs. 'Tis no' as if he doesna hae cloth to spare and wouldna give it gladly."

"'Tis no' for me to be asking," Sheena said.

"Och, now, who has more right than yerself, eh?" Gertie clucked. "'Tis his wife yer are, or hae yer forgotten that sae soon?"

"I didna forget."

Gertie didn't hear, or chose to ignore, the bitterness in Sheena's voice. "Well, then, yer must be dressing as befits the wife of a Highland laird. Great beastie that he is, Sir Jamie doesna ken the needs of a wife. Yer could start by insisting he send for yer own lovely things. I'm sure yer father would no' begrudge yer, even after what's happened."

"I'd rather no' be discussing this right now, Gertie, if you dinna mind."

"Of course, lassie. I'll be going."

"Gertie, wait." Sheena stopped her. "You said there are guests?"

"Aye, there are indeed. Keiths and MacDonoughs hae arrived, and Gregorys and Martins will nae doubt come 'afore the end of the day."

Sheena turned sickly pale. Those were clans aligned with the MacKinnions, clans Jamie could call on for war. So he had not attacked yet, but was instead planning a full-scale slaughter! Why else would he send for all those clans?

"What is amiss, lass?" Gertie asked worriedly.

"He . . . he's brought them all here to . . ." She stopped herself from going too far.

Gertie clucked again, misunderstanding Sheena's distress. "Och, you've naught to fear meeting friends of the MacKinnions. Why, Thais is sae eager to meet yer, 'twas she who sent me up here to see how soon yer'd be coming down."

"Thais?"

"Sir Jamie's younger sister," Gertie explained. "Fair fashed she was wi' him, too, for no' waiting till she and her husband arrived."

Sheena was going to be wretchedly sick. Not waiting? So he had attacked after all!

"Och, what did I say, lass?" Gertie was at her

side in an instant. "Yer wait right here, and I'll be getting Sir Jamie."

"He's *here?*"

"Where else would he be, wi' sae many wedding guests to attend?"

"Wedding . . ." Sheena was beside herself with relief. "Why did you no' say so, Gertie? I thought the guests were . . ."

"Och, the celebrating will go on for days. Sir Jamie didna tell yer he's invited one and all to meet his new bride?"

"Nay. After yesterday . . ."

"Dinna fash yerself about yesterday, lassie," Gertie said firmly. "Sir Jamie's no' going to let it spoil the wedding, and neither should yerself."

"When did Jamie return?"

"He didna leave the castle, except to see what could be done for Jock and Hamish. He wasna gone long."

"Did . . . Hamish . . .?"

Gertie patted his shoulder. "He's holding his own, bless him. He may recover. Now are yer sure about the green gown?"

"I'll wear the blue after all," Sheena conceded absentmindedly.

She had to talk to Jamie. This was a reprieve, but maybe only because so many guests had been invited and he could hardly turn them away. But when they left? She had to know what Jamie meant to do.

Chapter 33

JAMIE took a swig of ale, bracing himself against the turn in the conversation to his right. Colen and Alasdair MacDonough had warmed to their subject, and Jamie started to interrupt, but too late. At Colen's prodding, Alasdair admitted why he had broken his betrothal to Sheena. Colen's face reflected disbelief, then understanding, and finally humor. When Colen burst out laughing, it was more than Jamie could bear.

"I'm thinking you've said enough, MacDonough." Jamie's tone was sharp, surprising the older man.

"Och, Jamie, you dinna mean to say you've told no one of that time, not even your brother?"

"Never mind," Colen interjected. "I'm wanting to hear more of Jamie's stay at Tower Esk."

"Nay, lad, you'll have to hear that from your brother," Alasdair replied uncomfortably.

"Well, Jamie?"

Jamie was scowling. As if enough wasn't going

wrong with his life, he also had to contend with his brother's humor.

"There's nothing to tell, Colen. I met with Fergusson hospitality is all. Leave it be."

"In their dungeon?" Colen grinned. "And needing a lass to help you escape?"

Jamie's mien got even darker. "'Twas only fitting she aid me, since 'twas her fault I was there to begin with."

"But to end up in a Fergusson dungeon, Jamie?" Colen shook his head mockingly. "You must have been badly smitten even then, to play the fool so well."

Jamie nearly exploded, but his brother-in-law Ranald Keith had overheard and clapped him on the back. "What is this about a Fergusson dungeon, lad? Is that where you met your bride, then?"

Jamie glared at his brother. He quickly told the humiliating story, except for the part Niall had played, for he was still obliged to protect the lad. More humor was had at his expense, Colen delighting in all of it.

"She risked a great deal to avoid marriage to you, Jamie," Ranald said thoughtfully. "And yet she's wed to you after all. 'Tis no wonder the poor lass willna come down to celebrate her wedding."

"I wouldna call her a poor lass, Ranald Keith." Thais stuck up for her brother. "She's lucky to be having a man as fine as Jamie."

"So *you* think," Ranald retorted to his wife. "But what does she think, eh?"

"Aye, Jamie," Colen asked, serious then. "What does she think—now?"

Jamie sighed. "I could've sworn you werena going to hold a grudge, Colen. Are you still bitter over losing her?"

"No' bitter, Jamie," Colen replied. "But I did warn you no' to hurt her."

"And you think I have?"

"What happiness has she had since she wed you?"

Jamie smiled ruefully, remembering. "I'd like to think she had some, if only for a little while."

Colen reddened, understanding perfectly. "That is no' the answer to happiness, Jamie. She needs peace of mind. Can you give her that now, after all that's happened?"

"Och, now, listen to you two." Daphne came up behind Jamie and put her arms around his neck. "My two brothers fighting, and they canna even blame drink, early as it is. What is this fighting about? Tell me."

"I do believe the reason has decided to join us," Ranald said.

Across the hall, Sheena was making her way toward them, regal in her royal blue silk gown, with her hair swept back, the long tresses curling to her waist. Jamie's chest puffed with pride.

"Och, Jamie, you said she was a bonny lass, but you didna say she was the most bonny lass in all of Scotland," Ranald breathed in awe.

"Well now, will you look at this big beastie of a husband you have." Daphne grinned at her sister.

"'Tis lucky I am my Dobbin isna here yet, or he'd be drooling over his new sister-in-law, too."

"Mine can drool all he likes." Thais grinned, enjoying her husband's uncomfortable look. "Jamie will see that drooling is all he does."

Poor Ranald had never understood the penchant for teasing among Red Robbie MacKinnion's offspring. Nor was he really sure when to take Thais seriously. He glanced at her, and his eyes softened, as they always did, for he was quite in love with his lovely wife. The prettier of the two sisters, in his prejudiced opinion, with a golden tinge to her red hair that gave it a coppery hue and brown eyes that could tease, cajole, and flash with fire or love as the mood took her, Thais was beautiful. Aye, he loved Thais with a passion that surprised him at times. Yet after five years, of marriage, he still didn't know when she was jesting.

Ranald squeezed Thais' hand under the table, hoping it was not jealousy over her extraordinary sister-in-law that brought the sparkle to her eyes. "Extraordinary" was not even a good enough word to describe the beauty of the Fergusson lass. Skin so delicate, eyes so big and crystal blue, and that glorious hair, so darkly contrasting against her pearly skin. Jamie was indeed a lucky man.

Thais did not think Jamie so much lucky as deserving. She adored her older brother and wished for him anything he wished for himself. She would never be able to repay him for choosing Ranald of the Keith clan for her. Unlike Daphne, who was not satisfied with her husband, chosen by their father, Thais was completely contented with her life. She owed that to Jamie.

It pained Thais to see that Jamie was not as happy as he ought to be, and she was reminded of his first disastrous wedding. Yet he apparently did not feel he had made the wrong choice. That was plain to see in the way he looked at Sheena.

Thais was prepared to love her sister-in-law, simply because it was obvious that Jamie did. Whatever problems were causing the unhappiness between them could be mended. Nothing was impossible.

Daphne also wanted her brother's happiness. But, standing behind Jamie, she didn't see the tenderness in his eyes when his bride appeared. She knew only of the bad mood he had displayed the evening before and the whole of the morning, so as far as Daphne was concerned, Jamie had made a terrible choice. What had possessed him to marry a daughter of their lifelong enemy? The match was fated to fail. It couldn't possibly be otherwise. Colen knew it. Jamie likely knew it, too, or he wouldn't be so coldly reserved now the deed was done. What had happened yesterday only proved there could never be peace between them.

Daphne could see no way of making it better. There was certainly nothing she could do, so to get involved would be a pointless mistake. She couldn't even hope that her sister-in-law would warm to Jamie. Daphne had seen how miserable Sheena was the day before. She looked no happier today. The lass obviously hated Jamie, hated living in his home. They were doomed.

Well, Daphne could sympathize. She knew what it was like not to love her husband. But at least she didn't hate Dobbin. In fact they got along well, due mainly to their hardly ever speaking to each other. And after so long, she was used to his occasional painful ruttings, over as quickly as they began. Dobbin Martin was an insensitive brute, but Daphne still welcomed his obligatory visits, wanting desperately to have a child to fill the void in her life.

Unlike Alasdair, who sighed wistfully on Sheena's approach, Colen gritted his teeth. He had yet to speak to her alone since the wedding. He had yet to hear from her how miserable she was. But his eyes told him, and his heart ached for her. It was not that he still pined for her. But she had sworn she would marry only a man she loved. Yes, Colen ached in sympathy for her.

It was painful, taking sides. The soft spot he felt for Sheena and his love for his brother were tearing at him. He was angry, but that anger was directed at the man responsible for ending whatever small chance Sheena had had for happiness at Castle Kinnion.

Colen put the blame on Black Gawain, and he was furious that Jamie had not. The wedding, meant to end the feud, had only fueled it. And the worst was not over yet. There was still a chance that Jamie might seek retribution for the raid. Sheena's clan would be held responsible.

It was impossible to get Jamie to confide his intentions. He flatly refused to speak of them. But Colen was certain, more certain than he had ever been of anything, that if Jamie attacked the Fergussons, he would never have peace with Sheena, never have the love he had gambled for, the love he so desired.

Sheena, walking slowly toward her husband, his friends and family surrounding him, felt totally alone and despised. She feared these people, but she would not let them cow her. She held her head high, facing them boldly.

She reached the table, and Jamie rose. Sheena stood stiffly away from him, and he didn't extend his hand to her. His look was guarded, a little stern, revealing nothing.

It was Alasdair MacDonough who broke the silence, having risen along with the other men. "You're as sinfully beautiful as ever, lass," he said.

Sheena's eyes widened, confusion mingling with surprise. "You're no' still angry with me?"

"'Tis ony regret I'm feeling and 'tis growing worse by the second, now I've seen you again."

What could Sheena say? This was not the arrogant, conceited Alasdair she remembered. She began to feel her own regret, regret that fate had stopped her from marrying him instead.

"I'm sorry, Sir Alasdair," Sheena replied softly. "Truly, I wish—"

"Dinna be monopolizing her, Sir Alasdair." Thais cut Sheena short, fearing she was about to say something she shouldn't. "And you're a great lout, Jamie MacKinnion, to be standing here without making introductions."

Jamie gave his younger sister a sidelong glance of gratitude. "Sheena, this is my sister Thais, and her husband, Ranald Keith." Then he added, "And you've met my sister Daphne."

Sheena's cheeks took on a rosy flush, and she smiled hesitantly at Daphne. "I fear I was a wee bit bemused for the better part of yesterday, when we met."

"You dinna have to explain, Sheena." Daphne tried to put the poor girl at ease. "I can remember very little of my own wedding day except the terrible nervousness. I'm sure 'tis the way with most of us."

Thais took Sheena by the arm and led her over to the fire, murmuring something about getting better acquainted while the men amused themselves. Daphne followed, and Jamie's eyes followed the women. He was wary of Sheena's being alone with her sisters. There was no saying what she might tell them.

Ranald congratulated him again on his bride, and then half a dozen Gregorys arrived. The next hour was spent in heavy drinking despite the early hour, and Jamie was kept busy. Aunt Lydia had come down, bemoaning a nasty head, throbbing from the night before. She joined the women by the fireside. Jamie turned around to glance their way every few minutes and soon saw Sheena laughing with his sisters, apparently at ease and enjoying herself. The sight infuriated him. How dare she dismiss all that had happened?

He needed to talk to her, needed to set her straight. She was his wife. What happened outside the castle would not change that.

Chapter 34

T HE merrymaking continued throughout the day. Sheena was actually enjoying herself, especially so while Jamie was away. He left the hall without so much as a glance her way, and then returned a few hours later. He wore the same brooding face. Unapproachable was what he was, unapproachable when she needed to talk to him. She forced herself to forget about him and turn her attention to the company.

She found she liked Jamie's sisters very much, as she had liked Aunt Lydia from the first. What was it about these MacKinnion women that was so agreeable? Lydia was so warm and sympathetic. Daphne was more reserved, but charming and understanding. Thais, no older than Sheena, was vivacious, full of life and good cheer. Sheena found herself quite envious of Thais. And of the family. She wasn't used to a loving family. She had had Niall and her father but never the love of her sisters. The difference between these sisters and her own was appalling, making her wistful with longing. No wonder Jamie was tender with her at times. He had had so much practice with his two sisters.

"So my Dobbin has finally arrived."

When Daphne spoke, Sheena turned to the entrance and saw a big, brutish man with red hair and beard and eyebrows that were much too thick and bushy. Almost his whole face was covered with hair.

Sheena couldn't hide her surprise. "That's your husband?" She knew she was staring.

Daphne grinned good-naturedly, used to people's reaction to Dobbin Martin. "Och, now, we canna all have handsome devils for husbands. And mine's no' so bad. At least his temper doesna run amok, and his only real fault is his indulgence of his cousins—especially that one. She must have been waiting outside for Dobbin, knowing she would find welcome here only with Dobbin as her escort."

Sheena saw the woman standing a little behind him. Jessie Martin. She frowned. Having hoped she would never see that viper again, she was unpleasantly surprised.

And if that was not enough, Black Gawain appeared in the entrance. His face was more darkly set even than Jamie's, if that was possible. His anger stirred Sheena's own temper. Was he here to cause trouble? His eyes lit on her with a smoldering intensity that signaled the worst.

Sheena left the women by the fire and hurried to Jamie's side without considering that she might be rebuffed. She pulled him away from his conversation, away from the tables and any eaves-droppers. When she turned to face him, Jamie didn't look at all pleased.

Undaunted, Sheena let her anger spill forth. "Are you aware Black Gawain is here?"

"Is he?"

Jamie's casual response brought sparks to Sheena's eyes, and she demanded, "Are these guests here for our wedding or no'?"

"They are."

"Then have I no say who is invited to partake of the celebrating?"

"Dinna be a hypocrite, Sheena," Jamie replied coldly. "You've made it clear you've no reason to celebrate, so what does it matter if there is another here who feels the same way?"

"I dinna want him here, that is what matters! I canna stand the sight of him, Jamie. If no' for him . . . ."

She hesitated, and he demanded, "What?"

But she wouldn't admit that things might have been different between them if not for Gawain. She would have spent the night with Jamie, still in a haze of happiness, instead of crying her heart out alone. But she wouldn't tell him any of that, so she said instead, "If no' for Black Gawain, my cousin wouldna have been wounded. Do you think Iain survived the long trek home? He is probably dead even now!"

"And only fitting if so, considering I've two kins-men of my own sorely wounded," Jamie retorted cruelly before he could stop himself.

Sheena gasped. This was not the man she had come to know. Worse, it *was* the man she had been raised to fear. What was happening to him?

"What will you do, Jamie?" she asked, as mildly as she could.

But he had spent the whole day in a black mood and was not appeased by her sudden meekness. The fact was, he had made no decision about what to do, but he would keep that from her.

"Whatever I do, lass, you'll still be my wife. If you're no' clear about what that means, let me enlighten you. I'll no' stay away from our room again as I did last night. We will share that room—and more. Do you ken?"

Her chin came up stubbornly. If Jamie thought he could dominate her simply because he was her husband, he was about to learn differently.

"I ken." Her answer was controlled. "And now *you* ken. You think you have rights over me, but I'll no' honor them. I was made wife to you, but 'twas no' what I wanted, and in my mind those ties are severed as of now. So dinna expect me to ever call you husband, Jamie, for our marriage is a mockery."

Her words dissolved Jamie's anger, striking him with terrible pain until his heart felt wrenched from his chest. *He had lost her.* He knew it was probably too late to change that. Panicked, he knew it was his own fault.

"Sheena . . ."

She turned away, unable to listen anymore. What she had said had stunned her. She hadn't meant to be so . . . final. Her throat constricted. She hadn't meant what she'd said. But having said the words, she couldn't take them back.

She looked at him, at the soft blond waves of his hair curling on his neck, the strong, handsome face. Pain reflected in his hazel eyes. Did her eyes mirror his? But hers were even more revealing, filling with tears she couldn't stop.

"I'm sorry, Jamie. I fear we're both too stubborn."

She couldn't say more, and she couldn't stop crying, so she turned and walked swiftly from the hall.

Chapter 35

IF Jamie meant to put on a good front, to deceive his guests into thinking all was well, he failed miserably. Sheena did not return to the hall. And more than one person had seen her leaving shedding dismal tears.

How he wanted to go after her! Yet how could he? It had become a matter of pride and where pride was concerned, Jamie was too vulnerable. Pride had always mastered him, not the other way around. She had made their argument public.

It was all Jamie could do to wait until the hour when he could retire without notice. It grew quite late, but there were still many guests in the hall. The Gregorys and the Martins were stout drinkers and would no doubt be at it long into the night. Deciding there was no discourtesy in it, he rose to leave. He had had a few hefty tankards, but had been careful not to drink too much.

Jamie opened the door to his room. It was quite dark. The room was chilly, the fire out. She wasn't there. In a moment or two he had a blaze going, but it was still chilly. And empty.

He sat down on the bed with a sigh. Should he go searching for her? He should just let her stay wherever she was. There were any number of lasses who would warm his bed. Jessie, of course, had signaled that she was available again. She had ignored Black Gawain all evening, staying by her cousin, Dobbin, which put her closer to Jamie, as close as she could get. He could remember the warmth of Jessie's body, so soft and yielding. Never would he get anger from her, only heady passion.

"Who am I fooling?" Jamie muttered aloud in the cold room. He listened to the silence, then got up and left.

He tried the room he had put Sheena in before their wedding. And there she was, curled up in the small bed, fast asleep. She had no business being asleep, looking so peaceful.

He didn't wake her, just removed her covers gently and scooped her up in his arms. She made a faint noise of protest but remained asleep and snuggled into his shoulder as he carried her back to where she belonged.

Jamie laid her on the bed, then stood back ready for the fight to begin. But Sheena only stretched slightly without opening her eyes. Jamie grinned. She was making this very easy for him. He would have her at his mercy before she even woke up. And with that delightful thought, he quickly divested himself of his clothes.

He began by slowly easing her thin woolen shift up her legs, running his fingers along the smooth skin as he did, stopping whenever she made a noise, beginning again when she was quiet. How he delighted in the silken feel of her, her legs so shapely, so firm yet pliant.

When her shift couldn't be moved any farther without disturbing her, Jamie left it alone, gently lifting only the front above her waist. He then devoted his full attention to the tender warm nest between her legs, touching her ever so gently, his fingers teasing, beckoning a response.

It was long in coming, but when she began to respond, his fingers glided easily over the moist surface. She was ready for him, but he held back.

He knelt by her side and tugged her shift from under her hips, but she still didn't waken. He positioned himself between her legs, then swiftly pulled the shift up.

Sheena woke instantly, but before she could speak, he was pulling the shift over her head. Her cry of outrage was smothered as his mouth covered hers.

She tried to turn her head away, but he held her still, plundering her mouth with his fiery tongue. His pulsing manhood glided smoothly into her.

Sheena was shocked by the ease with which he entered her, filling her totally. More shocking was the way her body reacted, welcoming, arching toward him.

I canna! her mind screamed. I canna let him master my body!

299

But he was doing just that, and with such expertise. Sheena succumbed quickly. She wanted him. Despite everything, desire soared in her with a fluid rush. He was filling her, filling her to bursting. Nothing mattered but the heat inflaming her, and Jamie.

Release remained just out of reach, maddeningly so. Jamie wouldn't quicken his pace, and it was driving her crazy. He would bring her just so close, so near, then he would stop. Her entire body screamed for that last release. She moaned, her nails raking his back. But Jamie was determined to prolong this exquisite torture.

Finally she realized that Jamie was no longer kissing her. Her eyes flew open, and she found him staring at her with such a pained expression that she knew what he was doing to her was hurting him, as well.

Why? He told her soon enough, his voice beseeching yet insistent. "I'm your husband. Say it!"

Her thoughts were too jumbled for understanding, so she gladly told him what he wanted to hear.

"You're my husband."

"You'll never deny it again."

"Nay, never."

His body pummeled hers with a violence then that was sweetly savage, and Sheena thrilled to it, met it with equal fervor. She was starving, and he was the nourishment, and she could never get enough of him, never. . . .

To have thought intrude on that delicious languor was regrettable, but intrude it did, after the fury

300

was spent. When Jamie rolled over and pulled her body into the crook of his arm, when he began to move his fingers over her, caressing her with such tenderness, as if their lovemaking had settled everything between them, she couldn't hold back anymore. She spoke up quickly, before his hands had a chance to work their magic again.

"You took advantage of me, Jamie."

"Och, now, sweetheart, I didna do anything you didna want me to."

"You're wrong, Jamie. I dinna know why you're able to stir such passion in me with your touch, but there is a great difference in what I felt then and what I feel now. You can only rob me of my will for a short time. I have it back now. Nothing has changed."

"Ah, but it has, lass, it has," Jamie breathed softly. "You've learned you canna deny me, no matter your wanting to. Whatever the future brings, we will still have this. And I'll no' stop wanting you, Sheena." This was spoken solemnly, in earnest, almost like a threat. "And you may wish it otherwise, but you'll no' stop wanting me, either."

Chapter 36

THE loveliest, most wonderful feeling, to be bathed in soft cloud, as if you were floating high above the reality of the world in a mystical heaven. Sheena experienced that feeling as she walked along the battlements late in the afternoon. It had been that way most of the day, thick clouds coming down to surround the castle. At times she'd had to stop, unable to see a foot in front of her. And she could see nothing at all beyond the walls. Yet she could look down into the courtyard and see clearly, for, of course, the clouds did not gather there, only over it, like a ceiling.

She was watching another group of guests leaving. That was probably the last of them, except for the Martins, who intended to visit for a while. Jamie would be sorely displeased. He had wanted the festivities to continue for a week or more, but the prevailing atmosphere had not encouraged festivity. The guests had been quite uncomfortable amidst the hostilities of bride and groom.

It was Sheena's fault, she knew it. Jamie had tried to appear in good spirits that day. Perhaps he really was enjoying himself after his victory of the night before. But Sheena had made little effort.

The possibility that she might always want Jamie was absurd, wasn't it? Yet something had been proven the night before, and the truth of it was hard to bear.

She hated Jamie—didn't she? It certainly felt like hate. If it wasn't hate, what was it? How could she feel such pleasure from his touch? She couldn't reason it out.

Sheena heartily wished she could float away with the clouds and forget it all, her marriage, Jamie's claim on her, everything. Of course she couldn't. She would have to go back to the hall eventually and suffer through another painfully solemn meal. And then later—where could she hide that he couldn't find her? Perversely, a small voice asked if she really wanted to hide.

Sheena shivered in the cold and wrapped her cloak tighter as she watched the Keiths riding through the gate. Could they see to make their way down the mountainside? From her perch on the wall, she couldn't tell. She would miss Thais and her cheerful banter. But perhaps it was better that the guests were gone. Maybe Jamie would settle the matter that had cast the pall over their wedding. Settle it one way or another. She couldn't bear the suspense, the constant worry over her family.

"You should be leaving as well, 'afore there are more deaths because of you."

Sheena gasped. She didn't have to turn around. She knew that vengeful voice behind her. She ran, ran as fast as she could, before Black Gawain decided to help her leave. It would be so easy to claim that she had stumbled because of the thick clouds and fallen over the wall. An accident. Who could say it hadn't been accidental?

When she reached the warmth of the hall, she was still trembling. But she was safe there, and the trembling subsided. If she could say nothing else for Jamie, at least his presence made her feel secure.

Jamie didn't speak to her when she sat down by his side. His mood had indeed soured with the parting of nearly all his guests. He took no notice of her pallor, acknowledging her presence with a grunt and then resuming his conversation with Dobbin. At least Daphne and Lydia were there to keep her company, and to help her ignore the presence of Jessie, who was sitting next to Dobbin.

It might have continued fairly comfortably, each ignoring the other, if Black Gawain hadn't put in an appearance. He wasn't there just for the evening meal, Sheena sensed that. Her eyes were fastened on his face, mesmerized by the malevolence of him. Daphne was talking to her, but she didn't even hear. Reaching the table, Gawain stood directly behind Jamie's chair and announced as loudly as he could, "Hamish has succumbed to his wounds. He is dead."

Jamie turned around instantly. "Are you sure?" he asked simply, quietly.

Gawain nodded. "The question is, what will you be doing about it?"

It took great daring to demand that of James MacKinnion. Black Gawain was either a fool or simply beyond all caution.

It was Colen who shoved the question aside angrily. "Is that all you can think of when a kinsman has just died? Can he no' be buried first?"

"If your brother had been thinking of the clan, instead of his new bride, there would be no need for burying at all," was Gawain's blistering reply.

There were shocked mutterings. Was the fool looking to be buried himself? How did he dare cast aspersions against Jamie?

Quite slowly, Jamie stood, until his face was only inches above Gawain's, and very close. Gawain had to look up to meet those cold hazel eyes.

"For a tacksman, cousin, you take a lot upon yourself," Jamie said smoothly. "I'm thinking you forget whose blade it was that pierced a Fergusson, when they were one and all under my protection."

"And you forget I was provoked!" Gawain fumed.

Jamie's voice was but a whisper. Only Gawain heard him say, "No' forgetting, just doubting now—as I did then—that there was any provocation at all. Need I make myself clearer, Gawain, or do you see the action I should have taken was against you?"

Gawain lost some of his bluster. He turned quite pale, and Sheena would have given anything to know why. But she hadn't heard.

"Have a care, Gawain," Jamie added more loudly. "You would do well to leave my presence while I'm still inclined to let you."

Black Gawain saw the wisdom in that, but he couldn't resist a parting shot. "She's bewitched you, Jamie. You've no' seen things in perspective since she came here. Retaliation is called for, yet you let her sway you. She's turned you soft, man. There's no other explanation."

Jamie held himself in check to keep from responding. For the truth was, he still wasn't certain what had happened that day, his wedding day. It was time to be certain, though, time to stop procrastinating and do something. Black Gawain's accusation rang true, and Jamie resented it bitterly. Maybe he had let Sheena influence his judgment. There was no excuse for that, even if he hadn't been aware of it at the time.

"Jamie?"

He looked at Sheena but couldn't bear seeing fear in her eyes yet again. Besides, he needed space to breathe, to think. He couldn't do that with her asking questions he couldn't answer. Without another word to anyone, he left the hall.

It was the middle of the night when Jamie finally came to their room, and she was waiting for him. She found out what he'd decided on more easily than she wanted to. Her stomach twisted into a tight knot as she watched him gather weapons, knowing whom those weapons would be used against.

"So you've let him goad you into it?" Sheena whispered in a strained voice.

Jamie wouldn't look at her. "I've delayed long enough. It must be done."

She felt lifeless, dead, except for the pain that wouldn't stop.

"I'll no' be here when you return." Her words fell out of her, one over the other.

Jamie swung around, his eyes blazing. "You'll be here, Sheena, or you'll be wishing you were dead when I find you. And find you I will!"

She caught her breath. On top of everything else, he dared threaten her life! Life rushed back into her, and she flew off the chair where she had been sitting for hours, waiting for him.

"Wish I were dead? I wish I were dead now! Aye, dead, instead of married to you!"

"Careful, Sheena—"

"Or what?" she shouted. "You'll kill me? Better me than my kin!"

Jamie turned away. He had no intention of killing her kin! He'd meant only to talk to Dugald, but he was too angry to say so.

"I'll no' be swayed again!" he growled, more to himself than to her.

Sheena ground her fists into her temples in utter frustration. "I hate you for the fool you are, James MacKinnion," she hissed. "I'm my father's first-born! You know how he feels about me. Knowing that, how can you believe he would attack you, leaving me here to suffer for it? Don't you see?"

"You've no' suffered!"

"But he canna know whether I have or no'. He wouldna risk it! Can you no' see that?"

If Sheena had been distraught and crying, he might have relented and reassured her. But she was too angry to cry, and he was too angry to acknowledge the sense of what she said. Still, he couldn't leave her like that. He caught her to him, and his kiss was as furious as their tempers.

And then he shoved her from him, holding her at arm's length. "I'll be talking to Dugald first," Jamie told her curtly. "But I make no promises beyond that."

He gathered the last of his things and walked out of the room. Then, finally, tears came to Sheena. They racked her, the tears and her desolation.

Chapter 37

THE next morning, not even Daphne could bring Sheena out of her despondency. She sat in the hall by the great hearth, seeing nothing of what went on around her. Tortured images were all she could see, bloodied figures.

It was nearing noon when a voice broke through, a voice she despised. Jessie Martin was sitting across from her, a smugness and a strangeness about her. Sheena had no reason to hate Jessie Martin. Hadn't she once felt pity for the woman? Still, there was something so distasteful about Jessie.

"Did you say something?" Sheena asked civilly.

"The question was asked if you're no' ready to leave yet," Jessie answered.

"Was it?" Sheena sat back. "Why should I? Do I no' have everything I could want here, a fine home, a handsome—husband?"

Jessie's eyes narrowed at the thrust. "I would think your Fergusson pride couldna bear your

309

staying where you're no' wanted."

"And who doesna want me here?" Sheena inquired sweetly. "Jamie certainly does, very much so."

"But no one else does," Jessie said tightly. "They may no' admit it, but 'tis in their thoughts. You've changed Jamie. He's no longer the man he was, and you're resented for it."

"Liar!"

"She speaks the truth, Sheena."

She looked around to see that Black Gawain was standing behind her, and she felt cornered between them, suffocated.

"Jamie doesna care yet," Black Gawain continued. "The newness hasna worn off. But when it does, he'll hate you for what you've done. And it'll be too late by then. His kin will be set against him—and all because of you. But that is what you *really* want, isna it, Sheena Fergusson? You want him torn 'atween you and his kin."

Sheena couldn't find a quick answer, but they didn't wait for one. Both walked away abruptly, leaving her alone to ponder their vicious lies. Only . . . were they really lies? She probably was resented there. She was a Fergusson, the enemy. And look at what had happened since her wedding. Hadn't she blamed herself for the feud beginning again? Well, everyone else blamed her, too, no doubt.

She sat there in a daze for several minutes more, then got up slowly and left the hall. She walked to her room, where she changed to her old green gown, her movements unhurried, mechanical. When she was ready, she went to the courtyard, where she was given a horse as soon as she asked for one. The lad jumped to do her bidding. She had no problem at the gatehouse, either, the gatekeeper simply waving her through.

It was really too easy, she thought dismally as she guided her mare down the mountainside. Had she known how easy it would be, she'd have left the other day, when she had planned to, before Jamie had a chance to make love to her again. That way, she wouldn't have found out that even anger and hurt couldn't stop her from wanting him. Oh, how she wished she hadn't found that out!

Sheena rode blindly, her thoughts in a jumble, until she realized how dangerous that was and stopped to get her bearings. She found herself on a small plot of land in the middle of a recently harvested field. And then she found she was looking down into the face of a crofter.

"You dinna look well, lass," the man said with genuine concern.

"I'm fine—really," Sheena assured him, but she didn't feel fine. She felt all manner of things, but not fine.

"Sir Jamie's new bride?"

Why deny it? "I am."

The man nodded. "He'll be back 'afore long. Off to be meeting him, then, are yer?"

"I . . . I . . ."

"Here, now, yer really dinna look at all well, lass. Come inside and rest. My Jannet'll get yer a

311

dram of the potents."

Sheena let him lead her horse over to a small croft. He helped her down and ushered her inside. The croft was dark, with heavy cloths over the windows. There was a glowing fire in the center of the single room. The wicker door closed, and she was enveloped in a friendly warmth.

Jannet, a ruddy-faced woman, quickly set aside the meal she was grinding and came forward. "Och, Sir Jamie's bride! I saw yer at the wedding, but I didna think to be seeing yer again sae soon."

"She's out of sorts, Jannet, and could be using some of yer potents," the crofter explained.

"Och, yer poor wee thing," Jannet sympathized. "I'll be getting yer a dram, and yer'll come over by the fire to set a spell. 'Tis a chilly day to be out and about, and nae mistake."

Sheena sat by the fire on a stool and took the whiskey gladly. The crofter and his wife stood by anxiously. Sheena saw that the room was scantily furnished, with only two stools and a table, a box bed, meal kists, and a few utensils. A barren existence, yet the middle-aged couple seemed happy enough.

She wondered if they resented her, too, as Black Gawain claimed everyone did. They didn't seem unfriendly, yet they had probably known Hamish MacKinnion quite well.

"Why are you being so kind to me?" Sheena asked suddenly, her feelings brought to the surface.

The man was truly surprised. "And what else would we be?"

"But I'm a Fergusson," she said sharply. "You dinna have to pretend you don't know."

"Pretend, lass?" The man chuckled. "Do you really think I am?"

"But you must hate me. Others do."

"I dinna know about others, as yer say. I only know I judge each man on his own merits. Why should I be holding yer birth against yer? Yer a MacKinnion now, anyway. Yer'll bear the laird a son, and yer son will be laird one day. Yer one of us, lass, or dinna yer feel that way yet?"

Sheena didn't feel like that or believe she ever would. She felt alone, isolated, neither a MacKinnion nor a Fergusson. Thinking of it, she suddenly knew she could never go home, not as long as the feud continued, not bearing the MacKinnion name. Among Fergussons she would face exactly what she faced among MacKinnions. So where did that leave her?

No sooner had Jamie dismounted and handed his horse over to the stable lad than Jessie Martin sidled up to him, blocking his path. He was in no mood to be detained, and he didn't want a scene with Jessie while his men looked on. He was in no mood for anything except sleep after riding to Angusshire without stopping, and back without stopping, either.

What a disgusting waste of time it had been. He didn't know what he'd expected to accomplish by talking to Dugald. He had been received grudgingly, had listened to the man storm and bluster, and had come away without any resolutions. The problem was he didn't know Dugald Fergusson well enough to know whether he was an adept liar or was speaking the truth. Even in the midst of a powerful rage, he might have been acting.

Jamie didn't doubt Dugald's anger. For apparently Iain had indeed died on the way home, just as Sheena had feared. Jamie had left a generous settlement with Dugald to compensate, as was his custom in accidental deaths. But that had not appeased Dugald or his MacAfee cousin, who had insisted on being present during their meeting.

Jamie remembered Niall speaking of MacAfee with disgust, confessing that Sheena couldn't stand him, either. Jamie found himself thoroughly disliking William MacAfee, as well. Except for that tall, thin man, Jamie might have accepted Dugald's word that he hadn't raided the MacKinnion lands that night. But Sir William MacAfee had exuded an air of gloating satisfaction when Jamie mentioned the raid, an air that couldn't be denied. If only Jamie had been able to talk to Niall, but Niall had been nowhere in evidence.

Jamie did receive one promise, confirming Sheena's belief. Dugald swore he would not, could not, take action as long as Sheena was in Jamie's hands. But . . . truth or lie? Sweet Mary, he wished he could be sure! If only Jock had not sworn the raiders' plaid was green, gold, and gray. If ony Jock had not identified the cry as the Fergusson battle cry.

Jamie was no better settled on what he should

do. And he certainly wasn't looking forward to facing Sheena, being able to tell her only that he hadn't done anything yet. She would only demand to know what he planned, and he still couldn't tell her.

But just then he was facing Jessie Martin and not liking it one bit. "You make yourself free in my castle again," he said tersely.

She made a little moue as she moved closer. "You wouldna ask me to leave, not when my cousin is still here, would you?"

"You hide behind your cousin," Jamie replied curtly. "Just be sure you leave when he does."

"And who'll keep you company, now that your wife's rejected you?"

Jamie gripped her arm and shoved her away. "A wife canna reject her husband," he said tightly. "And you intrude in what is none of your concern."

"I dinna think she agrees," Jessie retorted, rubbing her arm. "A wife can reject her husband if she so chooses."

Jamie grunted. "She'll be coming around, once she's used to being married."

"Will she now?" Jessie taunted angrily. "How will she do that, Jamie, when she's no' even here."

A number of emotions crossed Jamie's face before he turned and made for the hall. But Jessie stopped him, her voice bitter, before he got very far.

"You'll waste your time looking for her. I'm no' the only one who saw your precious Sheena leave.

She's made her rejection of you a public matter, proclaiming to one and all she wants naught to do with you." Jamie turned and ran back toward the stable then, and Jessie shouted after him, "You canna still want her, Jamie! Have you no shame? No pride?"

But Jamie continued on, ignoring the outburst, and Jessie stomped off in the other direction. She would have to tell Black Gawain she had failed. Jamie was going after his foolish wife after all.

What an impossibly stubborn man. Couldn't he see the little Lowlander was no good for him? Couldn't he see what Jessie had to offer? He was blind—and that was his misfortune.

Jessie never should have stayed at Castle Kinnion, she chided herself, enduring Black Gawain's crude lovemaking just so she could be there. A waste of her time and talent. And Black Gawain didn't even care for Jessie. It was Sheena he had wanted from the start, until he learned she was a Fergusson. Sheena—always Sheena! Jessie worked herself into a blind rage, and as she stomped through the castle in search of Black Gawain, those she passed gave her a very wide berth.

Chapter 38

S HEENA was ready to mount her horse again
and return to the castle. But as she was leaving
the croft, Jamie galloped furiously toward her,
coming to a skidding halt in the yard. Hearing the
noise, the crofter and his wife came back out of
their hut. They could only stand there, mute in the
face of Jamie's black rage.

Sheena was equally mute and frightened. She
had confessed to Jannet that she meant to leave the
Highlands, and Jannet had effectively talked her
out of it. But Jamie couldn't know that, of course.
And he was in no mood to be told.

"Stopped to tarry on your way home, did you?"
Jamie said, his voice harsh and accusing. "'Tis well
you did, so I found you 'afore you left MacKinnion
land."

"Well for whom?" Sheena dared to ask.

Jamie's frown deepened, his eyes turning almost green, smoldering dangerously. "You
didna heed my warning, and now you dare to be

317

impudent, as well?"

"Jamie, I—"

"You mock me, you defy me, and you think nothing will come of it?" he raged, his anger robbing him of control.

"Jamie!"

"Nay!"

He moved his horse closer and caught her arm, pulling her. He wanted to shake her violently, but he only held her, his fingers biting. Seeing her wince didn't lessen his anger or make him feel better.

"You misused the feeling I have for you, Sheena. I am lenient with you, so you're thinking you can do as you please," he shouted, "You're my wife! There's no excuse that will appease me this time!"

Sheena yanked her arm away. Her chin went up stubbornly. "Then I'll no' give one!" she shouted back.

She would have liked to explain, was the truth. She would have told him she'd changed her mind. She had tried to tell him, but his tirade had made it impossible. Now she refused to try. She had her pride.

"I'll no' be taken back!" she said adamantly. "I'll no' live with such an arrogant, churlish knave!"

Jamie glowered at her for an eternity, his fists clenching. An ominous gleam entered his eyes, and some of the steam went out of her then. He was fighting for control and she knew it.

When he finally spoke, his voice was quiet, too

quiet. "I'm no' here to bring you back, Sheena."

Confusion took over. "I dinna ken."

"You're my wife—that hasna changed. But I'll no' be shamed by you again. You've abused me for the last time, Sheena. I dinna want you back." His mouth was a grim line. "That should make you happy. *I* certainly have failed to make you happy, Lord knows."

She felt a tightness in her chest, and her vision blurred. "You . . . you're letting me leave?" she said softly, close to choking on the words.

"Nay, Sheena." His voice was overly tight, as if it was all he could do to keep it under control. "I forbid that. You're a MacKinnion now, and you'll live on MacKinnion land. I'll have a dwelling built for you. You'll live there—alone, as is your wish. You can tend the land or no'. Whichever, I'll see you dinna starve."

She was incredulous. "Jamie, you canna mean this."

"I didna think I would ever say such a thing. But you've said from the beginning that you wanted naught to do with me. Finally, I believe you."

Sheena fought to keep back both tears and fury. How could he?

"You keep me as wife, but mean to deny me what that entails?" she stormed. "You think you can?"

"I know I can."

"I refuse! You canna treat me that way!" she cried. "I'll be going back to my father."

"You'll stay!" he thundered. "I'll give you this

warning just once. You go home to your father, and I'll tear his tower down piece by piece to find you. Heed me, Sheena MacKinnion, for I'm through with threats!"

Jamie had said all he was going to. He grabbed her horse's reins and rode off at a furious pace, her mare galloping along behind. The yellow-gold of Jamie's hair and the green and gold of his plaid became a blur as Sheena's tears came.

"Och, now, hinny, there's nae need for that." Jannet put her arm around Sheena and led her back inside their home. "Sir Jamie will be relenting, yer'll see. He's a temper is all, just like the auld laird, his father. But it willna last."

"Last!" Sheena echoed. "He's been in a temper since the day I met him."

"And has there been a reason for that?" Jannet asked wisely. Seeing the two of them fight with so much emotion had told her what she'd suspected was true.

Sheena didn't answer. She was devastated. She tried to tell herself that the ache she felt was only because of Jamie's anger, and because she wanted to go home and he was stopping her. But that wasn't the whole truth, and she knew it.

As Jannet tried to sooth her, insisting Sheena stay with them until Jamie came to his senses, all she could think of was that Jamie had left her, had ridden off and left her. And she didn't even know what had happened in Angusshire between the clans.

320

Chapter 39

S HEENA curled up by the fire, wrapped in her cloak and in a plaid lent by Jannet. It wasn't terribly windy outside, but there was still a draft running along the floor where she lay. At least she wouldn't be sleeping on the cold dirt floor, for there was a narrow strip of plank on the ground, the covering of a store.

Sheena had been surprised, never having seen a store inside a crofter's hut, but Roy explained that he had dug it for his wife. Jannet was from the south, where hot summers necessitated a cool place for keeping cream, butter, and fresh game. She had talked Roy into digging the hole before she learned that summers in the Highlands were not so hot as what she was used to.

Sheena was glad to have a smooth surface to lie on, even if sleep did elude her. Roy and Jannet were long since fast asleep in the far corner, Roy after securing the outside and checking his goats and sheep, Jannet after grinding meal for the following day.

They had been so kind to her, assuring her that Jamie wasn't as terrible as he seemed and that everything would work out for them. She was to remember that prophecy later.

She wasn't sure what they were, those first swirls of smoke. They seeped in through the roof, and she was staring right at them without comprehending. Impossible. Yet she had to believe it when flames appeared, eating a hole in the thatch.

Her first instinct was to flee, but that was stifled when she recalled the recent raid in which Jock's and Hamish's homes were fired. It could only be another raid. Sheena cursed the bastards for sneaking up on them, hoping to catch them all asleep. It was a dastardly thing to do, so devious, lacking any measure of honor.

Sheena was trying desperately to keep from panicking as she watched the hole in the roof getting bigger. They couldn't leave the hut—or could they? Could the raiders have started the fire and then ridden on? Or were they still outside?

A torch fell through the roof, and she quickly smothered it with the plaid. A torch! That was how the fire had started. So it *was* a raid! Jannet screamed, having wakened to a nightmare, and Sheena turned to see Roy grabbing for his weapons. She was sickened. She couldn't bear the thought of kind Roy going out there to meet his death. Yet they would all die if something wasn't done quickly.

She ran to the window, praying that the raiders

had gone on. But outside, in the glow from the fire, she saw five mounted men. They were just sitting there, waiting. Waiting until everyone inside had been burned alive.

At first the faces were a blur. All she could see was the color of their plaids. *Her colors*. Her mind would not accept what her eyes saw. But then she saw faces a little more clearly. She was such a fool not to have guessed before. William! That was William's face!

Part of the roof fell in, and Sheena screamed, stopping Roy as he was about to open the door. She rushed to him, pulling him back with all her strength.

"You canna, man! There's too many of them, and 'tis what they want. They're waiting for you!"

He pulled her fingers off his jerkin and said, "Get back, lass. Get under the bed wi' my Jannet. I'll hold them off until help comes. We're no' sae far from the castle."

"But there's five of them!" Sheena was crying. Couldn't he understand? "Jannet, tell him no' to do it! Have you no water? We can fight the fire!"

Jannet was coming forward with a tin of water. Sheena's skirt had just caught fire, and she doused it. She was calm, more so than either Sheena or her husband.

"She's right, Roy. Yer canna go out there."

"We've no' enough water, Jannet!"

"I know. But there's another way. We've the store. We've a better chance of surviving there than wi' you being cut to pieces outside. Do as I say, man."

"The fire will still reach us," he insisted, even as he let her pull him toward the plank in the floor.

"It may," she agreed, keeping her voice calm for their sake. "But no' as quickly. Now open the trap and get inside," she ordered as she splashed the rest of the water over the planks. "You, too, lassie. Quickly."

The space was tiny, with just enough room for one person to move between the shelves lining each wall. But it was also deep, with steps carved into the earth. Roy went down, Sheena followed. Jannet was the last to enter, closing the trapdoor above them with a sickening finality. They were crammed tightly into the hole, Roy pressed against the back wall, Jannet crouched on the stairs, Sheena in between them. It was very difficult to breathe.

"I told yer yer should've made the store bigger, Roy," Jannet joked, knowing how frightened her companions were.

"What difference does that make if we're sealed in a tomb?" Roy retorted.

The fire was burning too quickly. They heard it. Sheena couldn't believe help would come in time. But she had to believe it.

Roy was growing more and more agitated. "Enough, Jannet! They've gone by now. Let's go."

"Mayhap they have gone, but the fire hasna. We've nae choice but to wait till the flames die down some."

It might have worked out that way if part of the

324

roof hadn't fallen on the trapdoor instead of to the side of it. At the sound of the crash, Jannet tried to push open the door. It wouldn't budge. Through the cracks in the door there was only a white blaze. They couldn't see smoke, but they could smell it, taste it, and their eyes burned. Breathing was next to impossible.

How long could that little bit of water on the planks keep the fire back? How long before the boards caved in on them?

Sheena was asking herself why Jamie had left her to this. And she was grieving for Roy and Jannet. Poor souls, none of this was their fault.

Jamie was racing blindly down the mountainside. When he had been told of the fire and whose hut was being consumed, he couldn't believe it. He still wouldn't accept it, not even when he saw it for himself. The flames had lessened, but were still lapping greedily at anything that hadn't been destroyed. Jamie charged in, a man gone wild, burning himself as he tossed aside flaming wood and debris, praying, however futilely, that he would find Sheena alive, that she wouldn't be dead, as reason insisted she must be.

"Mayhap you ken how I felt when my sister died this way." Black Gawain's quiet voice penetrated Jamie's crazed state of mind.

"She's no' dead! And if you're no' here to help find her, then get out!"

Black Gawain stumbled outside, running into Colen, who had just arrived that minute. "He's lost his senses, lad. Try to get him out of there 'afore the walls cave in and we lose him, too."

Colen ignored Black Gawain, ordering the men he'd brought with him to help search. He followed them in. Gawain shook his head and left the scene. As much as he had hated Sheena, he wouldn't have wished that kind of death on her—not even to avenge his sister.

Every piece of rubble and scarred wood was moved. The search was for bodies now, for nothing could have lived through that fire. Jamie was nearly out of his mind, but the one little bit of sanity left demanded proof. He wouldn't believe she was dead until he had proof.

There was great excitement when the plank door was found, charred but intact. In his haste to reach the door, Jamie threw men aside. He lifted the door. Three bodies were there, cloths covering their faces, unmoving. Unmoving! Jamie couldn't move. He couldn't breathe. Then one of the bodies coughed, a tiny sound, and he couldn't move fast enough.

He lifted Jannet out and handed her to Colen, then took Sheena in his arms and carried her out of the house, leaving others to see to Roy. Tears coursed down his face as he set her down in the cool air away from the house. No one came near him. Those watching turned away as Jamie knelt by his wife and began shaking her, slapping her, all the while shouting prayers and curses, one after another.

The first thought Sheena had when feeling returned was that the flames must have reached them, for her lungs were on fire. Suddenly she was racked by coughing so violent she could hardly catch her breath. But she did manage to breathe a little, and the air was so cooling, soothing her raw throat and burning lungs.

Then she was crushed in someone's mighty arms and couldn't breathe again. She began to struggle, fighting, and the grip lessened a bit.

Colen approached, so relieved he felt giddy. He could well imagine what his brother was feeling.

"Jannet and Roy are alive," he informed Jamie. Then he delivered the bad news. "The croft below didna fair as well. Sheena and Roy and Jannet would be dead now, too, wi'out that place to hide. Do you know that?"

"I know."

"What possessed you to leave her here unprotected, I'd like to be knowing?"

Jamie looked at Colen over the top of Sheena's head, his face tormented. "Do you think I can ever forgive myself? I was so consumed with anger, lad, I didna think to post a watch over her. But that's no excuse. Because of my fool temper, she might have died."

Colen shook his head. "Then may I hope you'll make an effort to control your fool temper next time?"

"There'll be no next time," Jamie said quietly.

"Will we be riding directly this time? They canna be too far ahead," Colen said.

"Aye, as soon as I take Sheena to the castle."

There was nothing wrong with Sheena's hearing.

Joy at being alive fought with bitterness. She pushed Jamie away from her.

"You havena asked if I *want* to be taken to your castle." Her voice was only a whisper, and she rubbed at her burning eyes.

"Nay, I havena, nor do I intend to," was Jamie's reply. It left no room for argument. "Och, Sheena, forgive me. I know you feel this is all my fault, and I dinna shirk the blame. Can you no' see how sorry I am?"

"I see it—but it doesna help." She started to cry and hid her face in her hands. "You didna have to leave me here!"

Jamie gathered her to him again, and Colen discreetly left. "Hush, Sheena, hush." He rocked her. "Do you think I really wanted to leave you? The things I said to you today, I meant *none* of them. I was hurt. Do you ken, Sheena? I'm no' used to having my life controlled by another. But you control me, you do. You have the power to give me pain or joy, and when 'tis pain, I react badly. But no more, sweetheart. I swear I'll never put you from me again."

He was terrified, afraid that was not what she wanted to hear. What if she really wanted to hear that he would let her go? He could never do that, not even to make amends for what he'd done. Sheena was part of him, whether she accepted it or not, and he couldn't let her go.

But Jamie needn't have worried. The fight had gone out of Sheena—either because of his declaration or from exhaustion. She put her arms around him, leaning against him, and he nearly burst with joy.

"I'll take you home now, lass, and put you in my aunt's care until I return," he said gently.

Jamie carried her to his horse and held her ahead of him as they rode back to the castle. She was quiet all the way home, and he couldn't help wondering why.

In fact, Sheena was speechless because of the power he claimed she held over him. Power? She had always known she could arouse his anger easily. But for Jamie to be so deeply affected by her, that she could cause him pain or joy . . . Was it possible?

At the castle, Jamie dismounted and helped Sheena down, but he was not going to stay. He was anxious to be off, before she began pleading with him not to retaliate for the raid. He hailed a servant to bring his aunt, and others arrived. Black Gawain was dumbfounded to see Sheena alive. Jamie's men joined him, preparing to leave with him, all carrying weapons.

Sheena waited, expecting Jamie to escort her to her room. After she'd watched the activity for some time, she suddenly understood that he meant to go after the raiders, he and his men. She paled. He didn't know who the real raiders were yet! He still blamed her father.

"Jamie—"

"Dinna say it, Sheena," he said firmly. "Can you no' see I've no choice this time? You canna stop me."

"But I dinna want to stop you, Jamie."

He was taken aback, then looked at her suspiciously. "Why?" he asked. "Your kin didna know you were in the croft they burned. I didna think you would hold it against them."

"And I wouldna, if they *were* my kin. But it wasna Fergussons who came. I saw them, Jamie!"

Black Gawain was infuriated. "You're no' going to listen to her, are you?" he demanded. "She would say anything to save her kin!"

"Aye, I would." Sheena glared at Gawain. "But as it happens, I dinna have to, for they are no' the devils who came tonight. I saw the men who set the fire. I saw them clearly from the window 'afore the blaze forced us into the store. Aye, they wore my colors—but they werena Fergussons, *they were Jamesons!* 'Twas William Jameson I saw waiting to slaughter whoever tried to escape the fire. I saw him!"

Black Gawain laughed derisively. "You should have chosen another to blame, lass. Jameson is only a contemptible coward. All here know that. He wouldna have the nerve to attack a Mac-Kinnion."

"Then how does a coward attack when he feels he must?" she asked, and was pleased to see the bewilderment her question caused Gawain. "A coward would strike brutally and run—as did happen. Isna that what he'd do?"

"Who is to say your father is no' a coward?" Black Gawain returned quickly.

"I am!" she shouted. "We attacked you in the

summer, after you broke the peace in the spring. And we lost men in doing so, because we werena afraid to fight. But tell me this, was one fire set on those raids? Was one animal killed? Nay, because my father doesna fight that way."

"But a Fergusson plaid was found. Their cry was heard," Black Gawain insisted.

"You're no' listening to me, man," Sheena cried. "I told you Jameson wore my colors, no' his own. He wanted the blame placed on another clan, and he chose mine. That way, he's been able to attack MacKinnions repeatedly all these months and hasna suffered once for it. Sweet Mary, do you think I would have hidden inside a burning hut if I had seen my own kin outside that hut? You're hating the wrong clan for killing your sister, Black Gawain. And that's the truth."

"But why?" Gawain cried.

"Because of Libby Jameson," Jamie said, his voice hoarse. "Libby," he repeated.

"Aye." Sheena sighed. Thank the Lord, Jamie had guessed right. "I knew he meant to hurt you, Jamie, through me, when he locked me in his tower."

"Locked you?"

She grinned. "It was rescuing me you were doing, though you didna know it then. Sir William despises you. He tried to rape me, and when that failed, he lied to you about me. Anything to hurt you, because of his sister."

"And why did you no' tell me this 'afore?"

"You didna believe me about his lies, so how

could I tell you the rest?"

She was right. There was nothing he could say.

He caught her to him and kissed her hard. "You'll be here when I return?"

"I'll be here."

Black Gawain was already running for his horse.

Chapter 40

IN his eagerness to reach William Jameson, Black Gawain was riding far ahead of them. Jamie sympathized, but he knew the hothead would get himself killed if he arrived at Jameson's tower alone. He tried to catch up with Gawain, leaving Colen and the others to follow as best they could. Jamie almost closed the breach completely when they crossed the river near Sir William's land. There, as the two men raced up the bank toward a boundary tree, a crossbow stopped them short. Gawain's horse was pierced, throwing Gawain, who rolled pell-mell down the bank, landing in the river. Jamie's horse shied and just barely missed trampling Gawain as he passed. But before Jamie could even see where the arrow had come from, he took a quarrel in his chest. He fell, sliding a few feet, then lying still on the ground.

The man in the tree jumped to the ground and warily approached Jamie's still form, his crossbow at the ready. Part of a raiding party just returned, the man had been left to watch as a precaution, a precaution no one had taken very seriously. He had thought the task unnecessary. Why, the Mac-Kinnions had never suspected a thing. It was a waste of his time to be left watching.

But there was the great yellow-haired one himself, *The* MacKinnion. And he had downed him! There was no movement, no breathing. The man wasn't brave enough to touch The MacKinnion to see if he was turning cold. But surely no target had ever been struck more true. The square-headed arrow must have pierced the heart, for both jerkin and plaid were soaking red.

The other man, lying half in, half out of the water, was not worth bothering about. Jameson's man was eager to tell his laird whom he had killed. Just to be sure, he shot another quarrel into The MacKinnion before hurrying away to the tower.

They decided to wake Sheena as Jamie's body was being brought into their room, not before. Half asleep, she woke to all that blood. Screaming, she jumped from the bed just before Jamie was laid down on it. She screamed and screamed again, yanking at her hair until Daphne grabbed her, shaking her hard.

"He's no' dead, Sheena!" Daphne cried. "Listen to me now—he's no' dead!"

She tried to pull Sheena away from the bed, but Sheena resisted, staring at all that blood, at his pale face.

"But—"

"He's only wounded, lass. Now come away so he can be tended. You'll only be in the way."

Finally, Sheena got hold of herself. "I'll tend him," she said adamantly.

Daphne argued, "You're in no shape to be—"

"I said I'll tend him." Sheena's voice was hard. "He's my husband."

Daphne fell silent. It was then that Aunt Lydia came into the room and, seeing Jamie, began screaming worse than Sheena had done. She ran from the chamber, her shrieks echoing through the stone hallway.

"You managed to calm me," Sheena told Daphne quietly. "Go and calm your aunt. I'll manage here, with some help."

And she did. Despite the nausea that kept rising to her throat, despite the terror, she and the servants managed to get Jamie's clothing removed and his wounds bathed and bandaged. The arrows had already been expertly removed. The position of one wound made her wonder why Jamie was still alive. Had that arrow struck a rib? It must have. It had just barely missed the heart. But he *was* still breathing, *was* still alive—just. The other wound was in his side, in both sides, the arrow having, horribly, gone right through him.

Daphne returned, but Sheena wouldn't respond to her questions and there was nothing she could do, so she left and shooed the servants out, as well.

Alone, Sheena lay down beside Jamie, careful not to move the bed. Her eyes raked his face. She gently touched him. His skin was hot. His eyes remained closed. His breathing came hard. She touched his lips with a fingertip, then laid her cheek against his shoulder. She was consumed by emotions, and her tears fell on Jamie's skin.

"You're no' to die, MacKinnion. Do you hear me?" She pinched his arm, furious because he was frightening her so. "Do you? You're my husband. And I . . . I need you!" The words were torn from her, and she sobbed. "I love you, Jamie. You canna die! You canna!"

Much later, still sobbing, she fell asleep.

Dawn found her in a chair by the bed, watching Jamie. The heat of him had awakened her, and she'd spent the rest of the night bathing him with spring water. He was a little cooler.

"You're no' to pity him, you know."

Sheena gasped. She turned to see Lydia standing at the foot of the bed, having entered silently.

The old woman was wearing just her sleeping shift and a woolen cloak over her shoulders. She looked terrible, her eyes darkly ringed, her hair unkempt. Aunt Lydia, who was always so fastidious.

She didn't look at Sheena as she repeated, "You're no' to pity him. He doesna deserve it."

Sheena frowned, bewildered. "But I dinna pity him."

"Good. He did it himself, you see."

"Did what?"

"Killed himself, of course."

"Who did?" Sheena cried, suddenly alarmed.

"My father!" Lydia said, pointing a damning

336

finger at Jamie.

"What is wrong?" Sheena asked sharply. "Do you no' know your nephew?"

"Nephew? I have no nephew. My brother has no sons. Father would skelp him if he did, for Robbie's too young." Then Lydia frowned, uncertain suddenly. "But Father canna skelp him. He's dead now. Is Father no' dead?"

My God! "And how old are you, Lydia?"

"Eight," the old woman replied, her eyes still riveted on Jamie.

Sheena gripped the sides of her chair. This wasn't possible. And yet . . . hadn't Jamie told her that Lydia had not been quite right since she was a child and had seen Niall Fergusson kill her parents? But that was not at all what Lydia was saying.

"You saw your father die, Lydia?" Sheena asked her, gently and very carefully. "Do you remember it?"

"How could I forget?" Lydia answered. "But he shouldna have done it. And The Fergusson shouldna have come. He was a fool to think he could have her."

"Your mother?"

A single teardrop trickled down Lydia's cheek. She didn't appear to be hearing Sheena, and she looked so desolate. Sheena didn't have the heart to press her. Yet Lydia continued talking without prompting.

"He was a handsome man, The Fergusson, with that dark red hair and eyes so bright blue. My Uncle Donald was so furious when he took The

Fergusson away. He didna hurt him, did he? The Fergusson's only fault was loving her."

Didn't Lydia know that her Uncle Donald had killed Niall Fergusson all those years ago—killed him brutally? It was becoming clear that Sheena's grandfather Niall had loved Lydia's mother and had come here to meet her—a lovers' tryst? But Jamie had said Niall killed both his grandparents. How had that clandestine meeting turned into murder?

Lydia seemed to hear her thoughts. "My mother told me she was leaving. I wish she hadna, then I wouldna have followed her. But she didna want me to worry. She said she would send for me soon. They were going to France, she said. He had a family, too, that he was leaving. They couldna stay in Scotland after that.

"I cried, but she wouldna change her mind. I didna want her to go. I knew Father would be angry—and he was. He stopped them in the courtyard. 'Twas late. There was a bright moon, and I could see them from where I hid. They stood there arguing. Father was so angry—yet different. He didn't seem . . . right, and . . . he . . . he . . . ."

Lydia closed her eyes, awash with tears. She hugged herself, rocking, whimpering, seeing again what she had seen so long ago. Sheena visualized it, the husband confronting his wife and her lover, the rage and pain that must have consumed him if he'd loved her. Had he loved her? Or was she just a possession he wasn't willing to part with? Was it only pride?

It was better not to let Lydia tell any more of it. She was so distraught, there was no telling what reliving it would do to her.

Sheena put her arm around the older woman. "Lydia, come, let me take you back to your room."

"But I canna go. I must wait here. Mother will be coming back, now he's found them. I must tell her no' to worry. Father loves her. He will forgive her."

"Of course he will," Sheena encouraged, not knowing what else to say. "But you need to rest now, Lydia."

"Nay!" Lydia pushed Sheena away with surprising strength, her eyes wild. "He's drawn his dirk! The Fergusson has his own dirk. My mother's crying. They're fighting. The Fergusson drops his weapon . . . my father has it now . . . he's putting his own dirk away, holding The Fergusson's dirk, looking at it. He's looking at my mother. Nay! He's hitting her with it, he's stabbing her! The Fergusson canna stop him! Father pushes him away.

"She falls . . . God, the blood—all over, blood. Father shouts the alarm, but The Fergusson doesna run. He's staring at my mother. My father is staring at her, too, and—nay! He's buried the dirk in his own chest, *his own chest!* He's taking it out, and the blood is . . . the blood—everywhere! The dirk falls at the Fergusson's feet, but he doesna see it. Why does he no' run? My uncle is coming. . . ."

Sheena felt bile rise in her throat. That a young girl should have seen all that!

"Lydia, 'tis all right, 'tis over."

"It isna over. My uncle thinks The Fergusson killed them. I told him the truth, but he hit me and hit me and called me a liar. He'll no' hurt The Fergusson, will he? I canna tell anyone else. If I tell again, my mother willna come back. I must wait till she comes back."

Lydia was sobbing uncontrollably, and Sheena guided her gently from the room, soothing her as she would a child. Would Lydia ever be herself? Would the horror of that night stay with her now, or would she forget again?

Sheena saw Lydia to her room and helped the poor woman into bed, then called for one of Lydia's servants to sit with her. Lydia moved between being distraught and being entranced by some vision only she could see. Sheena didn't want to leave her like that, but Jamie came first. And Lydia's servant, Colleen, was really more friend than servant, so the suffering woman was in good hands.

Lydia wholly occupied Sheena's thoughts as she went back into the room she and Jamie shared, so it took her a moment to realize that something drastic had happened. Jamie's eyes were open. His eyes were open, and he was looking at her! Had he heard his aunt's story? And if so, how much? Sheena's mind raced. Would he ask her to tell him all of it, or did he understand everything? She returned his gaze, her breathing stopped, her heart pounding, and then, slowly, she began to relax. He wasn't going to speak of it, not then, and she wouldn't, either. They didn't speak at all, just stared at each other, their thoughts the same. All the years of killing and hatred caused by the enraged passions of one man. The saddest part was that the truth wouldn't make any difference now. People had been killed. The feud had happened. Nothing could change that. The horror could not be diminished.

The feud should never have begun, no matter whose fault it was, and after forty-seven years, it was time to put an end to it.

Chapter 41

J AMIE recovered nicely, taking full advantage of Sheena's ministrations. Once he'd learned she had tended him from the start, he insisted she continue. Sheena didn't mind, of course, even knowing that Jamie was well enough to leave his bed. It was a surprise when she entered one day and found him completely dressed, standing by the fire.

"You know, do you no', that a new feud has begun—with Jamesons?"

Sheena nodded. Colen had told her what had happened after Jamie and Black Gawain were taken back to Castle Kinnion. Colen had attacked Jameson's tower, but he couldn't breach it, needing a bigger force than he had. Surprisingly, Jamie decided not to take the tower. True, there were deaths for Jameson to atone for, but Jamie didn't want to wipe out a whole clan. The enemy was known. He could be dealt with in customary fashion, with periodic raids. And he could no longer hide his activities.

Black Gawain had been furious. Having suffered a broken arm that day, he could do no fighting for a while. But he had sworn he would kill Jameson. He and Jamie had argued over it, and Gawain had left the castle in a rage. He had yet to return.

"You agree there's reason for this new feud?" Jamie asked her, his meaning clear.

Sheena smiled at him. He seemed to need her approval, and she did agree, knowing Jamie was set against a bloody revenge.

"A Scotsman will always raid, whether enemy or—friend," she replied lightly, then laughed. A scowl crossed Jamie's face, for her father had just raided Jamie, lifting several of his prized horses right from under his nose. Dugald was demanding ransom, and a handsome ransom at that.

"You think it amusing, eh, your father's catching me unawares?"

"I think he'll be recouping all his losses from this past summer. 'Tis only fair, the breaking of the peace no' being his fault."

Jamie grunted. "I suppose you'd like to come along when I pay the ransom?"

"Can I?" she asked hopefully, her eyes sparkling.

He hesitated only a moment. "Aye, if you can see to it this doesna happen again."

"I think I can manage that. But what of Black Gawain? You do see that what he did was intentional?"

"He's gone, Sheena. Leaving the country, I'm told. His man just brought me the news."

Sheena wasn't really surprised. "He suspected you'd take action against him sooner or later because of Iain?"

"I suppose. He sent a message for you. He asks you to forgive him—'for all things.' What does he mean by that?"

"We had several confrontations, he and I," Sheena murmured evasively, feeling no need to elaborate. "He hated me when he learned who I was. That was only to be expected, Gawain thinking what he did about the feud and my family."

Jamie was satisfied with that. "Will you be asking me to search him out?" he asked, worried.

"I dinna think so. He's set his own punishment, banishing himself."

"But will your father agree that 'tis enough?"

"He's a fair man, Jamie. I think he'll agree. Besides," she added with a grin, "he'll be so happy, gloating when he accepts your ransom, he'll probably no' even ask about Black Gawain." Jamie gave her a sour look, but laughed despite himself.

Then an awkward silence fell between them. In all the days since he had been hurt, they had not once talked of themselves. Sheena wasn't ready to. She was still getting used to the fact that she loved this man. It wasn't supposed to happen, but it had. Only, he had never claimed the same feeling. Wanting her was all he had ever admitted to, and she knew that wouldn't satisfy her.

The tension was broken by Daphne's arrival. She was so pleased to see Jamie up and about that she teased him.

"Well, well, so that great hulking body wasna rotting after all!" She laughed at his look and said, "Now I've no excuse to stay longer. I'll tell my Dobbin I'll be leaving with him."

"So soon?" Sheena asked.

Daphne laughed. "I've my own castle to be seeing to, you know. Though I canna say this visit hasna been interesting. 'Tis no' every day my brother takes a wife he doesna know what to do with."

Jamie actually blushed, and Sheena and Daphne grinned at each other, which caused him to glower. "When are you leaving?" he asked pointedly.

"Today, and we'll be taking Jessie with us, you'll be glad to know," she added. "She's overstayed her welcome, I do believe."

"Indeed she has," Sheena retorted.

Daphne grinned at her again before saying softly, "Jamie, you'll be surprised to hear Aunt Lydia has expressed a wish to visit me. If you dinna object, she can come with us today."

Had his sister gone mad? "Lydia—leave Castle Kinnion? But she has never left here in all these years!"

"I know. Is it no' wonderful? She claims I do much more entertaining than you do, and 'tis time she met new people, time she found . . . a husband."

"What?"

Daphne giggled. "Can you imagine our aunt wanting a husband at her age? High time, I guess."

"'Tis absurd," Jamie grumbled, but his sister

rambled on.

"And I'll be seeing she finds one, too, though I think she'll manage on her own. These days there's a peace about her that makes her glow."

Sheena and Jamie smiled at each other. As Sheena had hoped, Jamie's aunt didn't remember any of her confession. But there was still a great difference in Lydia, as if the unburdening of the tragedy, even though she had blocked it out again, had brought her peace.

"Well, I dinna object," Jamie said. "But 'twill seem strange with her gone, and no mistake."

"I doubt you'll be missing her *too* much," Daphne replied knowingly. "And you've much to do, now you're finally up and about. 'Tis no' like you to pamper yourself. I was beginning to wonder if you'd ever get out of bed."

Jamie kept his voice deliberately casual. "I had a dream, you see, when I was recovering."

"Did you now?" Daphne asked, exasperated by his mysteriousness.

He ignored her and continued, "I dreamed my wife said she loved me. Maybe I stayed abed so long hoping to have the dream repeated."

Sheena flushed a glowing pink as Jamie's eyes locked with hers. Could he really have heard her that night when the fever was on him? She couldn't take her eyes from his.

"Och, well, I can see when I'm in the way," Daphne said. "I'll be going now. Take care of your precious jewel, laddie," she warned her brother sternly.

She kissed them both and was quickly gone. With the closing of the door, Sheena grew exceedingly uncomfortable. Jamie's eyes were still on her, and she finally lowered her gaze.

"It was a lovely dream, Sheena."

"Was it?" she asked, not knowing what else to say.

Jamie frowned. She was going to make this difficult. How could he ask her what he needed to know if she turned away from him like that? He shouldn't have waited so long, he knew that.

He was not a man for tender words, nor did expressing his feelings come easy for him in any case. He had known for a very long time what was in his heart, but he hadn't got the words out when he'd had the chance. Now there could be no more waiting. He had to know.

"Can you love me, Sheena?"

There. It was done.

Sheena didn't know what to do. Should she tell him the truth? Tell him she already loved him? But she was afraid to make herself that vulnerable. This powerful feeling was new to her, and it was frightening. So instead of answering, she asked him the same question.

"Can you love me?"

He went to her and cupped her face in both of his large hands. His kiss was tender, yet so full of love, like the man she had come to know. Sheena was left breathless, clinging to him.

"Do I have to be telling you, Sheena? Did it ever really need saying?"

"Aye, it did," she replied solemnly.

"Sweet Mary!" he sighed. "I love you. There! Now dinna expect me to say it again." Then he inquired nervously, "And you?"

Sheena gave him a brilliant smile. "I love you, Jamie. I do."

He laughed with relief and joy, holding her tightly. "Och, sweetheart, you canna know how happy you've made me."

"I'm no' feeling so poorly myself," she teased him, as happy as she had ever been.

Chapter 42

THEY sat at the laird's table in the great hall at Tower Esk. The meal was nearly over. It had been a pleasant time—and a great relief to see Jamie and her father getting along so well. Still, Sheena was anxious to retire to the guest chamber she and Jamie had been given.

They would be leaving Tower Esk in the morning. Sheena had seen so little of Jamie during their visit, and she was feelng a bit jealous. It was not the same as when they were at Castle Kinnion, where he felt more at ease. After wanting for so long to get back to her home, now she wanted only to return to her *new* home.

Would it lessen in time, she wondered, this wanting to be with him every moment? Well, the desire didn't worry her. Wanting to be with him was not a bad feeling at all!

Sheena touched his bare knee below his plaid. Jamie grinned, his eyes twinkling.

"Do you know what you're about, lass?" He

leaned over to whisper in her ear.

"Aye, I think I do." She grinned as she moved her hand upward along his leg.

Jamie caught her hand, then stood up abruptly. He made the appropriate excuses before escorting Sheena out of the hall.

Once out of sight of the others, they ran like children, laughing all the way to their room. Inside, behind the closed door, Jamie tumbled Sheena to the bed. Their passion was wild and tender and, as always, wonderful.

"If it wasna so cold, I'd take you to your little pool in the morning," he told her between kisses. "For memory's sake."

Sheena sat up abruptly and demanded, "Who told you about that? Niall?"

"Nay, lass. Your brother's told me many things, but he didna have to tell me about the pool in the glen. I saw you there myself, in the spring."

"You *saw* me?" she gasped, blushing. "Jamie, you didna!"

"I did." He teased her without mercy. "And may I say, sweetheart, there was never a more bonny kelpie than you were that day. Truly, I didna think you were real."

"But . . . you saw me!"

Her indignation only spurred him on. "Just like this," he said, kissing her bare breasts. "The image of you in that pool never left me. Now do you see why I was so surprised the day I found you in Colen's room? I'd had no luck finding you, and suddenly there you were—with my brother."

"Finding me?"

"Aye, lass. You never left my mind. I came back many times, hoping to see you again. Did you never wonder why I was alone when your father's men found me?"

Her eyes widened. "Then you were captured because you came looking for me?"

"Aye."

She considered that for a while, then said, "Serves you right! You came to spy on me!"

"If I had found you, I assure you I wouldna have settled for just spying," he told her.

She giggled. She just couldn't stay angry very long anymore. Especially when he was kissing her all over, as he was doing just then.

"You're a devil, Jamie, but then, I always knew that."

"Did you now?" he murmured, glancing up.

"Aye. And I wish you had found me again at the pool," she added impulsively. "I wouldna have known who you were, and you wouldna have known who I was, and we might have been making love that much sooner."

Jamie chuckled, delighted. "Och, sweetheart, but I do love you."

"And I thought you wouldna say that again." She grinned.

"Well, I *like* saying it. But no' as much as I like showing you. Can I show you again?"

Sheena sighed happily and wrapped her arms around him. "If you dinna, Jamie MacKinnion, I'll be greatly disappointed, and no mistake."

The publishers hope that this
Large Print Book has brought
you pleasurable reading.
Each title is designed to make
the text as easy to see as possible.
G. K. Hall Large Print Books are
available from your library and
your local bookstore. Or you can
receive information on upcoming
and current Large Print Books by
mail and order directly from the
publisher. Just send your name
and address to:

G. K. Hall & Co.
70 Lincoln Street
Boston, Mass. 02111

or call, toll-free:

1-800-343-2806

A note on the text
Large print edition designed by
Bernadette Strickland
Composed in 16 pt. Times Roman
on a Mergenthaler 202
by Compset Inc., Beverly MA